A
CLEARING
IN THE
FOREST

A
ℭLEARING
IN THE
ℱOREST

JOURNEYS FROM AYRDEN

KIM LOVE STUMP

A Clearing in the Forest

Journeys From Ayrden

Map by Gillis Björk
www.gillisbjork.com

Published by Foxcroft Publishing
1043 Morehead Street
Suite 105
Charlotte, NC 28204

Library of Congress Control Number
2016909002

ISBN 978-0-9975914-0-8 (hardcover)
ISBN 978-0-9975914-1-5 (paperback)

Comments about *A Clearing in the Forest* and requests for author appearances may be addressed directly to Kim Love Stump at www.kimlovestump.com.

To my husband, Tim,
who always thought I should,
and to my children, Stuart and Bo,
who always believed I would.
All love and joy and gratitude for journeying with me.

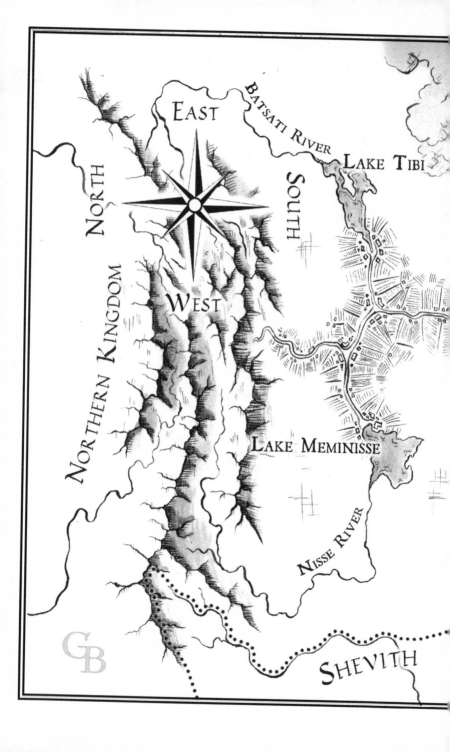

THE FOREST

To
CHEHALEM

THE CLEARING

To Shahar

PALACE OF
AYRDEN

SOUTH
GARDEN

To
BERYLLIOS

The KINGDOM of
AYRDEN

Proclamation of Ayrden

Be it known to All—

The Sovereigns of Ayrden

Shall not be deemed worthy to rule

By birthright alone.

Each royal descendant of Ayrden

Shall embark upon a Journey

During that descendant's sixteenth year

Or forever give up any claim to the Throne.

Each descendant shall Journey forth,

Alone and unarmed,

Carrying one day's provision Only.

Upon a Sovereign's death,

The Throne shall pass to the eldest descendant

Who from His or Her Journey Hath returned.

If there be not such a One,

The deceased Sovereign's eldest sibling,

Requisite Journey complete,

Shall assume the Throne.

This is an Edict in Perpetuity decreed by the

First King of Ayrden.

CONTENTS

CHAPTER 1

THE SUMMONS OF STANDING

Princess Adriana kept her hand steady as she lifted the slim onyx cylinder from the castle courier's outstretched palm. But she could not keep her heart from pounding or her throat from squeezing shut, making it difficult to swallow. Her Summons of Standing had arrived. The small parchment scroll contained within ordered her to proceed at once to the King's Throne Room.

Adriana hurried down the long stone corridor. She had been expecting the summons for days, both dreading and anticipating what it would reveal. She was not concerned over her reception by the King—she was the beloved eldest child, in her opinion her father's favorite, and the apple of the kingdom's eye.

But this audience would set the course of her life.

A CLEARING IN THE FOREST

If any of her Teachers deemed her unworthy to embark upon the Journey of her sixteenth year, the lifetime of preparation and training she had undergone would be for naught. Though she would not be banished from Ayrden, she would never rule. And the thought of what might have been had she worked harder or longer or smarter would be a bitter dose of daily humility. Even good news, that her Teachers considered her competent to embark upon the Journey, brought with it the anxiety of traveling alone into the unknown.

After passing along numerous corridors, the princess arrived at the solid gold doors of the Throne Room. She stopped, smoothed the skirt of her brocade dress, and took a deep breath. Pushing a lock of hair behind her ear, she turned toward one of the sentries.

She was surprised to see it was Emaht, her fencing Teacher, who also served as an early morning guard.

"Emaht," Adriana said, "you are back. Does that mean Sarian is well today?"

"Yes, Beloved of the King." Emaht gave a low bow. "She is much improved. The Healer says she shall soon deliver our precious child."

"I'm so glad for you both. I will be sad to miss the festivities." Her voice caught a bit as she thought of what lay ahead. "If I have already left," she added.

"Princess, the festivities for our precious one will be

as nothing compared to your homecoming. I am confident you are ready for your Journey. And that you will return."

Adriana smiled. At least one tutor considered her prepared.

"You know my mind too well, Teacher, and I have no interest in debating you on my preparedness. My luck in fencing with you is limited, as you well know."

In all the years Emaht had taught fencing to the princess and her brothers and sisters, none had ever defeated him.

"True. But do not forget:

> *Today's outcome need not be the same*
> *as the days' that have gone before.*

"Thank you for those words of encouragement," the princess said with a laugh. "Now, you had better announce me to the King, or I'll get no credit for being so prompt in responding to my father's summons."

With that both of the guards pulled open the gold doors and called with one voice, "Presenting Her Royal Highness, Princess Adriana of Ayrden."

The room opened before her in all its splendor. The floor was made of emeralds the color of new grass, and the walls were covered in the whitest of marble. Overhead, sapphires and diamonds alternately filtered and focused the sun's rays. In the center of the far wall stood the golden throne, studded with rubies and flanked by expansive window openings that framed the mountains and rivers of

Ayrden like master paintings.

Adriana swept through the doors toward her father, the King, and the dais on which he stood. But when she saw his eyes fall upon her and the joy of his expression, she quickened her step until she was running across the emerald floor.

With a hearty laugh and a tender father's kiss to her cheek, the King wrapped her tightly in his arms before putting her at arm's length and looking closely at her face. "Beloved, you are worried and afraid of what lies before you?" he asked, concern evident in his voice.

Adriana gave a small sigh. "Everyone seems to know me so well."

"Ah, that is because we love you so well, and have been so well loved by you, my dear. Here, sit down. We need to talk," the King said.

Large cushions of the most lovely and beautiful silks surrounded the King's throne. Adriana dropped to one of the cushions and rested her head on her father's knee. For a time there was complete silence in the Throne Room. Except for the two of them, the room was empty. All of the guards and attendants were elsewhere in the castle, and a quietness settled over her that she had not expected. Her father's strong fingers gently caressed her dark hair, repeatedly stroking it away from her temple and smoothing it as it cascaded in curls down her back.

She wondered if this could be a preamble for the devastating news that she would not to be allowed to go.

The King finally spoke. "The Teachers all say you are sufficiently prepared to embark upon your Journey."

Adriana's heart at once began to gallop.

"I know you have questions," the King said, "but I can answer very few of them. As you know, each ruler's Journey is his or her own and is of very little benefit to anyone else. What I encountered on my Journey will not be what you experience. Telling you my story will only set expectations that will alter your judgment. However, I can advise you that when you are worried you will not make your best decisions and that, in the end, the Journey is all about the decisions you choose to make."

He tilted her face up toward his and said with a trace of a smile, "Your first decision is when you will leave. Have you thought about that yet?"

"I have thought of little else for days, perhaps weeks," Adriana said. "Is there a time that the Wise Ones say is better than another?"

The King replied, "They have studied this question for centuries, of course. But no, the Wise Ones find nothing that indicates one season is preferable, nor that a particular date after your sixteenth birthday is better than any other. It's no secret that I left the day I turned sixteen, yet my father almost ran out of time. He left the week before his seventeenth birthday. And his mother, your great-grandmother, left a month or so after her sixteenth birthday—the specific date was not deemed important enough to record."

"Father," Adriana said, "the three of you returned. But not everyone does."

The King sighed before saying slowly, "True, not everyone returns. Did you know that I was not the eldest?"

Adriana's eyes widened and she shifted her gaze to her father's face. Her aunts and uncles lived in various cities of the kingdom, but they were an important part of the royal family and came often to the Palace of Ayrden to visit. Yet never had Adriana heard of an aunt or uncle older than her father, the King. "An older brother or sister? What happened?"

The King placed a hand alongside his daughter's cheek. "I had an older brother, Kelak, two years my senior. We were playmates and rivals, best friends and vigorous competitors. He set out on his Journey in the middle of his sixteenth year. Every day I would go to the edge of the castle estate, where his path led him into the forest, and watch for him. I would stand so still and quiet that even the animals soon forgot there was a human presence in their midst. I would listen so hard." The King's gaze lifted from Adriana's face and seemed to focus on the forest that edged the vast lawn of the estate, barely visible in the distance through the massive window opening. "Sometimes I was sure I could hear his horse's hooves, or the sound of his voice. But he never returned. And then, when I went on my own Journey, I thought somehow that I might find him and bring him back with me. That perhaps we would rule together. But I never even saw him. And he has never been seen or heard from again."

The King's gaze returned to his daughter's upturned face. "But enough about all these people of the past, even me. Tomorrow is your sixteenth birthday. As I told you, I have spoken to the Teachers. All of them say you have mastered the skills requisite for the Journey. Starting tomorrow your decision is twofold: Will you go? And if so, when?

"I love you, Adriana, and I will miss you while you are away. But I will be waiting for your return, and I am confident that you shall."

CHAPTER 2

A GOLDEN BALL

Adriana awoke to sunshine and the singing of birds. The cloudless sky was hyacinth blue. *What a glorious day for a birthday*, she thought. A tingle of excitement fluttered through her body. She danced over to one of the turret windows. Flinging it open, she breathed in the fragrance of honeysuckle and lilac as she surveyed the expanse of green lawn below her window. Gleaming white tents and gazebos were being erected, and lengthy garlands of flowers lay everywhere on the grass, waiting to be draped around the structures.

"Sixteen today!" she whispered to herself. Determining to put away any thought of her approaching departure, Adriana vowed she would simply enjoy this day, deliberately drinking in all the wonder of her birthday and the accompanying festivities.

A GOLDEN BALL

That plan was soon interrupted by a knock on the door that heralded the arrival of her serving maids. Even before a happy birthday wish was expressed, Banah, the oldest of her maids, asked, "Princess, do you require your clothing for the Journey or birthday attire?"

Adriana watched as Banah glided across the floor, leading a procession of maids toward a large dressing screen standing in the corner. Irritated at the intrusion, Adriana nevertheless asked politely, "Do you mean my clothing for the Journey was prepared without my knowledge?"

"But of course, Princess. I have seen the clothes. I assure you they will fit you perfectly, and they are mandated to be so simple there was no need for you to be consulted." Banah's expression as she stopped to gaze at Adriana was almost catlike, with her tilted head and raised eyebrows.

"Still," Adriana continued, "I would at least have appreciated the opportunity to choose the fabric."

Banah's mouth stretched into a thin smile. "Princess Adriana," she said softly, "there was nothing to choose. The clothes are of the material dictated by the first King of Ayrden. They will be perfect. But most importantly, they are ready, so you may leave when you choose."

The princess gave a small, rueful laugh. "I'm sorry, Banah. I suppose I am more in the dark regarding this Journey than I am aware. Is there anything else I should know?"

"Not that I can tell you," replied Banah, returning Adriana's gaze with unblinking gray eyes. "However, I'm sure this day will be very enlightening. Now, do you wish to wear your yellow silk dress with the pearls or the pink one? The seamstresses added fresh rosebuds to the hem just this morning. They thought that would be a nice touch for your birthday."

Adriana ran lightly down the wide white marble steps toward the terrace, where her entire family would gather for breakfast. However, at the bottom of the staircase, she impulsively turned into the Room of the Ancestors, the hem of her dress scattering a few fresh, fragrant rose petals onto the floor. The room was silent and empty of furniture. Only the full-length portraits of the past rulers of Ayrden occupied it. Adriana slowly walked the circumference, pausing in front of each of the portraits of successfully returned ancestors. Some smiled, while others glared. She stopped in front of her grandfather's painting. In the portrait he bore a striking resemblance to her father, except that he looked so solemn. There was not even a hint of a smile on his face and, though it was probably her imagination, she thought he looked concerned. Sunlight filtered through the leaves of the nearby trees as Adriana dropped into the patch of sunlight on the floor below her grandfather's image. She could feel the top of her head warming from the sun's rays and a sudden inspiration came to her. Filled with excitement and sudden purpose, Adriana jumped up and ran from the room.

She arrived at the terrace breakfast table as her twin sisters, Emma and Ella, the youngest members of the family, were being settled on either side of her mother. "Good morning, Mother," Adriana said as she kissed her on the cheek.

The large stone table was laden with platters of food and pitchers of juices. Seated around the table were her parents and all five of her siblings, as well as several aunts and uncles already arrived for her birthday. Adriana walked around the table toward her usual seat between her two brothers, Alexander and Ty. Alexander, who was a mere thirteen months younger than she, tossed a ball to her, calling, "Catch! And Happy Birthday!"

"Alexander!" the Queen exclaimed. "Do not throw balls at the table. How many times do I have to tell you?"

"Sorry, Mother," Alexander said, seeming not at all perturbed. "But that's my present to Adriana, and you know I always like to be the first to give her a gift."

"Far too true, little brother," said Adriana as she slipped into her chair, weighing the ball in her hand and gazing at it with interest. "I only hope this year's gift is more to my liking than your present to me last year."

"What! You didn't like the sweet little pet I gave you?" Alexander asked with mock innocence.

"Alexander, I hardly think a snake qualifies as a sweet little pet, do you?" Adriana replied. "Even though the thing wasn't poisonous, it also wasn't exactly the kind of gift I expected to find first thing in the morning, on my pillow no less!"

"I did better this year!" Alexander said. "I actually think you'll find this a very appropriate gift. Given at a very appropriate time."

"Oh, just ignore his talking and open it, Adriana!" urged Bess, their thirteen-year-old sister.

"Yes, yes, open it, open it," chorused the twins.

Adriana laughed and continued examining the ball in her hand, turning it with curiosity. "I will open it . . . if it opens . . . and if . . . I can find out how to open it."

Adriana looked up from studying the ball. Everyone around the table was watching with expectation etched across their faces. Alexander winked at his father, who was looking on with amusement.

"Oh, Adriana, look!" exclaimed Bess from her place on the other side of Alexander. "You've gotten gold from the ball all over your hands!"

"Honestly, Alexander," Adriana said with annoyance, "can't you give a normal gift for once?" Adriana looked from her hands, covered in gold powder, to the ball itself, which now clearly showed elaborately lettered words all across its circumference:

In the stable you will find
a brilliant steed to calm your mind.

"Is this a joke, Alexander?"

"You know I'd never spoil a well-laid plan by telling you that! Ready to go to the stable to see your steed?" Alexander teased.

"My steed! I feel like that's code for something I'm not going to like."

"Only one way to find out, Princess!" the King said, standing up. "All of you finish breakfast while we walk down to the stables. We'll be back shortly."

"I want to go!" Bess said. She jumped up and hurried off with Adriana and Alexander while the King followed behind them.

The stables were full of activity when the four royals arrived. Horses and chariots were being dispatched to gather guests for the evening festivities, while other horses were being led out to the lush green pastures in order to empty the stalls for the horses of those arriving.

"Happy Birthday, Princess!" called Beecher, the riding

Teacher. His face was weathered and old, but his smile was gleeful and young. "What in all of Ayrden are you doing down at the stables on your birthday? Don't you have more important things to be doing? Picking out your ball gown for the evening or something?"

Adriana smiled at him. "I'm so glad you're here, Beecher. If Alexander's hidden something disgusting in your barn, I'll let you deal with him. My golden ball says there is something 'brilliant' here for me."

"Well, come in and see what you find then." Beecher grinned as he stepped aside.

No sooner had Adriana walked into the barn than she stopped. A huge black stallion stood alone in the breezeway, a wide-bowed ribbon looking ridiculously out of place around his neck.

"Alexander!" Adriana gasped. "Seriously? Seriously?" She spun around to face her brother. "It is Sultan, isn't it? You're giving him to me? Is this one of your jokes?"

The King and Alexander stood smiling at Adriana, but Bess looked dumbfounded. "A-A-Alexander," Bess stuttered. "You can't give Sultan to Adriana, *you* need him—I mean you *will* need him—next year, you'll need him for *your* Journey. What are you doing?"

Ignoring both of his sisters, Alexander walked up to Sultan and ran one hand down the horse's neck and the other down his nose. Sultan sank to one knee, bowing to

Adriana like a submissive prince from a far-off land.

"You don't have a horse that can see you through your Journey, Adriana," Alexander said, his face and voice growing serious. "Sultan's ready now, even though I have to wait at least another thirteen months. And depending on when you leave, I have time to show you all the things I've taught him to do. Bowing is just a birthday trick."

Adriana hugged her brother tight and whispered in his ear, "There may be a little problem with that timing, but I'll tell you about it when we're alone."

Turning to Sultan, Adriana put her hand on his withers and then looked back to her father and Bess. "I'll need to put on riding clothes if Alexander is going to take Sultan and me through our paces. Come on, Bess, let's go back so I can change. Beecher, will you saddle Sultan and bring him up to the castle, please? And Alexander, thank you."

CHAPTER 3

THE PRONOUNCEMENT OF THE GIFTS

W hat do you think?" Alexander asked, looking up at Adriana as she sat astride Sultan after her ride.

Adriana grinned. "I think I'm never going to remember all the tricks you've taught him, though they're certainly wonderful! He's amazing, Alex, really. Thank you more than I can say."

"Enough already," Alexander said with a wave of his hand that set Sultan prancing in place. "Just be sure you make it back with him. We sort of have a connection."

"I'll do my best, little brother," the princess said as she gave Sultan the subtle signal to drop his head into a forward attacker's chest and shove him back.

Alexander stumbled backward. "Hey, no fair using his

tricks against the trainer."

With a quick double snap of his fingers, Alexander had Sultan on his hind legs and Adriana sitting in a sudden heap on the grass at her brother's feet.

Adriana jumped up, anger making her eyes glitter. She approached Alexander on sure and steady feet, hands taut and ready to do battle.

Alexander sighed. He might be good, even excellent, at training horses and be a good deal taller and heavier than his sister, but she was practically lethal in hand-to-hand, particularly when she was angry. "Sorry," Alexander said, raising both hands in a show of surrender. Adriana paused, and Sultan, who had been carefully watching Alexander, suddenly collapsed to the grass and lay still.

"I forgot to show you this one. Sultan has to be looking, of course, but if he sees you raise both hands"—Alexander again raised both hands, palms out, in front of him—"he falls to the ground and lies still until you give him a signal."

"And what is the signal to bring him to life again, pray tell?" Adriana asked, her voice still showing her annoyance at Alexander's previous trick.

"Up." At Alexander's single word, Sultan rose from the grass and stood.

"Hmm. Easy enough, I guess. Do you have more tricks to play on me, or are you ready to hear my plan?"

"No more tricks today. Go ahead and tell me."

"I'm leaving tomorrow morning at first light. I don't want to miss tonight, or I'd go right now. Before I came to breakfast this morning, I spent some time in the Room of the Ancestors. You know Grandfather almost left his Journey until too late. That's not going to happen to me. I've decided to go tomorrow. With good fortune, I'll be back before you turn sixteen and you can take Sultan on your Journey as well."

They began walking on foot back toward the stables, Sultan following neither Adriana nor Alexander, but placing himself in the space between the two.

The knock on Adriana's chamber door came after the moon had risen and the guests had assembled. "Are you ready?" the King called.

"Indeed!" Adriana replied as Banah opened the door. Adriana gave her father a kiss on the cheek.

"Ah. You look beautiful, beautiful," the King said as he looked down at Adriana.

Her dark hair was studded with diamonds and tiny white, star-shaped flowers, and her cheeks glowed with excitement. She spun on one slipper-clad foot and sent the long sweeping skirt of her white brocade ball gown swirling.

THE PRONOUNCEMENT OF THE GIFTS

With a regal bow and an offer of his arm, the King escorted Adriana to the partygoers awaiting her arrival. When they exited the doors onto the wide terrace running the length of the castle, the King paused. The musicians began playing a song written just for the occasion. It made Adriana think of sunshine and joy and excitement all at the same time. "Happy sixteenth! Happy sixteenth!" rang out from the hundreds of guests gathered below the terrace until the cries swelled into cheering and applause.

The King stepped aside and, holding only Adriana's left hand, looked on fondly as she made a deep curtsy of thanks to her guests.

The evening was spectacular. Adriana and the King began the dancing, and Adriana's favorite delicacies were served to all during the dinner. As Adriana sat at the head table in the place of honor, zing—a sparkling sweet and tangy silver drink she was particularly fond of—was poured into tall fluted glasses for toasts. Well-wishes for the Journey and funny stories of the princess's past exploits were told to the amusement of all until a breeze began to blow through the tents and gazebos.

The breeze increased in strength. Then, one by one, the three Gifters stood, their long pale hair blowing around their thin faces and ruffling their gossamer robes. With expectancy Adriana leaned forward. As the eldest in her generation and thus the first potential heir to reach sixteen in her lifetime, she had never seen the Gifters make their Pronouncement of the Gifts.

"It is time—" began the oldest of the three in a deep melodious voice.

"To reveal to you—" continued the youngest.

"The gifts we bestowed upon you at your birth," concluded the third Gifter.

Together, the three spoke in unison, "We gave you courage and fidelity and kindness. They were ours to give and we gave them freely to you." Their voices together were like the sound of a complex piece of music that carries a single melody even with many instruments playing at once.

"But be forewarned—" continued the youngest Gifter as she raised her hands high above her head.

"Your greatest strengths—" said the oldest.

"Can hinder you more than your weaknesses," said the middle Gifter.

"You must marshal your gifts for the good," they concluded in unison.

The breeze stilled, and the three Gifters each raised a glass of zing from their respective places in the midst of the gathering. "To Princess Adriana. May you return."

The entire assembly raised their glasses, and then, first one by one, then two by two, and finally table by table, they all stood, raising their glasses and crying out in unison, "To Princess Adriana. May you return. To Princess Adriana.

THE PRONOUNCEMENT OF THE GIFTS

May you return. To Princess Adriana. May you return!"

Although the dancing and festivities went on until the night was late and the moon had moved to the far side of the sky, for Adriana her birthday had turned from a celebration to a preparation. She danced and laughed and moved about the guests, but her consuming thought for the rest of the night was, *What if I don't return? What happens to me if I'm not able to return?*

CHAPTER 4

TY'S DRAWING

ourage, fidelity, and kindness, Adriana thought as she stood in her room the next day watching the dark sky lighten in the predawn. *Are they enough?* she wondered. *Enough to get me through this Journey?*

She was disappointed. She thought her gifts would have been bigger, bolder, more impressive to both her and those who heard the pronouncement. Oh, courage was good. Of a truth, great. And she assumed her departure so soon after her sixteenth birthday would be evidence of that courage to the citizens of Ayrden. But her hammering heart and the persistent feeling that an unseen hand was squeezing her throat was not how she had ever imagined courage feeling.

And fidelity and kindness? Lovely gifts for when she was a crowned ruler. Fidelity would produce strong and trustworthy alliances, and what subject wouldn't appreciate kindness from a regent? But on this Journey? Would either be of use at all?

Her reverie was interrupted by a quick, cursory knock as Banah entered the room. She carried Adriana's clothes for the Journey over one arm. Her face showed surprise. She had obviously expected to find Adriana still sleeping.

"Your clothes as you requested last evening, Princess," Banah said with a slight curtsy. She glided across the room and hung the clothes behind the dressing screen.

"Thank you," Adriana said, stepping behind the screen and fingering the lightweight ivory tunic and breeches and the buttery soft leather boots. *Quite a change from last night's ball gown and slippers,* she thought.

She quickly put on the clothes and stepped back out. "Banah, didn't I see you bring in an outer garment?"

Banah jumped up from the stool on which she'd been sitting, almost dropping the cape she was still holding. "It's right here, Princess." She drew the moss green velvet cape around Adriana and fastened it at her throat.

Banah stepped back and surveyed Adriana coldly. "You should appreciate the opportunity to go on this Journey, Princess. Not everyone is so fortunate."

Adriana was nonplussed. Though Banah was never warm toward Adriana, or anyone else for that matter, she was unfailingly proper. Her statement seemed to border on rudeness. Not sure how to reply, Adriana chose to ignore the comment.

She turned and picked up seven sealed envelopes, each addressed to a member of her immediate family. "I'll not be saying good-bye to my family this morning, so if you would please deliver these at breakfast, I'd be most grateful." Then, deciding to put her gift of kindness to work, she added, "Thank you, Banah."

Adriana walked softly down the stairs and through the silent castle. The clothes felt foreign, but they were comfortable and they also somehow made her feel free. And though that aspect of the Journey had not occurred to her before, she realized that on this Journey she would be free in ways she had never been before. There would be no lessons to attend and no parents to please. For the first time in weeks she felt happy rather than nervous at the thought of what lay in front of her.

She exited the castle to find Beecher standing beside a fully saddled and bridled Sultan in the almost-light.

"Princess, as requested, he's saddled and ready to go. Your day's provision is packed and in the bag," Beecher said, patting the small leather bag hanging on one side of the saddle.

"Thank you, Beecher. He's a fabulous animal and I'm glad to have him. Take care of Alexander while I'm gone. I dare say he'll be a bit lonely with Sultan and me both absent."

"Absolutely. Don't you be worrying about anything back here. Ready for a leg up?" Beecher stretched out his hands.

But just as Adriana was about to mount, she saw her brother Ty running out the castle door and down the stairs to the lawn.

"Ty, what are you doing up? It's not even first light yet. And you're barefoot as well," Adriana said with concern as he stopped beside her and grabbed her hand.

Ty, saying not a word, pushed a piece of parchment into her hand. It was a drawing of last night's Pronouncement of the Gifts. But the breeze, instead of being invisible, was drawn with silver-winged warriors circling and moving through the air, swords and daggers drawn in preparation.

As always, there was enough reality to his drawing to make Adriana wonder if Ty was a See-er, one who saw both the visible and the invisible realms, and occasionally the future as well. Or perhaps he was just a little boy with a vivid imagination. It was a hard thing to discern, as Ty, though nine years old, had never spoken.

Kneeling down so she could look into his face, Adriana touched his cheek gently. "The drawing is nice, Ty. I'd like to think that my gifts have some power to protect me, since I can take neither sword nor dagger for my Journey. Thank you for showing this to me." She handed him back the drawing, then pulled him close and kissed his temple, holding him to her for a moment before standing and accepting Beecher's help in mounting Sultan.

She turned Sultan toward the woods lining the back of the castle grounds where she'd been assured the path for her Journey would open before her. But because she did not look back, she did not see that Ty's drawing had two sides. While the drawing she had seen was colored in silver and white, the other side was bitterly black and bloodred.

CHAPTER 5

Making a Way

Not at all sure how the path was supposed to open before her, Adriana cantered Sultan across the vast expanse of lawn. She scanned the woods for any entrance the entire time she rode toward them, but she saw nothing. When she finally arrived at their edge, the castle was far in the distance behind her.

She turned Sultan parallel to the forest's edge and rode alongside it for several minutes, wondering what to do. There was no one to ask now, and over and over she'd been assured that the way would merely open before her.

But there was no path. Her eyes swept the towering trees and the dense underbrush at the edge of what seemed an impenetrable forest, and she rode. On and on she rode.

Finally she stopped and rode a distance away from the forest before turning Sultan to directly face it. She sat comfortably but looked with confusion at her first apparent task of the Journey.

How was she to get the path to open before her? What had she been taught? What lessons had she learned that might apply to this situation? She bit her lip nervously and once again surveyed the line of the forest where it met the cleanly groomed grass of the castle lawn.

"Father said I'll not make my best decisions if I'm worried," she muttered under her breath. "Well, I am worried. What if my Journey never begins?" She blew her breath out through pursed lips.

"Today's outcome need not be the same as the days' that have gone before," Emaht had said. Surely she wasn't to do this day after day, she thought with frustration.

And at just that moment a fragment of her mother's teaching came to her:

Your belief makes a way.

That might apply. But I did believe it would be here waiting for me, she thought, *and there is no path.* However, she realized, that wasn't precisely what she'd been told. The oft-repeated phrase was actually, "The way will open before you." *If I believed that, what would I do?* Adriana asked herself.

The answer was suddenly obvious to her and, summoning all the courage she possessed, she urged Sultan to a full gallop straight toward the thick forest. They drew closer and closer and still there was no opening, yet she kept riding. Wasn't that the point? *My belief will make a way; my belief will make a way*, she chanted to herself in time to the pounding of Sultan's hooves. And just before she absolutely had to make a decision to stop or turn, the way opened.

They were in! Sultan's stride lengthened and, like a boat plowing through the water, the woods simply gave way and parted in front of them. Adriana rode like this for some distance before glancing over her shoulder to see that just behind them the woods had returned to their place, erasing the path on which they were riding.

Amazing.

Could she turn back, even if she wanted to? Fear rose in her throat. How long could they go on like this? Was this what the Journey was supposed to be like?

She slowed Sultan, and the woods kept parting and opening and disappearing in an almost hypnotic way. She slowed again, sparing Sultan's energy, as it occurred to her that it was still early and she had no idea what needs might arise as the day progressed.

She slowed Sultan still more, testing to see if the woods continued to part. They did. So Adriana slowed Sultan to a walk and at that moment the path unfurled before them, mysteriously winding through the woods even as it still closed behind them as they proceeded.

Adriana rode Sultan along the path the rest of the

morning. They stopped twice and drank from crystal springs that sporadically bubbled up along their way. It was approaching high light when the path ended in a large clearing. The ground was covered in a thick carpet of sunlit grass.

As the path had closed behind them, there was no apparent exit from the clearing, but by now Adriana was more relaxed. The way would open or they would open a way, she concluded. Regardless, the sun was fully overhead and she was hungry.

Adriana dismounted and removed Sultan's tack, freeing him to graze in the verdant grass. Taking her lunch to the edge of the clearing, Adriana took off her cape and spread it on the ground before sitting on it and opening the leather bag Beecher had pointed out before she'd left home.

Two large slices of dense soda bread, two apples, a hunk of white cheese, a large cluster of purple grapes, and a small bottle of zing rested inside. She smiled. Her single day's provision might be modest, but, as with the lavish feast last night, it consisted of some of her favorite foods. She popped two grapes into her mouth in quick succession and picked up one of the bread slices. Then she paused.

Wait—how would she find food once this meager provision was gone? So far she'd seen nothing that looked edible on her way through the woods. How much of this should she eat? Half of it? Less, so there would be food left for tomorrow? She sighed before breaking the soda bread slice in half and putting the other half and the cluster of grapes back in the bag. She would settle for a quarter of the bread and an apple for this meal and see what happened after that, she decided. She bit into the rosy apple. It was delicious, and the few small sips of zing she allowed herself were cool and refreshing.

The clearing was oddly still. None of the usual birdsong or rustling of small animals filled the silence. There wasn't even a breeze to stir the leaves high overhead. Sultan grazed close to her as she ate. When she'd finished most of what she considered her lunch portion, she offered Sultan the last few bites of apple and settled her back against a tree. The sun was warm, and she was content to rest for a bit. A combination of excitement and fear had kept her from sleeping most of the night, and she'd risen well before first light. She felt her eyes grow heavy and let herself slip away into sleep.

CHAPTER 6

CHOICES THREE

Adriana awoke sometime later, disoriented and confused, her heart pounding. Discordant sounds filled the air and the ground itself seemed to be shaking. Snatching up her cloak, she saddled, bridled, and mounted Sultan as quickly as she was able. She was having a difficult time deciphering what the raucous sounds were—animal or human or something else altogether—when they stopped and a profusion of leaves and twigs and small branches began to fall around her and litter the grass.

The huge trees along the perimeter of the clearing, at least all of them that Adriana could see, were shaking and bending in every direction. Then, as if an invisible hand were plucking them up like so many flowers, certain trees began to uproot, falling in every direction. Sultan pranced in an anxious dance of uncertainty beneath her. Adriana was undecided. Should they remain here in the center of the clearing as far away from the forest destruction as possible? Or should she be looking for cover?

Then, as quickly as the chaos started, the pockmarked ground under the uprooted trees began to smooth and pave itself. Adriana watched in amazement as a broad, twisting path of smooth gold appeared on her right, and a narrow path of the greenest grass she'd ever seen appeared on her left. The animal-like noises and the sounds of the violent ripping and shredding of tree roots and branches had completely subsided; now there were barely audible sounds of grass and trees and shrubs growing and changing shape before her eyes. A tinkling noise came from behind her, and she turned just in time to see polished gemstones clicking into place, creating the most beautiful road imaginable. A mosaic way of crystalline diamonds, sapphires, and emeralds glowed bright in the reflecting light.

The trees left standing along the three emerging paths changed as well. They grew taller and thicker, sprouting distinctive leaves. Along the golden path, dark trees grew clusters of silvery green leaves as a carpet of white and yellow flowers sprang from the ground and spread beneath as ground cover.

The grass path stretched into a dense wood of towering oaks, their trunks turning a burnished red as they climbed into a canopy of vibrant orange and yellow leaves.

The trees lining the gemstone path had arching branches

like weeping willows. The shimmering limbs curved in heavy abundance toward the ground, brushing a profusion of spring flowers that had appeared there. The tree limbs and leaves made a tinkling sound as a light breeze fluttered through their branches.

Three fully formed paths now led out of the clearing into the unknown. Adriana rode the circumference of the clearing on Sultan. It was impossible to see farther than a dozen stallion strides down any one of them.

She was undecided. First she'd had no path into the forest at all, now she had to choose which of the paths to take. *The Journey is all about the decisions you choose to make*, she remembered her father saying.

There was no doubt that the sheer beauty of the gemstone path drew her. Everything was a delight to her eyes and music to her ears. She was tempted to take this bejeweled path that reminded her of home, but she tried to imagine the benefits of the other two as well.

The path of gold was broad and sunny, summery-looking. She could envision the fruit trees in such a place, weighed down with delicious fruit around every bend, like the abundance of Ayrden, perhaps.

The grass path was narrow, but it was lush and coolly shaded, the most familiar on this journey of the unexpected and new.

She resolutely turned Sultan toward the prosaic path

of grass. While the history of Ayrden was replete with heirs who had accumulated great wealth on their Journeys, perhaps more likely on the path of gold or precious gems, she had Sultan to consider. He could eat the grass, and the footing would be better for him as well. Decision made, she rode out of the clearing, down the grassy path, and around the bend into the unknown.

CHAPTER 7

THE TREES OF CHEHALEM

Adriana was concerned. She had been riding through the Land of Green, as she had begun to call it, for two days, and she had seen no one and heard nothing. The only sound was the quiet padding of Sultan's hooves on the grass. As for food, she had eaten the last crumb of soda bread yesterday at last light. She had been hungry when she finally fell asleep under a tree by a spring where they had stopped to spend the night, and she was hungrier still when she awoke at first light. She talked to Sultan simply to hear some kind of noise and keep herself from worrying.

"The sun's past high light, boy. The next spring we find, we'll stop and drink. Even if it's not just like home, this Land of Green is beautiful, isn't it?"

The unrelenting silence pressed in again as they

continued down the path.

"Wait! Wait!"

Adriana whirled Sultan around to face the sound that had come from behind them, even as he shied from the unfamiliar voice. Adriana scanned the thick barrier of trees that lined the sides of the path, looking for the person who had spoken. She saw no one.

Wait, was the trunk of that tree moving? Was that a face? Adriana blinked. Maybe she was hallucinating because she was so hungry. But no, as she looked more closely, she could actually see the shape of a person in the tree trunk. There was a head and a face and arms crossed over a chest with hands clasped. But that was a tree, not a person. Wasn't it?

As Adriana watched transfixed, a lovely female face began to emerge. A bare shoulder, and then hands and arms followed as a humanesque form parted from the tree. Within moments a magnificent being stood in front of Adriana. She had been part of the tree, of that Adriana was sure. Red hair flowed in a myriad of smooth braids down the tree being's back, and her smooth face and arms were the color of stained mahogany. A soft robe the color of fall's burnt orange leaves wrapped and folded over one shoulder before it fell to the ground, covering her body.

"Thank you for stopping," the figure said in a measured, melodious voice. She took a small bow in Adriana's direction before stretching her arms and lifting them above her head. "My goodness, I'm glad you've arrived. Word came to us days ago that you had attained the clearing. Of course that didn't necessarily mean anything, as you might have never reached us." At Adriana's quizzical look, the figure continued explaining. "Because you might have chosen a different path. Or you might have changed your mind about continuing."

Adriana walked Sultan closer and reached out one hand, thinking perhaps the being would take it and kiss it, as had sometimes happened when she visited far corners of the kingdom with her father, or perhaps take it and press it between her two hands as was done among friends in Ayrden.

But the figure hastened backward. "Ah, no! You must not touch me. There is a very strict code of conduct. We mustn't touch. It would present—problems for you." Her voice was kind, but cautionary. "My apologies. I haven't even told you my name. I am Redbud, your Guide while you travel here in Chehalem."

"And I am Princess Adriana of Ayrden."

"Lovely to meet you, Princess. Welcome to Chehalem. Are you hungry?"

"Starving! I finished the last scrap of my food last night. Sultan—this is Sultan, by the way." Adriana patted his neck and continued, "He's getting by fine on the grass for now, but I don't recognize anything that is edible for me."

A smile spread across Redbud's face. "No one told you you'd need to catch your food?"

"No. But I haven't seen anything to catch. Are we fishing? Or trapping?"

Redbud's puzzled expression was followed by a shrug. "I don't know what fishing is, or trapping. But I can teach you to catch something to eat easily enough. Follow me."

With that Redbud turned and walked down the path in a smooth and elegant manner as Adriana followed on Sultan. Redbud's robe billowed behind her in shifting colors of orange and salmon. Watching her from behind, Adriana realized that Redbud must be almost ten feet tall.

She eventually glided to a stop where the path sliced between fields of flowers, barely waving in the slight breeze. "There you go, all the food you could possibly want," Redbud said as she pointed across the fields.

The flowers were unlike any Adriana had ever seen. Five feet tall with red stems, violet leaves, and green center pods, they were not particularly attractive, though they were distinctive.

"Do I pick them? What part of them do I eat?"

"No, no. I told you, you'll have to catch your food. Though it's not terribly difficult. Here, you do it like this." Redbud waded into the field, letting her hands gently run across the tops of the flowers. Pods began to gradually open, emitting a delicious yeasty smell. Round balls of vibrant blue studded with lime green nodules rose into the air like wafting smoke and floated off in the breeze. Redbud caught one and returned to Adriana, twisting the fruit in her hands so that it separated into two halves. "Here, a snack for you."

Adriana was surprised when the halves dropped like a common fruit into her hand. She thought it tasted faintly like the raisin bread that Banah baked and another of the serving maids would sometimes bring her as a breakfast treat, but the fragrance was different, more earthy and dark. Each side yielded two bites and, while welcome, they did not begin to quell her hunger.

"Your turn to give it a try," Redbud said with a lilt in her voice.

Adriana dismounted and walked to the edge of the flower field. She had been right; Redbud towered over her, almost twice her height. As Adriana waded into the flowers, attempting to mimic what she had seen Redbud do just moments before, she could barely reach the tops of the flowers, making running her hands across the pods virtually impossible. When she did finally manage to free a pod, it floated up and out of her reach before she could catch it.

"Redbud," Adriana said, turning toward her Guide, "is

this going to work for me?"

"You'll never know unless you keep trying. I told you I could teach you to catch food; I did not say it would be particularly easy."

"Well, you said it wasn't terribly difficult!" Adriana could feel her frustration growing alongside her hunger.

"Princess, it's not. It's neither particularly easy nor terribly difficult. It lies, like most things, in between, needing both a bit of ingenuity and a bit of effort."

"Perhaps if I rode Sultan through the field?"

"An interesting idea and one certainly worth trying."

Still feeling somewhat annoyed, Adriana remounted Sultan. Guiding him with her legs alone, she walked him into the field. The flowers were now a bit too low for her to reach easily, but by leaning to one side, Adriana was able to both release and catch one of the floating pods. It opened easily in her hands, and this time the flavor was totally different, sweet and crisp, almost like an apple.

"Redbud, these are amazing. They don't taste the same at all!"

"Of course not. That would be quite boring. Perhaps you could use your saddlebag to capture more than just one at a time?" Redbud called back from the edge of the field.

Adriana nudged Sultan deeper into the flowers and tried a variety of ways to release and catch the food. As the bag filled and her confidence grew, so did her amusement with the entire process. She began riding Sultan in lazy circles and serpentines through the flowers, releasing the pods as they cantered in one direction and catching them on the return.

The air was full of the yeasty fragrance and bright with blue and green floating pods when Adriana returned to Redbud. "That was fun. Would you like one?" Adriana asked as she pulled a pod from the saddlebag and bit into what tasted like nuts and fruit.

"No, but thank you very much for the offer. It's actually not necessary for me to eat while I'm away from the trees. Would you like to sit over there to eat, or would you prefer to keep going?" Redbud pointed down the road to where Adriana could see a low stone table that sat underneath a spreading tree, beside a spring of water.

"Let's sit. And perhaps you can tell me how you knew I'd reached the clearing?" Adriana asked with curiosity and warmth.

Once they were settled at the table, Redbud explained to Adriana the way of Chehalem news. Information actually passed from and through the trees. The trees that lined Chehalem saw her enter the clearing and, as the wind blew, the knowledge held in their leaves passed along to the leaves of neighboring trees as they touched in the breeze. The news of her arrival had traveled, leaf to leaf and tree to tree, more quickly than Adriana might have imagined, to where Redbud slept in her chosen tree.

"So," Redbud concluded, "I knew when you'd arrived, and I knew when you'd chosen the path into Chehalem. I was actually quite excited. It is the first time I've ever had the pleasure of being a Guide."

"So you know things just by touching leaves?"

"Yes. We actually fully know everything that we touch or that touches us. Additionally, when I am separate from the tree and in this form, I not only receive knowledge from what touches me, but I also pass knowledge to anyone I touch, tree being or human. And it's knowledge unabridged. If I touched you, then you would know everything I know, and that, as I said, would be problematic for you."

"I don't really understand why, but I appreciate your protection, I guess. Do you know what I am supposed to do here, Redbud? Do I have a mission to accomplish? I've felt a bit foolish just riding along the path not knowing where I was or what I was looking for."

Redbud tipped her head to one side and fixed her gaze on Adriana. "I have suppositions regarding what you are to accomplish here, suppositions I have deduced from what I know of you and your family and the happenings of Chehalem over the centuries, but to tell you would create false goals. What you need to accomplish depends totally upon where you choose to go and what you choose to do, within Chehalem and without."

"Interesting. You sound like my father. So now I guess I need to make a decision about whether we stay here for the remainder of the day or ride on, do I not? Well then, let's be going. I have gathered enough food for the rest of the day, and I would like to see what other surprises Chehalem holds."

CHAPTER 8

THE WOULD-BE KING

When Adriana awoke it was not yet first light and Redbud, tucked into the tree behind and above her, still slept. Adriana decided to go catch breakfast before Redbud awoke so they could make an early start. They had covered very little ground yesterday before stopping for the night.

She quietly fastened her cloak around her shoulders and pulled on her boots. Trying not to wake Redbud, she only bridled Sultan before mounting him bareback. As she rode off down the path toward the field of food, she glanced back at Redbud, her shape barely discernible in the tree.

It was not as close to first light as Adriana had supposed, and the trail remained dark as she and Sultan ambled along. Also, the field was farther than she expected, and the landmarks she had picked out yesterday were difficult to see in the gloominess. It was not until the sun cast its first warming rays on Chehalem that Adriana realized her mistake. She had ridden in the wrong direction. Before her stood a cabin she had never seen. She surveyed the weathered hovel, which looked derelict and empty. A few rough, uneven steps led to a tiny porch and a door with numerous locks and dead bolts.

Suddenly someone jerked Adriana off Sultan. She hit the ground with a thud so hard she had to struggle to fill her lungs with air once again. Her assailant, whoever it was, began dragging her by her hair and one arm across the uneven ground and up the stairs. All she could see were legs encased in filthy fabric. Her hip hit the edge of each step, sending flicks of searing pain through her body as she tried in vain to free herself.

Sultan whinnied and followed to the foot of the stairs, seeming to wait for a signal. Unfortunately, Adriana was too busy trying to fight off the person dragging her to think to give Sultan any signals at all. In a mere ten ticks Adriana found herself inside the cabin. Her attacker threw her onto the cabin floor where rough boards scratched her cheek, drawing blood. The sound of dead bolts shooting through their locks tightened the vise of fear around her throat.

Adriana jumped up and took a hand-to-hand stance,

ready to deal with her captor. But when he turned around, she was facing her father. Her hands dropped to her sides.

"You're safe now, but that was close," he said.

Upon hearing him speak, Adriana realized she had made yet another mistake. This man was most certainly not her father, but his features were eerily similar to the King's.

"Who are you?" Adriana asked.

"My name is Kelak, prince of Ayrden."

Adriana was dumbfounded. It was her father's eldest brother. It had to be. He looked much like the King, but on closer inspection Adriana could clearly see the differences. Kelak was quite pale and his hair was long and unkempt. Where her father had a ready smile and laugh lines around his mouth and eyes, Kelak wore a grimace as he squinted at Adriana through narrowed eyes, lines of suspicion etching his face. "And who are you?"

"I am Adriana, princess of Ayrden. I think I know who you are. You're my father's brother. He told me about you."

"Your father?" Kelak exploded, spittle forming at the corners of his mouth. "Dressed as you are, claiming to be who you say you are—this would mean your father returned from his Journey. That is impossible."

"No, of a truth. I am from Ayrden. The King, your brother, is my father. Just before I left on my Journey he told me about you. That you had not returned. How he waited for you at the edge of the forest day after day until he went on his own Journey. How he had looked for you while he was away but never saw you. It made him sad. I think he believes you are—I mean, I think he believed— you were . . . dead."

"I am not dead!" Kelak took a step closer to Adriana, thrusting his face close to hers.

"Well, obviously not, Uncle. I just meant that since you had not returned in all these years, it was a logical— but very sad—assumption," Adriana said, attempting to appease him, unsure how she should handle the situation. "It's been a very long time," she said in a hesitant voice. "Why are you still here?"

"Because it's safe."

Adriana looked around the small, dirty room. "Safe from what?"

Kelak looked at her as if she were the one deranged. "Safe from them!" He pointed outside, then scuttled to a grimy window and peered through it in every direction before going to the next small window to do the same.

"Safe from them who?" Adriana asked, standing still but following him with her eyes.

"The trees," he hissed. "Haven't you seen them? How long have you been here?"

"I have met Redbud, but she is not exactly a tree, she's more of a woman. And I've been here several days. Do you know how long you have been here?"

The would-be King of Ayrden sat down in the sole chair in the room, crossed his arms, and looked at Adriana haughtily. "I've been here ever since I entered the forest on my Journey. I've created a life for myself, and I've kept myself safe. Isn't that enough?"

"I don't know," Adriana said, but she hoped not. In truth, for herself, she was sure not. But she kept silent. Her uncle, the King's eldest brother, seemed dangerous, more dangerous than she ever would have expected, and more desperate, too.

Adriana stayed with Kelak all that morning, not because she wished to, but rather because each time she suggested she depart, Kelak resisted. He countered her every reason, entreating her to stay.

When Adriana suggested she should really be going now that the morning was well under way, that Redbud would be concerned about her whereabouts, Kelak replied, "If Redbud is really so all-knowing, she will certainly understand your remaining with your uncle. Why, we're just now getting acquainted. Please stay."

Adriana silently acquiesced. Redbud probably did know where she was at the moment. Whether Redbud would understand how she felt about remaining inside this cramped space with a frightening and volatile uncle, she was less sure.

In response to Adriana's next suggestion, that she should check on Sultan to make sure he had plenty of water, Kelak scoffed. "You think I would build an abode away from a spring? The loveliest spring in Chehalem is just behind us. No need to leave on that account."

And indeed, when Adriana looked out the small window at the back of the cabin, she could see the spring and Sultan standing nearby.

But it was when Adriana suggested she leave to release and catch some breakfast for the two of them that Kelak cut off all conversation of her leaving. "Enough! It is not safe to be out in Chehalem during the day. I harvest my food after last light. It's why I pulled you inside. I assure you, you were in grave danger, even more so because you were so ignorant of it. Sit down there by the fire, and we will have some breakfast."

Adriana pulled off her soft, thick cape and folded it into a square, making a cushion for herself. Placing it by the small fire, she sat down and watched as her uncle pulled pods one by one from a small saddlebag much like her own. When she saw it, she realized she had forgotten to bring hers along when she had left Redbud sleeping. What had she been thinking, slipping off alone like that? Why hadn't she waited for Redbud to awake? Why had she been so impatient to prove herself to her Guide, to show off her newfound knowledge and ability? Adriana continued to mentally castigate herself as Kelak opened the pods one at a time, laying them on the small, warped table, until he had a dozen pieces lying before him.

He paused and looked at Adriana sitting by the hearth. His eyes narrowed. Then a slow, small smile stretched across his face. To Adriana it looked uncomfortable, as if he had not smiled in a very long time.

"Where have my manners gone?" he asked. "Here, come take the chair while I go collect some springwater for us. I traditionally do that before first light as well, but I will be quick."

He moved the single chair to the table and stood behind it. "Come, come. We will eat and talk. I have not given you much of a welcome thus far. It has been far too long since I have . . . entertained." He emitted an odd, guttural sound. Whether he intended it to be a chuckle or a grunt, Adriana was not sure.

She rose from the dwindling fire and made her way slowly across the small space. She sat in the chair and Kelak pushed it gently toward the table. "I will be back in two ticks," he said as he strode across to the door and then outside.

Adriana was unsure of what to do. If she ran out the door now, she was confident she could get away. Once in the open, a snap of her fingers would bring Sultan to her and two short whistles would bring him at a full gallop. But what if Kelak was correct and Chehalem held dangers, from trees or some other source? Redbud had said nothing about that, but Redbud herself had most certainly come from a tree. And while Redbud was her Guide, perhaps there were other trees, or tree creatures, that were dangerous.

Dangerous, Adriana thought. More dangerous than her uncle? And what of her father, the King? Would he not be delighted if she not only returned but also brought his beloved and long-lost brother with her? The victorious princess leading home the prince of Ayrden long presumed dead. Before she could decide whether to go or stay, the door swung open and Kelak entered.

"Your horse is a bit skittish of people, isn't he?" Kelak asked. He carried two small pitchers made of chalkstone to the table and sat one at either end. "I need to build another chair, so when you visit again we can both sit." Kelak drank from his rounded gray pitcher and took a bite of pod. "Huh, cheese and crackers, not my favorite, but filling. You do know the pods have a variety of flavors?"

Adriana nodded and bit into a pod; it tasted of pears and honey, quite delicious. She followed the bite with a sip of water from the chalkstone pitcher sitting on the table in front of her. "Yes, my Guide showed me the field of food and taught me about the pods yesterday. Do you have a

Guide?"

"No," Kelak answered shortly. He changed the subject. "Tell me about your father, and your family," he said, his tone changing from curt to kind.

Adriana found herself distrusting the kindness in his voice, but she nonetheless replied politely, "He is well. The kingdom remains at peace, as it has been for many generations. My mother is Tallia, from the neighboring kingdom of Shevith. Do you know of it?" Just speaking of her parents made Adriana miss them, and she felt her heart begin to speed up.

"Yes." But Kelak said nothing more. He stood at the other end of the small table, watching Adriana eat.

Since Kelak seemed to be waiting for her to continue, she went on. "I am the eldest of my father's children. I turned sixteen less than seven lights ago." Adriana's mind reeled at that thought. Less than seven first lights ago, she was waking in her castle bedroom, listening to the birds sing. Less than seven first lights ago, she had awoken safe, and sure of her safety. Pushing thoughts of home aside, she continued, "I have two brothers, Alexander and Ty, and three sisters, Bess and the twins, Emma and Ella. The twins are the youngest, only three years old." Adriana waited for Kelak to say something, to steer the conversation in one direction or another, but he remained silent. "The day after my birthday ball I left before first light. What of

53

you, Uncle? How soon after your sixteenth birthday did you leave?" Adriana wiped a hand across her forehead; a fine beading of sweat dampened her temples and her heart began to gallop.

Kelak's gaze was fixated on her face. "Soon thereafter."

"So, then, you heard from the Gifters? That was a surprise to me. Not quite what I expected." Adriana felt she was speaking too slowly and her mouth tasted odd. Perhaps the chalkstone of the pitcher was overly flavoring the springwater. "What were your gifts, Uncle?"

What looked to be a genuine smile crossed Kelak's face. "Discipline and desire."

"Only two?" Adriana's throat felt constricted, and she swallowed another sip of water. "Are there not—" She wiped the back of one hand across her eyes. It was increasingly difficult for her to focus, but she completed her question, "Traditionally three?"

"Yes." Kelak's voice was light and almost melodious as he finished his sentence. "My first gift—was cunning." It was the last thing Adriana heard him say before her arms fell uselessly to her sides and her head hit the table.

CHAPTER 9

TRAPPED

Adriana opened her eyes but could see nothing. She lay on her side, head bent at an awkward angle. She could feel the soft thickness of her cloak under her bruised cheek, but she couldn't feel her arms or feet, which frightened her. Her head and body ached. She felt as if she had been trampled by one of the renowned plowing oxen of Ayrden.

She tried to move and realized she was bound hand-to-foot—her hands tied behind her back, her feet bound together and then secured to whatever was restraining her hands. She hoped her feet and arms were merely numb from the restraints. She was unable to move without excruciating pain shooting through her arched back. She fought panic. What had happened? She remembered arriving at the cabin along with first light, Kelak tossing her to the floor and locking the door, sitting by the fire watching him, eating at the table, and then—nothing. No, wait. She remembered them talking, about the Gifters. What was it he said? His gifts, what were they?

Adriana blinked her eyes in frustration, trying to see into the darkness, trying to think. Was it actually dark or had she somehow been blinded? She felt nauseated.

Nauseated, that was it! Kelak must have put some kind of potion or poison in her water. It had tasted bitter. She remembered that now. She had thought it was the chalkstone of the pitcher leaching into the water that produced the odd taste.

Fighting both nausea and panic, Adriana slowed her breathing as she had been taught by Emaht. Her fencing Teacher had explained it as a way to focus the heart and mind and hand for battle. At the moment, she could use some strength for all three, though doing battle in her current position was impossible. Her breathing slowed and deepened, her head began to clear, and her eyes began to focus. Good. She had not been blinded.

The windows were barely visible, mere squares of lighter darkness, but she could orient herself from them enough to surmise her back was to the fireplace. Was Kelak somewhere in the room? Adriana listened closely for any sound. Nothing. Her eyes strained to find his shape in the darkness. No sign of him.

Adriana let out a sigh. She must have slept through the entire day and into the night. She supposed Kelak was out gathering food. He had seemed to regard foraging at night as a mandatory discipline.

Discipline! Suddenly the conversation about the Gifters returned to Adriana in its entirety. *Discipline and desire and cunning*, she thought with disgust. The idea of a birthday banquet in her uncle's honor with the Gifters making pronouncements and guests making toasts to his well-being and success made Ayrden, for the first time in Adriana's life, seem like a foreign and perhaps unwelcome place. Could cunning really be used for the good of a kingdom? Was that even a genuine gift?

Adriana began to struggle against the ties binding her hands and feet. They held fast, and Adriana's panic was replaced by anger—anger at her predicament, at her uncle, at her folly. Why had she not left the cabin when the chance afforded itself?

She continued to strain against the thin ties cutting into her wrists, fury mounting as she pondered the uselessness of her training. At home in Ayrden, she had believed lessons in fencing and riding and morality would somehow make her Journey a success. Make it easy. She had believed in her lessons, her Teachers, her life. She would blush at her foolishness if she were not so furious. Why had Emaht even taught her fencing when she was required to leave for this Journey without a weapon? How could Prelechett have taught her a code of philosophy that encouraged love and care of one's family, when what she was going to find in Chehalem was duplicity and fraud and danger at the hands of an uncle?

But what else did she have? It was the training she had been given. It was practically all she had brought along on this Journey. And lying on the floor of this common cabin, trussed like one of Ayrden's vanquished foes of old, her training and gifts were all she had to bring to the predicament. And in fairness, Emaht's training, which she had just put into practice, had provided her with a dose of strength for heart and mind. Regardless, what was she to do now?

Before Adriana could formulate a plan, she heard noises. Several thuds on the door were followed by the screech of a rusty metal bolt sliding across its hasp. After several repetitions of thudding and screeching, Kelak opened the door and entered. His eyes searched for her in the darkness.

When Kelak saw Adriana, he said, "Ah, so you are awake. Lovely. I have not used lusweed in quite some time. You slept so long I thought it might have killed you."

He sounded unconcerned, lightly curious, as if he were recounting something as trivial as the flavor of a particular pod.

He stepped over her toward the fireplace, out of her sight. She could hear firewood dropping to the floor and scratching in the embers. The sound of first one and then another small twig catching light was audible in the silence before the soft crackling of the fire began anew.

Kelak appeared again, squatting down in front of her so he could look in her face. "So, what do you think, Princess? Should I kill you, take your horse, and continue upon my own Journey? He doesn't seem to like me much, that horse of yours, so I am not at all sure that would be such a good idea. He might do me harm. I remember tales of Ayrden's horses from the Days of War. The stable master had a clever way with the horses—trained them to deal with Ayrden's enemies on their own.

"Or I could keep you here for company. I have had no one to converse with in quite some time. What do you think of that? You seemed interesting enough yesterday while we supped." A malevolent grin spread across his face.

Oh, Wise Ones of Ayrden, Adriana thought. *He looks like he is devising a plan. What is he going to do?* She fought the urge to fight against the restraints that held her arms and legs fast. And then, as if Prelechett were in this very hovel with her, Adriana heard,

> *Serenity, in the face of danger,*
> *is strength.*

Kelak appeared to hear nothing. He continued his grinning scrutiny of her, the fingers of one hand drumming his lips.

Before Adriana could calculate what his response might be, she said, in as serene a voice as possible, "Whatever you think best, Uncle Kelak."

He stopped all movement and simply stared at her. His hands fell from his face and he stood. "I brought some food," he said shortly.

As Kelak prepared pods across the small room, Adriana wondered at what had just happened. Had she shamed him? Reminded him that they were related by blood and lineage? Whatever had happened, she was relieved. She relaxed a bit as she watched him break open three of the bright blue and green orbs. As the yeasty smell of the opened pods wafted her way, she wondered about Redbud. Where was she? And what did she know of Adriana's predicament? Had the surrounding trees reported back that she had been thrown into the cabin against her will? Was Redbud mounting a rescue? Was that part of her role as Guide? Adriana seemed to have nothing but questions.

Kelak turned and Adriana saw a knife in his hand. He scuttled toward her and Adriana tensed. She silently began to chant to herself, *Serenity is strength. Serenity is strength.* He stepped over her once again and disappeared from her view. She closed her eyes.

TRAPPED

Adriana felt the sudden letting-go of the tether that bound her feet to her hands and she moaned in pain as her back cramped with the release from the awkward position she had been in for many hours. She brought her knees to her chest, curling into herself to try to relieve the pain, willing herself not to scream.

Kelak watched her writhing on the floor for a moment before putting the knife in the small sheath on his belt and moving back to the table.

Feeling began to return to Adriana's feet and legs. The needle-sharp prickling sensation was almost as painful as the cramping in her back. Though her feet were still tied together and her hands still bound behind her, she was grateful for even this partial release. *Serenity is strength*, she repeated once more to herself before saying through teeth clenched in pain, "Thank you, Uncle Kelak."

He shrugged, his back to her as he ate his breakfast.

"Here," he said flatly, tossing a half-eaten pod in her direction. "I cannot abide the taste of this one."

Humiliated to be crawling on her belly like a beaten dog, Adriana nevertheless inched her way toward the discarded scrap of food. She ate it as best she was able without the use of her hands.

It smelled of earthy darkness and tasted like raisin bread. It was the first food that Redbud had given Adriana when she was free and had a world of discovery in front of her. It had reminded her then, as it did now, of the bread the serving maids would sometimes bring her as a special treat, freshly baked by Banah. Of a truth, it reminded her of home.

She finished the scrap of pod and turned her face away from Kelak, hiding the warm, salty tears that crept down her cheeks.

CHAPTER 10

GIFTED WITH KINDNESS

Thus began a weary series of long days and nights of captivity for Adriana. Each day was much the same. When Kelak left to forage in the darkness, Adriana would sleep by the dwindling fire. He always left her bound hand-to-foot, though never as tightly as that first night. When he returned, most often arriving well before first light, he would eat. After he finished, he would give Adriana a bite or two.

Twice each day, before first light and when last light had passed, he would take her outside to relieve herself. But he was never farther than an arm's length away, and always he stood ready with the small knife drawn. It was on those trips outside, always in darkness, always in silence, that Adriana, with her hands free but her legs hobbled like an unschooled donkey, would search for Sultan and any sign of Redbud.

She often spotted Sultan standing statue-still on the other side of the spring, the moonlight and starshine reflecting off his black coat, somehow still clean and glossy. But Redbud, Adriana never saw. Whether that was because Redbud's form was hidden in one of the trees surrounding the spring and therefore invisible in the darkness, or because she was in truth absent, Adriana was not sure.

All through the light hours, while Kelak slept, Adriana planned ways of escape, but the reality of the situation made each of her plans impossible to implement. Eventually she settled on a tactic that stemmed from a proverb of Ayrden:

Civility calms an angry heart,

and kindness breaks the heart of stone.

Her ability to fight or run was limited by the restraints Kelak constantly kept on her and by the knife he kept handy. All her freedom was contained in her mind and attitude. But the Gifters had graced her with kindness. Surely she could bring Kelak to reason and win him over through this gift of hers, she thought, so that he would soon release her.

Therefore, Adriana was ever polite. She offered a thank-you for each small morsel of food he deigned to share with her, a pleasant word each time they returned from outside. Each time he released her hands, for even a short period, she made sure to do a kindness. She picked a flower for him or straightened his chair. Always, she was cheerful and pleasant. Kelak did not deserve such treatment, but it made Adriana feel more like herself as she daily found opportunities to hone her gift of kindness, even in such distressing circumstances.

Over time, a great deal of time, it worked. Adriana gained some small freedoms. Kelak took the hand restraints off her while he was awake and they were inside the cabin. He included Adriana at the table, eventually even building a chair for her, and shared his meals with her, though the portions he gave her remained meager.

Over these meals, Kelak shared fragments of his Journey story with her, which Adriana pieced together over time. His Journey had begun much later in his sixteenth year than hers, and more easily as well. His path into Chehalem was straightforward. There had been no closed forest, no clearing, no choice of path to take. He had ridden from the kingdom grounds straight into the green land of Chehalem. He had ridden and ridden and ridden, meeting no one. When he had long exhausted his one day's provision and could take the hunger no longer, he took a chance on a benign-looking berry growing along the path. Unfortunately, it had been the fruit of the lusweed. When he awoke from his accidental and self-inflicted poisoning, his horse was gone. He wandered on foot until he found a spring, where he built his first crude shelter. He never explained how he learned of the field of food and the edible pods.

On a morning when Kelak was particularly talkative, he gave a disjointed account of numerous attacks by the trees, but it seemed to Adriana there were significant omissions. As usual, when she attempted to draw out more details, Kelak became evasive.

Their conversations, however, were not limited to Kelak and his experiences on his Journey. He was very interested in Ayrden and his family, what had become of them, and who held which positions in the kingdom.

"Tell me, Princess," Kelak asked one day over their morning meal, "is Beecher still stable master of Ayrden?"

"He is. He taught me to ride. In truth, he has taught each of my brothers and sisters to ride as well, though that only took a day or so for my brother Alexander." Adriana paused. While she was committed to her strategy of kindness and civility, she loathed giving Kelak too much information. She feared he would put his cunning to work and use it against her in some way.

In order to forestall his probing further about Alexander, she asked, "Was Beecher stable master when you left on your Journey?"

"Yes, he had just taken over from his father. He was barely older than I, but he was quick to please my mother, the Queen, and he was a decent horse trainer. I presumed he would prosper. And what of the other Teachers? Who taught you fencing?"

"Emaht."

"I don't recognize that name. Is he the son of Turr?"

"No. But Turr was my earliest fencing Teacher. Did he teach you as well?" Adriana tried once again to direct the conversation toward gaining information while giving away as little as possible.

"Yes, but tell me about this Emaht," Kelak commanded, gesturing in an imperious manner.

"He is ten years my senior, married to Sarian. They were expecting their first child to be born soon after I left on my Journey." Adriana paused, forcing her mind away from what she was missing at home.

"Enough of his family information," Kelak scoffed. "What of his skill?"

"It is phenomenal. He came from the Kingdom of Shevith. He was an orphan, reared by the fencing master there. My mother sent for him once Turr grew weary of giving lessons. Emaht won the title over several other contenders. No one in all the kingdom has ever beaten him with a sword of any kind, be it foil or broadsword."

"Interesting."

Before Kelak could ask more questions, Adrianna asked, "Did you have a favorite skill, Uncle? Fencing, hand-to-hand, horses?"

A CLEARING IN THE FOREST

"I was accomplished in all my lessons, but fencing was my strongest. It's unfortunate I must keep you in restraints—I could enjoy fencing again."

Adriana felt a sense of relief. While in Ayrden all competitions were fought to victory without bloodshed, she had a feeling of dread that Kelak might be prone to fight to the death.

Whether it was cunning or mere desire for conversation, Kelak also spent considerable time telling stories about his childhood in the kingdom. It was the telling of these stories that brought confusion to Adriana regarding her feelings toward her uncle.

Back home in Ayrden, the day before her sixteenth birthday, her father had said, "We were playmates and rivals, best friends and vigorous competitors," with love and longing in his voice. The stories Kelak told brought to life the words her father used to describe the relationship between them.

Kelak told of competing against her father in all they did: riding, fencing, swimming, even eating. One amusing anecdote he told and retold was of her father's horse balking at a last jump as the two boys raced their horses across the fields and streams of Ayrden. Her father landed face-first in the mud. Kelak passed him with a clean jump over the same fence and a raucous cheer. A swim in the lake had followed. In retaliation, her father had climbed out of the lake first, dressed quickly, and, before Kelak realized what was happening, took all of Kelak's garments but his underclothes. Telling of his long and breezy ride back to the stables made Kelak laugh, and his face reminded her more and more of her father's with each retelling of the story.

The stories made her wish for the landmarks of her home and family, but more, they made her desire to somehow bring Kelak back to her father, to the brother who had loved him so much. It was that tension of wanting to escape from Kelak and yet also wanting to return with him to Ayrden that caused Adriana confusion when she thought about her escape and departure from Kelak's rough cabin. For although Adriana had no idea how it would be accomplished, she was convinced she would escape and resume her Journey. That belief was bolstered on the first day Kelak freed her from the foot-to-hand restraints while he slept and she had her first sighting of Redbud.

CHAPTER 11

AN ALLY BEARING LEAVES

On a morning when Kelak was particularly gregarious, he paused as he refastened Adriana's hand restraints after their early morning meal.

"I think I will not bind you hand-to-foot today," he said to Adriana as he finished tying her hands behind her back. "Can I trust you?"

Adriana thought of the pleasure of not being bound in the uncomfortable position and smiled. "Of course you can trust me, Uncle. Thank you so very much."

"Fine, just the feet and hand restraints then." Kelak checked the metal shackles around her feet, ensuring they were secure. "But I'll sleep in front of the door. And the windows, even if you did somehow manage to get free, are too small for you to escape, I believe." Kelak looked Adriana up and down. Though her slim body had grown ever thinner from the meager portions of food, he was right, the windows were still too small to be useful.

Kelak stirred up the fire, wrapped himself in his cloak, moved his pallet to the door, and lay down to sleep. Adriana sat by the fire and waited.

Once she was sure Kelak was asleep, she inched her way quietly to the window. There, finally able to see outside during the light hours, she glimpsed Redbud standing near Sultan on the far side of the spring. She seemed to be looking toward the cabin, so Adriana moved about in front of the grimy window as much as she dared with Kelak sleeping across the room, attempting to draw Redbud's attention. Kelak made a rustling noise in his sleep. Adriana froze in front of the window and Redbud turned away. As soon as Kelak was sleeping quietly again, Adriana once more began moving in front of the window, first swaying and then bobbing up and down, careful to keep her feet as still as possible to prevent the rough boards from squeaking under her feet or the metal shackles from clinking together.

But Redbud had disappeared. Sultan stood alone by the spring. Adriana was dismayed. Had Redbud not seen her after all? Did Redbud not know she was a prisoner in this shack? Why was Redbud not doing something?

Adriana again heard a rustling noise behind her, and she turned with dread toward the door where her uncle slept. But the noise was not coming from an awakening

Kelak. Rather, a small hairless animal was pushing its way in through a crack between the wall and the door.

The creature resembled a mouse, or perhaps a squirrel, with large, bulging eyes, its pink skin hairless and wrinkled. A long, whiplike tail was revealed as the small animal pulled itself completely inside the cabin. Adriana drew back, not at all sure how to respond. Other than Sultan, it was the first sign of animal life she had seen around the cabin, much less inside it.

The small creature soundlessly skirted Kelak as he slept and dropped a bright green leaf at Adriana's feet. Standing on its back legs before Adriana, it gazed up at her with its bulging eyes, picked up the leaf, and dropped it once more at her feet before scampering quietly across the floor and disappearing through the same small crack through which it had entered.

Adriana was confused. She squatted down to inspect the leaf. It appeared to be simply that, a broad green leaf. She knelt, without making a noise, in order to inspect it more closely. Nothing but a leaf. With her hands tethered behind her, Adriana could not turn the leaf over with her hands, so she used her mouth and tongue to flip the leaf to its other side. Nothing but a leaf. She sighed. She remembered what her Guide had told her about the way the trees passed news through the forest. Was Redbud trying to send her a message? If so, it was not working.

AN ALLY BEARING LEAVES

Adriana wasn't able to gain knowledge through touch alone like Redbud and the trees. Could Redbud write? How else was Adriana ever to know what was going on outside these four rough walls?

She returned to the window. Redbud was once again standing on the far side of the spring. Adriana shook her head back and forth, trying to indicate her lack of understanding. Redbud again disappeared from view.

Over and over throughout the day, as Kelak slept, the small creature quietly wormed its way through the narrow opening and dropped leaf after leaf at Adriana's feet. There were broad leaves, thin, narrow leaves, tiny, prickly leaves, glossy leaves, and finally one so large the little creature entered first and pulled the leaf in behind him through the crack by the door. At each new leaf's arrival, Adriana did the same thing. She inspected it and turned it over to see if anything was written on it. She made sure to touch it, in case she was somehow able to receive information like the trees, but to no avail.

Adriana was frustrated but hopeful. She finally felt as if she had an ally. However, as last light approached, she also grew frightened. The pile of leaves by the window where she had been standing all day had grown quite noticeable. What would Kelak say when he awoke? Would he be suspicious and return her to the foot-to-hand restraint? Her jaw clenched and her back cramped at the thought.

Then, just as Kelak began stirring, Adriana thought to grab her cloak and drop it over the leaves. With her hands tied behind her it was difficult to tell if she had managed to cover the leaves, so she quickly sat down on the cloak, leaned her back against the wall under the window, and closed her eyes. When Kelak arose he seemed to notice nothing unusual.

He replaced the foot-to-hand restraints before he left for the night, so Adriana painstakingly blew the leaves across the floor and into the fire once he had departed. There, the leaves dried and withered in silence before finally curling in upon themselves and disintegrating into nothing but smoke. By the time Kelak returned from foraging, Adriana had eliminated all evidence, but she was bone weary.

Hoping for another daytime reprieve from the foot-to-hand restraints, Adriana attempted to engage Kelak in even more conversation than usual once they were both settled at the small table with the food pods before them.

"Uncle Kelak, is there ever a season when you cannot harvest the pods?"

Kelak pulled back slightly and looked at her across the small table before answering. "No. Haven't you noticed there are no seasons here in Chehalem?"

"Actually, I had not." Adriana's mouth filled with the chalky taste of dread. She had not realized it until that moment, but she had been lulling herself into a sense of complacency regarding the passage of time. She had rationalized that as long as it was still summer, surely not too many moon cycles were passing. She thought of Alexander and her promise to return Sultan before he left on his own Journey. She could feel her complacency being replaced by urgency, but she could think of nothing else to do in this moment but continue with her plan to promote conversation.

"That's very good for you then . . . that you . . . I mean, we, don't have to worry about storing food for the bare months. What were your favorite foods when you were in Ayrden?"

"Everything. I was only sixteen when I left; I was always hungry. Breakfast was my favorite, I suppose. All the platters of meats and cheeses and breads. Particularly the bread. The abundance is what I miss." Kelak sounded wistful.

"It's not too late to return, Uncle," Adriana said. Her newfound sense of urgency made her press the point, although she could see his eyes narrow in a way that normally would have caused her to pause. "We could join together. I imagine it would be much safer if we attempted our Journeys that way. Though so little is known about the histories of the Journeys. I have never heard of two heirs attempting their Journeys together. Perhaps we could be the first. We could both ride Sultan—he's strong enough. And who knows what we might discover? We could return to Ayrden as victors."

Adriana knew she was saying too much, pressing too hard, but she was still surprised when Kelak exploded in violent anger. Turning over the table in one swift motion and throwing his chair across the room where it broke against the stone of the fireplace, he screamed, "Be silent! I have no intention of continuing! I have no reason to return! Do you understand me? Be silent!"

Kelak grabbed Adriana by the arm, jerked her to her feet, and refastened all the restraints, tightening the rope connecting her feet and hands so severely she almost cried out.

Once Kelak had finished he leaned down, drawing so close to her she could hardly focus on his face. "You are proving to be a good deal of trouble to me, Princess. And I am no longer so amused by you. Take care if you value your life."

Within minutes the cabin was quiet and Kelak was on his pallet across the room. Even after he fell asleep he was restless and Adriana was afraid to move, lest she make a noise and rouse him.

She had been weary before he arrived back from foraging; now she was exhausted and depleted. However, while in days past she might have wanted to weep from weariness and frustration at her foolishness, a core of resolve and confidence was building inside her. Redbud knew she was here. Sultan was close by. She had tried kindness and civility and patience. It was time for a different tactic.

CHAPTER 12

FEATHERS AND BEES

While Kelak slept, Adriana reviewed her situation. She started with the day she turned sixteen, searching for some spark of inspiration that would show her the way of escape. During the banquet to celebrate her coming-of-age, the Gifters had said, "We gave you courage and fidelity and kindness. They were ours to give and we gave them freely to you." Well, she had tried kindness, to no avail.

What else had they said? Adriana recalled the Gifters' concluding warning: "But be forewarned, your greatest strengths can hinder you more than your weaknesses."

With a sigh Adriana acknowledged to herself the truth of that proclamation. A foolish dose of courage had landed her in Kelak's grasp to begin with, when she'd headed off on her own before Redbud awoke. And it was courage, again bordering on recklessness, that had made her press

Kelak to join with her and continue on his Journey.

Her fidelity, first to her father and then in some odd way to Kelak himself, had kept her here far too long. And while kindness had worked to improve her situation, as she lay on the floor, bound as tightly as she had ever been, she accepted that kindness was not going to lead to freedom.

Thinking back on the banquet and the Gifters' final proclamation, "You must marshal your gifts for the good," Adriana wondered how exactly she was to do that. Then with sudden clarity it struck her, as she lay helpless and humiliated on the floor of the meager cabin, that marshaling her gifts for the good meant for the good of the Kingdom of Ayrden. Not for the good of her father or herself or any one individual, but for the good of the entire kingdom.

Taking Kelak back with her could be the very worst thing for the people of Ayrden. If Kelak returned, he would have successfully completed the only necessary element to rule—he would have returned from his Journey. He would be the eldest and the rightful ruler of all the kingdom, would he not? Her father would no longer be King. And although under her father's rule all his siblings who had returned from their Journeys had authority over various regions, this was not a binding rule of Ayrden. Indeed, if Kelak returned and was made King, he could dictate anything he chose. The thought horrified Adriana.

She desperately needed to escape and escape alone. And as soon as possible.

She turned her cheek restlessly against her cloak. While her clothes were filthy and stank of the sweat of fear and her unwashed body, the cloak, which she rarely wore outside, retained its plush softness and rich green color. She thought of what other strengths she might bring to her quest to escape.

She was very good at hand-to-hand, or at least she had been. She looked at her arms, awkwardly cinched behind her back, and grimaced with disgust. She was probably as weak as a newborn foal and her limbs just as spindly, given the lengthy days of bondage she had endured. But, and she smiled as she thought of this, her ability in hand-to-hand had never been about strength.

Her tutor, Shenak, had sized her up at their first lesson, the day after she turned five, and developed his strategy for her. "Ye will neigh be big and brawny, Princess," he had said in his thick Northern Kingdom drawl. Eyeing her small stature and fine bones, he asked doubtfully, "Are ye quick?" He stuck his meaty hand out toward her, palm up, obviously waiting for her to slap it with her own small hand.

As Adriana had looked up into his face, she began, "Well, I"—and then,— while he was still looking into her green eyes waiting for her next words, she brought her hand up, then down, in one fluid motion to squarely slap his palm—"think so."

Shenak had been delighted, and from that time on he had tailored all of Adriana's hand-to-hand classes around her agility, speed, and ability to surprise her opponents. While Adriana pondered how she might best use these skills to escape, she noticed for the first time a faint crinkling noise as she moved her face over the cloak. She rubbed her cheek a little harder against its softness, listening closely. There it was again, in the corner of her cloak. She assumed one of the leaves, diligently brought to her the day before by the small and unusual creature, had gotten caught in the seam.

And then, as if her very thoughts had summoned him, the little creature once again squeezed into the cabin through the crack by the door. Once inside he stood upright, his long tail whipping around behind him as he surveyed first Kelak, asleep across the room, and then Adriana, prostrate and bound. He scampered across the floor toward Adriana, his sharp pink nails making just the tiniest of clicking sounds.

When he stopped and squatted back on his hind feet, Adriana had to actually look up slightly to see what he held in his mouth. This time, instead of a leaf, he clenched a bright indigo bird's feather between his sharp, pointed teeth. The hairless creature leaned in toward Adriana and brushed her face with the feather. It was soft and smelled

81

oddly of oranges but conveyed nothing else. Adriana shook her head once the animal pulled back to look at her.

Dropping the feather and leaving it behind, he scampered off across the floor and out the crack by the door. Just in case her little ally continued to bring feathers, as he had done leaves the day before, Adriana used her nose and mouth and chin to push the feather under her cloak, noticing once again the odd crinkling sound. Over and over through the light hours, while Kelak slept, the sharp little nose and the bulging eyes would appear at the crack and another type of feather would be hauled inside. Small feathers of bright blue and red and orange were followed by larger feathers of more muted colors. By high light, Adriana gave up hoping any of them would be able to convey a message. Having slept so little over the past day, she closed her eyes and gave herself over to sleep.

She soon drifted into a dream where she was a bird, with mottled feathers of blue and orange and green covering her wings. In flight, she rose higher and higher, first flying over the weather-beaten cabin and then circling the field of food before flying along the path she had ridden into Chehalem. But just as she was about to reach the clearing, she stalled. Her bird wings turned into spindly arms uselessly flailing the air and she began to fall, faster and faster.

Adriana jerked awake, piercing her cheek on a large gray-

and-black-striped feather that her little ally was holding in front of her face. She stifled a cry, more surprised than pained. And then it happened.

She could see Redbud's face as clearly as if she were standing right in front of Adriana. It was as if Adriana were a large gray-and-white bird, perched on Redbud's arm. Redbud's eyes were focused and intent and her mouth moved, but Adriana could hear no words, make out no sound. The image faded, but for the next few breaths, with every beat of her heart, the image reappeared.

Adriana's face must have conveyed her amazement and excitement, for the little creature began to leap around in circles, landing with a click of toenails and a quiet thud, as he spun first in one direction and then in another. Across the room Kelak stirred. Adriana and the little creature froze in place until Kelak stopped moving and the sounds of his sleep-heavy breathing filled the room once again.

For the first time, Adriana nodded her head and smiled. Her little ally cocked his head. Adriana lifted up the corner of the cloak with her teeth to show the pile of feathers below. Sitting up on his back legs, her helper looked quizzical, cocking his head first in one direction and then the other as his two eyes, one green and the other blue, looked from Adriana's face to the pile of feathers beneath the cloak.

Fearing to speak, and doubtful the animal would

understand her anyway, Adriana tried to mimic picking up a feather and using the sharp end to prick her skin again. Perhaps another of the feathers would give voice to Redbud. Surely that was what the leaves yesterday and these feathers today were all about. Redbud was trying to send her a message.

Adriana grew increasingly excited as she thought of the possibilities. Redbud might be explaining how Adriana could free herself from the restraints, or how she could overwhelm Kelak and escape, or perhaps Redbud was mounting a rescue and wanted to give Adriana the details.

She picked up a feather with her mouth and mimicked jabbing it. Still the creature looked confused. Pushing the cloak farther away, Adriana tried—and failed—to position one of the pointy ends of the feathers so that it pierced her skin. However, it was enough to get the idea across to her willing little helper.

The small animal burrowed under Adriana's chin. His hairless body felt surprisingly human, while his nose had the cold, wet feel of a cat's. He pulled out the first indigo blue feather he had brought in that day and jabbed the pointed end in the direction of Adriana's face. It hit her neck, barely making a scratch. But within three ticks Adriana could see Redbud's face, upon which the rays of first light were shining. Again Redbud's lips moved, which Adriana could see clearly, but there was no sound to be heard.

Adriana's face must have conveyed disappointment because the little creature pulled another feather out, this one a long, broad, white feather. With a quick jab the feather pierced the skin behind Adriana's ear, and she saw with startling clarity Redbud's face. Again Redbud was serious, intent on relaying some message, but again, no sound could be heard. Redbud's face appeared and reappeared with every beat of Adriana's heart for quite some time before finally fading away.

Adriana's little ally chose another feather, apparently eager to do it all over again, but Adriana shook her head. It was obvious the feathers could convey an image, but it was not enough. Adriana was encouraged but unwilling to continue the experiment. Clearly visible scratches and punctures might make Kelak suspicious, and Adriana wanted to avoid that at all costs.

The small creature pulled out a variety of feathers, but each time Adriana shook her head. He finally stopped and stared at her. Then, finding the striped feather that had first given face to Redbud, and picking it up in his mouth with his pointed yellowed teeth, the animal left Adriana where she lay on the floor and slipped out of the cabin once again.

Adriana pulled her cloak back over the pile of feathers, rested her cheek on the softness, and wondered what her next move should be. As she waited for Kelak to awake, waited for her little ally to return, waited for a plan to make itself evident to her, she drifted back into sleep.

Buzzing bees worked their way into Adriana's dream. She was small and young, only three, perhaps, and her mother, the Queen, was saying in a hushed voice, "Dearest, move slowly and quietly. You want to be careful not to startle them. Their sting is quite painful and they are easily incited to strike."

It was a memory being replayed inside her dream world. She and her mother were walking hand in hand on their way to the first supper of spring, which had been laid out under the early flowering trees of the South Garden, and they had just happened upon a fallen bees' nest. Hundreds of bees were angrily circling around the trunk of a nearby tree and the ground underneath. The Queen's dress, as pink and bright as any flower, drew the bees' attention and Adriana watched and listened, fascinated by their small striped bodies and their loud buzz as they swarmed over the pair of them. The Queen and Adriana backed away and were almost clear of the colony when Adriana was stung. Heeding her mother's injunction, she made not a sound, though the needle-sharp stinger remained in her arm, and the bee's poison as it traveled through her blood caused the welt to throb with pain.

It was not until they were completely clear of the swarm that the Queen realized Adriana had been stung. Arriving at the South Garden, she called at once for the Healers, who removed the stinger and applied a poultice to stop the pain. But Adriana had remained forever wary of bees of any kind.

The buzzing continued, swarming and incessant, intruding on her dream until she awoke. Opening her eyes Adriana saw a bee, larger and more vibrantly hued than any she had ever seen, buzzing around her head. It circled, looking ready to strike. Bound, Adriana could do nothing. She shut her eyes and waited for the sting.

The bee landed on her cheek, and Adriana braced herself for the pain she knew was coming. She felt the plunge of the stinger right beside her left eye.

But instead of pain, a feeling of liquid warmth ran through her, coursing through her body with every beat of her heart. Then, floating right in front of her face, she saw a vision of Redbud. Her earnest brown eyes and clear mahogany skin shone. She was speaking with earnest solemnity.

And Adriana could hear every word.

CHAPTER 13

CALCULATED COURAGE

Princess Adriana, I am so relieved you are alive. I had almost begun to believe you were not," Redbud said with intensity. "Listen carefully to me. As your Guide I cannot rescue you. As much as I wish to do so, it is simply not permitted by the laws of Chehalem."

Disappointment welled up in Adriana's throat. What was going to happen to her, then? If Redbud couldn't rescue her, then how was she to escape, bound as she was, weak as she was?

Redbud continued, her voice pulsing through Adriana. "I can, however, assist you in your efforts and will most certainly guide you on your way once you have escaped. Plan for your escape to take place during the cycle of light. Your uncle dares not go abroad then. And I cannot separate from the trees during the cycle of darkness. Sultan never wanders. He is at the ready. I wait each evening in the tree where we first supped, beside the stone table. If you can make it there by first light, then we will be . . ." Redbud's voice became indistinct, though Adriana could see her lips continuing to move as she relayed her message.

With the very next beat of Adriana's heart, bits of what she had already heard began resounding once again through her body. "Plan for your escape . . . the cycle of light . . . at the ready . . . the tree where we first . . . table. If you can . . . light then we will be . . ."

Adriana could have screamed with frustration. *If I can get there by first light, then what? We will be what? Safe? Prepared?* Bits and pieces of Redbud's message continued to replay in her mind for quite some time until both the voice and the image faded away. But Adriana could glean no additional information.

The bee, forgotten by Adriana until she heard it buzzing once again, landed in front of her on the floor. Perhaps a second sting by the bee would enable her to hear the remainder of the message. She looked at the brightly striped yellow-and-red bee with hope. But it rose on its iridescent wings and disappeared through the narrow opening by the door.

Adriana sighed. From her position on the floor she noticed that last light was approaching. The urgency of

A CLEARING IN THE FOREST

Redbud's message was contagious. Adriana did not yet have a plan, but it was obvious to her that she needed to develop one so she could be ready to escape as soon as an opportunity presented itself.

When Kelak awoke, Adriana watched everything he did, searching for a way of escape. As always, Kelak first went from window to window to peer outside. He opened a few pods, occasionally using his small knife before sheathing it alongside his belt, and placed the pods on the table before releasing Adriana from the hand-to-foot restraints and the tether binding her hands. He mentioned nothing of his fury from the night before, even when he moved the sole chair around to his place at the table. Adriana ate standing.

She was glad to be on her feet. It made her feel primed to seize whatever opportunity might come her way. Kelak finally stood and prepared to take Adriana outside to relieve herself. Then, as he always did, just before he unbolted the door, he turned to Adriana and said, "Remember, silence while we are outside." He pulled out the knife, pushed open the door, and let Adriana shuffle out in front of him toward the spring.

Adriana's senses were on high alert. She could see Sultan, standing as always across the spring. She assessed how long it would take for him to reach her if she gave a double whistle, which would bring him to her at a gallop. Too long for her to be safe from Kelak and his knife, she decided.

Noting the uneven footing around the spring, Adriana realized she could probably knock Kelak off his feet using only surprise and a well-timed blow, but with the shackles on her feet she could neither run nor ride. And while the darkness might give her brief cover, it would also give Kelak far too much time to find her. As Redbud had suggested, any attack would need to take place after Kelak returned from foraging.

As they reentered the cabin, Adriana gazed with longing down the path that led toward Redbud. Kelak bound Adriana once again and stirred up the fire. She was listening to the crackle of the fresh twigs hitting the glowing embers when an idea for escape came fully formed into her mind. Of course, the fire!

Kelak checked all the restraints before slipping out the door with his saddlebag slung across his chest, his knife nestled alongside his belt. From her position on the floor, Adriana closed her eyes and strained to capture every sound he made as he left. One, two, three, four bolts were shot home from the outside. The door creaked as Kelak pushed against it in order to line up the rough-hewn door for the last metal latch to slide into its place against the rusty hasp. Adriana could hear two footfalls as Kelak crossed the small porch, then three as he walked down the uneven steps.

Adriana counted her breaths, playing out her plan in

her mind, giving Kelak time to be out of earshot before she put it into action. When she was convinced he was well along the path, Adriana slid backward toward the fire.

Her plan was to first burn the hand-to-foot tether. Without catching herself on fire. Her first attempt resulted in burning a hole through her breeches and her second in singeing the back of her hands. But on her third attempt the acrid smell of burning was not accompanied by searing pain. She was hopeful that what was burning was the rope. Adriana continued to rock back and forth, in and out of the fire as best she was able, all the while pulling against the rope with her hands and feet. Her back grew hotter and hotter, and just as she knew she could not bear much more, she felt the first give in the rope.

"Yes!" she exclaimed, forcing herself to endure the heat of the fire a few ticks longer. Finally she rocked away, rolling quickly to her other side, trying to arch her back away from her tunic, grown painfully hot. She pulled until her hands were raw and her feet were bruised, even through her soft boots, but the rope held.

It was time to marshal every bit of strength she had. She rolled back to the fire and began again.

Finally, the binding rope gave way. Adriana was free from the worst of her restraints. The success renewed her fervor, and she assessed the best way to burn off the leather strap that bound her hands together. She thought with longing of the thick iron pokers that stood beside each hearth in Ayrden. That would have worked well and also served as a weapon, but Kelak had nothing like that in his cabin.

Adriana clenched her eyes shut. *Think!* For this plan to work, she had to be free of her hand restraints before Kelak returned. She calmed herself by breathing as Emaht had taught her. Then she began cataloging her various classes and Teachers, searching for a way to free her hands. The leather binding her hands made her think of riding: stirrup leathers and leather reins and the farrier's leather apron. Wait—the farrier's leather apron.

A memory of watching Beecher instructing a farrier's apprentice rose to the surface of her mind. Why would she be thinking of that? The burn in his leather apron, of course, that was it.

The apprentice had a habit of letting the horseshoe, molten red from the fire, touch his apron in the same spot just before he placed the semicircle of lead on the anvil to hammer it into shape. Beecher had corrected him: "Go straight from the fire to the anvil. Ye'll not be burning through that apron the first time or two, but ye'll be scarring your leg for life when you do. And rest assured it will burn through. Not even leather can resist the heat of the fire forever."

Adriana looked down and eyed her leg chains. Did she

93

have time to heat her leg shackles and burn through the strap tying her wrists together? A quick glance out the window showed nothing but deepest darkness. She had nothing to lose and freedom to gain.

Getting on her knees, she backed her legs into the fire, keeping her boots up and away from the flames even as she let the center of the metal shackles rest in the hottest part of the fire. When the center links were glowing red and the brackets around her feet were uncomfortably warm, she lay on her stomach and with some trepidation brought her feet up so the chain could touch the tether binding her hands. She managed to avoid touching the burning hot shackles, but she could feel the heat. More importantly, she could smell the pungent burning of the leather. It took a dozen trips into the fire before the leather gave way and she was able to break her hands free.

She looked at what remained of the leather roping. The pieces were too short and weak to be useful, she decided, and she tossed them into the fire before realizing the smell might attract Kelak's attention when he returned. But the leather was already smoking. She hoped Kelak would not take notice as he approached the cabin. Glancing out the window, Adriana could tell the darkest part of night had passed.

The now-cold metal of her last remaining restraint dragging on the floor, Adriana walked close enough to press her face to the window and search for Sultan in the darkness. Once she saw the gleam of his flank in the dim glow of the crescent moon, she gave two short whistles.

As if he had been waiting for just that signal, Sultan bounded through the spring at a full gallop before pulling up at the window, where he stood nose-to-nose with Adriana. Only the dirty glass separated them.

"Good boy," Adriana said with a catch in her voice. "As soon as Kelak arrives back, we are leaving. I need you to be ready."

Adriana walked over to the table and poured a chalkstone goblet of springwater that she drank down in one swallow. All the exertion by the fire had made her thirsty, and hungry as well, but there was no food in the cabin. She drank another goblet of water.

Pulling her cloak around her shoulders, she stationed herself by the door. The cabin was dim, though not dark. She had kept the fire burning as hot as possible, and it was still flaming brightly.

She thought her plan elegantly simple. As soon as Kelak stepped into the cabin, Adriana was going to move behind him, throw him to the floor, get out the door as quickly as possible, and lock it from the outside. Surely that would work. It had to work.

Adriana thought of spreading out the fire to dim the cabin further and better conceal herself. But, concerned Kelak might return before she could reposition herself by the door, she stood fast, waiting, going through her plan in her mind. She pushed aside all the questions of doubt that swirled just outside her focus. She smiled as she remembered Prelechett's comments on focus, one of her favorite lessons:

> FOCUS: First
> Only
> Commit
> Unwavering
> Sole

In this situation, the *first* thing necessary for escape was to take Kelak by surprise. The *only* thing necessary for success was to escape. She was *committed* to this plan. There was no going back. The time for escape was now. Regardless of what happened once the plan was put in motion, she would be *unwavering* in her attempt to escape. Escape was the *sole* occupation of Adriana's mind.

Adriana was so intent on her plan, she heard Kelak's footfalls on the hard-packed ground before he even reached the first step. She counted his steps on the stairs: three. Counted his steps on the porch: two. Counted the bolts sliding free: four. Heard the door shift as Kelak pressed against it, and then the last bolt screeched free and slid across its rusty fastening.

The door swung open.

And Kelak strode inside.

CHAPTER 14

PAKTOS

Adriana was shocked by how fast Kelak came into the cabin. He must have suspected something was amiss. Perhaps he had smelled the burning leather. She stepped behind him to the door, unlocked and standing open. He was out of arm's reach, so she could not take him to the ground. *Fine, change of plan*, she decided quickly. She would merely escape and lock the door.

But at her movement, the drag of the metal chain across the floor alerted Kelak to her position. He whirled around, grabbing for her as Adriana leaped for the door. He managed only to grasp a handful of her cloak. She spun around, ducking under the cloak and toward him. From this position there was just enough slack in the chain for her to kick Kelak behind his knee. As he fell back, she rose up and threw her elbow into his throat.

He went down with a thud, holding her cloak all the tighter. Adriana tried but was not able to unfasten it from around her neck, so she grabbed it with both hands, trying to pull it from Kelak's grasp to free herself.

As Adriana strained toward the door with her body and pulled with all her strength, the bottom hem tore away in Kelak's hands. The sudden loosening of tension caused Adriana to tumble backward across the floor. She jumped to her feet, adrenaline pouring through her body, and backed toward the door. Knees bent, poised for hand-to-hand, she was ready to deflect the knife she assumed Kelak would have drawn.

Instead, he held a creased and crumpled piece of parchment. He looked from it to Adriana with a stricken look on his face. "What is this? Why was this in your cloak? Who put it there? I said, 'Who put it there?' Answer me!"

Adriana had not an inkling as to where the parchment had come from or what might be written on it. But she took his bewilderment as her opportunity to back out the door and slam it closed. She barely managed to get the first bolt shot home when Kelak's shoulder hit the door.

He was coming after her.

As she shoved frantically at first one bolt then another, Adriana gave two short whistles. She immediately heard Sultan approaching from the back of the cabin. Kelak continued to batter against the door as she slid one more bolt into place.

Would Kelak break through the door before she was able to even get out of the clearing? She'd been able to fasten the first bolt securely, but the other two she latched were barely inside their brackets. Adriana hoped the door would hold fast until first light, when Kelak would not dare to leave. That was all the time she needed. She hoped.

Adriana jumped over the three steps. She threw her arms around Sultan's neck for the briefest moment before crossing the clearing with him by her side. Walking proved awkward and slow, with the chain dragging and catching on the uneven ground. If only her legs were free, she would be astride Sultan riding far and fast from this place.

She could hear Kelak screaming and pounding on the door. "Did you plant this note? Tell me! What do you know of this note?" And then, just as the sounds of his screaming and pounding were fading from earshot, came "Why did you never tell me Banah was alive?"

Banah? The name came as such a surprise to Adriana that she actually stopped. "Banah?" she repeated out loud, looking at Sultan as if he might answer her. "What does Banah have to do with this?"

Shaking her head in confusion, Adriana tried to walk faster down the path. Her sole focus was escape, she reminded herself. Her uncle was gifted in cunning. He might say anything, for any reason at all.

A Clearing in the Forest

The path remained in partial darkness for longer than Adriana would have expected. The woods were quiet, the only sounds the soft pad of Sultan's hooves and the muffled clank of the chains between Adriana's feet. Nevertheless, she glanced behind her with frequency, frustrated by her slowness and fearful of her uncle's possible appearance.

Then, over the rise, she saw it. Light broke through the inky darkness, lightening the sky to the palest shades of pink and blue. Adriana sighed in relief, a smile creasing her face.

As the path became more visible and the trees distinguishable in first light, Adriana realized her slow pace meant she would not reach the table where Redbud and she had eaten their first meal together for quite some time. When she saw a spring by the side of the path, she knelt to drink. She wished she could stop and rest but knew she needed to press on to put as much distance as possible between herself and Kelak.

Adriana anticipated seeing Redbud at any moment. Surely she would be pleased at Adriana's escape, even if Adriana had not been able to make it to the stone table by first light. *Now that day has come*, she thought, *Redbud should be making her way toward the cabin*. Therefore it was a shock when Adriana followed a sharp bend in the path and, instead of finding Redbud hurrying toward her, found her way blocked by a multilimbed tree creature. Unlike

Redbud, whose appearance was that of an extremely tall, exotic human, this creature looked much more like an actual tree.

It, or he, had large, hooded, lizardlike eyes over branchlike lips. He, or it, towered over Adriana, would even have towered over Redbud had she been there. Multiple thick, short limbs swung by its sides, each tipped with a wicked-looking talon.

Adriana's mouth went dry and she could feel Sultan tense beside her.

When the tree spoke, its voice was deep and raspy but perfectly understandable. "What is a heart for?" The creature looked at Adriana with unblinking eyes.

Adriana's heart pounded so hard and fast she felt sure it could be seen through her tunic. Was this tree the type her uncle had waged war against? Had he been right after all? Correct that Chehalem was dangerous, the trees lethal? How was she to respond?

If she confessed her heart was necessary for her to live and the creature meant her harm, then perhaps he would rake one of those talons down her breastbone and take a peek. She decided to be evasive.

"A heart is for pumping blood."

"Blood? What is that? And what is blood for?"

Adriana looked at the creature's thick, strong legs and razor-sharp talons. If it pursued her, she doubted she could outrun it, and, even if she could, she knew she would never run to Kelak for safety, regardless of the circumstance.

Courage and truth, she told herself. A proverb of Ayrden rose to the surface of her mind:

> *Courage untested is a bird without wings;*
> *and a truth untold is a well found dry.*

"My heart is here," Adriana said with all the courage she could muster as she placed her right hand over her pounding heart. "It pumps blood through my body. It is one of the things that keep me alive."

The tree being did not advance. Instead, it nodded, and the short spiky green fronds on its head covered and uncovered its unblinking eyes. "And how does a heart break?"

Adriana was confused. Was the tree asking a literal question or a figurative one?

"A broken heart means someone is very sad. It's not really their heart that is broken, though that is what we say in Ayrden. It is more"—Adriana struggled for the right words—"more like being so sad, because of someone, you feel sick. All over sick, like your heart can barely keep you alive."

"Thank you. I don't really understand that, but it is more than I knew before. Why are you wearing jewelry on your feet? Doesn't it make it very difficult to walk?" The tree's gruff voice poured out of him without a pause, making it difficult for Adriana to keep up with his thoughts.

"Jewelry?" Adriana looked down at her feet. The chain of her shackles lay on the mossy path. She supposed it could have looked like a necklace, if it were placed around the tree creature's neck. "Oh, no, this is not jewelry. But you are right, it does make it very difficult to walk."

The entire conversation seemed absurd to Adriana. She still had no idea whether the creature was friend or foe. He had not threatened her, though he had seemed threatening when she'd happened upon him. She wondered if she should continue on around him, wait for him to pass her by, or perhaps ask his permission to proceed. She hesitated.

Before Adriana could decide on a course of action, she heard a voice from behind the creature say, "Excuse me, Paktos. I am in a bit of a hurry this morning."

The tree creature turned, revealing Redbud striding down the path. Her salmon robes flowed behind her as she advanced toward them.

At the sight of Adriana, she stopped. A smile spread over Redbud's face. She clapped her hands together and held them to her chest.

"Princess! You escaped! I am so relieved. Have you met Paktos?" Redbud gestured toward the towering tree creature. "He is quite friendly; I am sure he has already engaged you in conversation. Paktos," Redbud said, turning her head to look up at him, "this is Princess Adriana of

Ayrden." Redbud gestured toward Adriana. "She is the one we have been trying to communicate with in Kelak's cabin."

At the mention of Kelak, Paktos made a loud rumbling, rending sound. Adriana stepped back.

"Do not concern yourself, Princess. Paktos's anger is not directed at you. If we have time, I will explain later. As for now, I believe we need to remove your chains. It will be impossible for you to ride until you are unbound."

Redbud approached and knelt in front of Adriana, assessing the shackles. "Paktos," Redbud called. "Come take a look, would you? Do you think you might be able to cut this metal with your talons?"

The ground vibrated as Paktos approached. Adriana stood as if rooted to the spot while the two tree beings knelt in front of her, testing the strength of the chain and examining the locks on the ankle manacles.

The sound Paktos made was between a cough and a chuckle, rolling out of his mouth along with the clean smell of cedar. "Might I? I dare say I can. But I am not supposed to touch her, is that correct? Not even with my talons?"

"That is right," Redbud replied. "How clever of you to remember that. Can you do it?"

"I believe so," Paktos said. "Can we tuck a bit of her cloak at the top of the manacle? I'll slip a talon in between it and the chain, and it should slice through the metal without my touching her. I should be done in a rustle."

"Excellent plan, Paktos." Redbud gathered the ragged hem of Adriana's cloak, stuffed a bit of it into the top of the ankle manacle, and looked up at Adriana. "Stay perfectly still," she warned.

With a quick motion of one of Paktos's short arms, Adriana felt the shackle open and fall away. He and Redbud repeated the procedure on the other foot, and Adriana was free.

"Oh, thank you so much!" Adriana said. She stepped back and looked in amazement at her boots, singed black by the fire from the cabin but free of all restraints. She was unbound for the first time in many moon cycles. Free to continue on her Journey, or perhaps even return to Ayrden this very day.

Adriana smiled as she turned to Sultan, ran a hand down his muzzle to drop him to one knee, and jumped on his back. Sultan arose, poised and ready for Adriana's next signal.

Redbud turned to Paktos. "You may want to stay here for the cycle of light. With first light having arrived, I doubt Kelak dares venture forth, even to track Adriana down, but if he should, your presence would certainly give him pause."

Paktos once again made a loud, rending sound before

saying, "I will stay here until I have to return into the forest at last light. Do not fear. He will not pass me this day during the light hours."

Relief flooded Adriana. "Thank you," she and Redbud said at the same moment.

They both laughed, and then Redbud turned to face Adriana. "Princess, let us go. There is much for us to discuss."

CHAPTER 15

REVELATIONS

Adriana, mounted on Sultan's bare back, progressed with Redbud down the path.

"I believe the priority of the morning is to feed you, Princess," Redbud said. "You remind me of a twig stripped bare of bark, you are so pale and thin."

"Food would be wonderful," Adriana agreed. "But Redbud, what am I to do then? Can I leave? Should I leave? Is my Journey over? Do I return to Ayrden from here? And what of my uncle Kelak? He kept screaming something about Banah from the cabin. Do you know anything about that? He never mentioned her name, not the entire time I was in the cabin with him.

"And is Chehalem actually dangerous? It is clear he thinks so. And why did you wait so long to try to send me a message? Ah, I have so many questions. Can you answer them?"

Redbud's face revealed nothing. She continued on, gliding toward the field of food, which had just become visible in the distance.

"Princess, I can answer many of your questions. However, only you yourself can determine the trajectory of your Journey. Let me gather some food for you first. I will do it for you, as I know you must be exhausted. I will certainly reveal to you what I know. But while we are still on our way, tell me what your uncle himself told you about his time here in Chehalem."

Adriana relayed all the information she could remember Kelak telling her about his arrival in Chehalem: the hunger, the lusweed, his horse disappearing, his battles with the trees.

"And in the cabin, at your escape? What happened there?" Redbud asked, turning to look at Adriana.

Adriana hurried through the story of her escape, concluding with Kelak's frantic screams about the parchment.

Redbud listened in silence. Adriana was just finishing as they arrived at the field of food.

Redbud nodded and waded into the edge of the field. Catching a single pod and floating it to Adriana to break open and eat, Redbud began speaking. "Princess, your uncle has told you some truthful things, some indisputable lies, and some other things that, though undoubtedly his perceptions, are absolutely not reality. As I told you when we met, as a tree being I know far more than what I alone see and hear. I also know virtually all that my fellow trees of Chehalem experience. It is a collective knowing."

Redbud continued to release and catch pods one at a time as she talked. She held them below Adriana where she sat on Sultan, in order that she might catch the pods as they rose into the air, break them open, and eat. "It is a truth that your uncle ran out of food and, being hungry, ate the berries of the lusweed. They are poisonous and caused him to lose consciousness for an entire day and night. However, when he awoke, his horse had most certainly not disappeared, but was standing right by him, as was his Guide, Parapak. Unfortunately, Kelak panicked. Whether it was the lusweed still coursing through him or merely fear"—Redbud shrugged as she released another pod for Adriana to catch—"Kelak pulled a sword from his horse's saddle and ran his Guide through. Parapak was dead before he touched the ground. Parapak and Paktos—"

Adriana interrupted, "That is impossible, Redbud. We are not allowed to journey forth with a weapon. Only a day's provision."

"Princess, I can see the scene replayed at any moment I choose. I assure you, your uncle had a sword. He used it to kill Parapak. After another day or so, he used it to kill his own horse for food. He most definitely had a sword.

"As tree beings we have no guile. I could not lie to you, even if I wished to do so. We simply do not know how. It has made dealing with your uncle somewhat . . . complicated. We believe not only what we see, but what we hear as well. For many nights after you were taken prisoner, when we could see nothing but could hear whatever sounds were made, your uncle walked the path to the field bemoaning that he had killed you. I—we all—believed him. It is simply our way. That is why I did not begin trying to communicate with you until the very first day I saw your face in the window."

Adriana felt sick. Whether it was too many pods of food after such a long time of meager portions or the events that Redbud was revealing to her, she was not sure. "Thank you, Redbud. I don't care for any more food."

As they walked away from the field toward the stone table, Adriana asked, "And the battles that Kelak spoke of? Did the trees wage war on him to revenge Parapak?"

"As I was about to say, Parapak and Paktos are part of the same family, and you saw the anger Paktos still has toward your uncle. But no, we do not wage war. We only defend as best we are able. Which is to say, we might be able to defend ourselves in the day, but at night we are bound to the trees in which we sleep. Your uncle was clever. He watched for the trees that housed us, and once night fell he destroyed a tree and the being in it, often by fire, occasionally by hacking the tree to bits using his sword. Eventually he made a mistake and first light caught him still outside. He was surrounded by several large tree beings and attempted to attack them with his sword, but they were successfully able to take it from him and bury it deep in the woods. We have left him mostly on his own since then, not showing ourselves."

"Then how did he ever discover the field of food?" Adriana asked.

"Some of the other Guides-in-Waiting told him. It was decided that perhaps once he saw we meant him no harm, but rather could and wanted to be helpful, he would relent from his war against us. Needless to say, he did not understand the gesture. Though he has most certainly made use of the information."

Adriana nodded. "And his comments about Banah? Do you know anything at all about that?"

"Very little. When he first arrived in Chehalem, before he encountered Parapak, he wept as he rode. Wait, let me tell you exactly." Redbud closed her eyes. "There it is." She paused, eyes still closed, standing motionless. She opened her eyes and gazed at Adriana. "Over and over he said the same thing: 'My heart, it is breaking. Banah, where did you go? How could you have left me?' It was the same refrain for days, even after he killed Parapak."

A CLEARING IN THE FOREST

"Unbelievable," Adriana said, shaking her head.

"You do not believe me, Princess Adriana?" Redbud asked, concern in her voice.

"Oh, of course I believe you, Redbud. I simply meant . . ." Adriana understood for the first time how literally the tree beings of Chehalem took all that was said. "I simply meant it is difficult to imagine how Banah was involved with him before he left on his Journey. She is, I mean, was my chief serving maid in Ayrden. But I think she came to the palace from Shevith, the land of my mother. I cannot imagine how she and Kelak would have even known each other."

The two arrived at the stone table and Adriana saw Sultan's saddle, dry and intact, lying underneath it.

"Redbud, what were you trying to tell me in your message about the stone table? You said, 'If you are able to get to the stone table by first light, then . . .' I am afraid the rest was too muddled and indistinct for me to understand."

"Ah. I said, 'then you will have time to continue or return.' Nevertheless, you still have enough light hours to decide whether to continue on your Journey in Chehalem or return to the clearing. It seems to me you have three choices, any of which you may choose, one of which will no longer necessitate my long-term assistance."

Redbud gestured beyond the table, and Adriana noticed for the first time another path, different from the one that had led to Kelak's cabin, winding its way through the woods. "First, that is another path in the land of Chehalem. You may certainly choose to proceed thereon. You might encounter your uncle on it, but I doubt it. He has not done very much exploring since he arrived. Second, you can obviously return down the path from which we have come. You have now eaten, and there is more than sufficient time in the cycle of light for you to pass Kelak's cabin and ride farther into Chehalem. Or, finally . . ." Redbud pointed down the path where Adriana had first entered Chehalem. "You may leave Chehalem altogether."

"Well, what should I do?" Adriana asked as she dismounted Sultan and gazed around at her options.

"Princess, I am your Guide, not a director of your Journey. Regardless of which of the three you choose, I will go with you at least as far as the trees around the clearing. If and when you leave Chehalem, however, I cannot exit with you."

"But what am I *supposed* to do?" Adriana asked.

"That I cannot tell you. It is your Journey; it is for you to decide."

Adriana made a frustrated sound, walked to the table, and bent to retrieve the saddle. Regardless of what she decided, she would be riding. Redbud stood in silence as Adriana began to saddle Sultan and mulled over her decision.

A CLEARING IN THE FOREST

Adriana again recalled Emaht saying, "Today's outcome need not be the same as the days' that have gone before," but she had no inclination to return to Kelak and try for a different outcome. In truth, she was not willing to pass Kelak's cabin and risk being caught up in another of his cunning schemes.

Adriana looked down the second path of Chehalem. It looked much like the one that had led to Kelak. Where did it go? She shook her head. She would never feel safe in Chehalem as long as there was a possibility that Kelak could find her. It had taken too much time to escape from him the first time.

By the time Sultan was saddled and Adriana was astride, she was resolute. "I am leaving Chehalem," Adriana said to Redbud. "So far this Journey has not been at all what I expected. But as you say, it is my Journey, and I have made my decision."

Adriana turned Sultan toward the path that would lead them back to the clearing. "Upon my entrance into Chehalem, I rode for almost two days before I met you. Perhaps we could make the clearing by last light if I gallop. If I do, can you keep up?" At this Redbud smiled and nodded. "Perhaps I will be home to Ayrden before dinner," Adriana said before setting off.

Though Adriana pushed Sultan for speed, she was the one that tired well before the clearing was visible. Redbud wisely suggested they stop for the night. Though it made Adriana nervous to think about Kelak following after her, once the cycle of dark began, she knew she had little choice. She was exhausted.

Redbud showed Adriana a small cave, just off the path, beside which a magnificent sequoia grew. After Adriana ate a few of the pods Redbud had brought along for her, Adriana stationed Sultan in front of the small entrance to the cave.

"You will be in the tree beside me, then?" Adriana asked Redbud.

"Yes, and I will wait until the last moment to join with it. This time, at first light, be sure to wait for me before setting out," Redbud said.

"Of that you need have no fear. I will stay snug in the cave until I see you have awoken. Good night, Redbud."

"Dreams of truth and happiness to you, Princess."

Adriana settled in the cave, hugged her knees to her chest, and pulled her cloak tightly around her. She gazed out the cave's small entrance. She could see Sultan's hooves, a bit of his forelegs, and the thick folds of Redbud's dress where it brushed the tops of her feet. Adriana closed her eyes and rested her head against the smooth rock, drifting off to sleep far faster than she imagined possible.

"Princess Adriana, wake up. We can leave now." Adriana opened her eyes to find Redbud's face and shoulders filling the opening of the cave.

After crawling out, Adriana stood and stretched her arms above her head. "Oh, Redbud. I feel so much better. And what a beautiful day."

After a quick meal, Adriana mounted Sultan. "How far away do you think the clearing is?"

"Actually, not far. I could just see it from the sequoia tree," Redbud replied. "We should be there before high light, even going at a modest pace."

"Wonderful!" Adriana exclaimed, barely refraining from kicking Sultan into a gallop. As Adriana contemplated leaving Chehalem, a few remaining questions arose. "Redbud, what if Uncle Kelak is not able to escape from the cabin? I did lock him in, though not very securely."

"You need not concern yourself with that, Princess. Your uncle battered the door open from the inside yesterday."

"Really? How do you know . . ." Adriana's voice trailed off as she thought of the leaves rustling and rubbing their messages, tree to tree, in the breeze. "And is he coming after me?" Adriana could feel her throat tighten at the thought.

"It is my understanding that he did attempt to do so, but not until darkness fell. And he never reached the cave where you were sleeping, as it was apparently farther than he dared to go."

"And the parchment? Did you learn anything about the parchment he said he pulled from the hem of my cloak?"

"No. I know only that as he walked through the night he muttered about finding you, about going home—to Ayrden, the listening trees presumed—and about Banah being alive." Redbud paused. "And Princess, we believe he also spoke of killing you. He said, 'I knew I should have killed her when I had the chance. It would have been so easy. If only I had known.' The trees along the way said he was most definitely looking for you. It appears you made a wise decision to leave Chehalem instead of continuing."

When moments later they rounded a bend and Adriana could see the lush grass of the clearing, she had mixed feelings. She was relieved to be leaving Chehalem and glad she had made that decision. But she was regretful that she would not be able to spend more time with Redbud, see more of the land, and befriend the odd but intriguing creatures of Chehalem.

Adriana stopped Sultan a few strides away from the clearing. "You're sure you cannot go with me, Redbud? We have plenty of trees in Ayrden. I'm sure one of them would make a splendid home for you."

"It does not work that way, Princess. Safe travels on all your paths."

A Clearing in the Forest

"Thank you, Redbud. But I hope the next path leads me back to Ayrden. Thank you for being my Guide in Chehalem. Perhaps someday you will meet my brothers and sisters. I myself am very grateful to have met you."

Redbud bowed and extended her hands, as if she were presenting an invisible gift, without taking her eyes off Adriana. "Safe travels on all your paths, Princess," Redbud repeated.

Sultan took the last few steps toward the clearing and Adriana turned back to look at Redbud one last time. But her gaze backward coincided with Sultan's forward movement into the clearing and, like a curtain being pulled across a stage, the trees on either side of the path closed with a sudden, heavy movement, completely obscuring Redbud from view.

The path was gone—and Redbud with it.

CHAPTER 16

THE SILVER ARCHWAY

Adriana sat cross-legged in the center of the clearing, looking from one possible path to the other. The path home to Ayrden was absent, just as it had been the last time she'd been in the clearing. She had chosen the prosaic path of grass over both the shiny gold one and the sparkling one of multicolored jewels. Now those were her only two choices. All around the clearing, the dense forest created an impassable barricade. The path to Chehalem, as well as the path home to Ayrden, remained closed, as if they had never existed at all.

What had she learned in Chehalem, if anything, that would make a difference to the Kingdom of Ayrden when, if, she was able to return? She shook her head. Chehalem, Kelak, Redbud—all that was in the past. She sensed she was standing in the gap between what had been, just moments

119

before, and what would be, as soon as she made her choice.

Adriana rose and walked across the clearing to survey the path of precious jewels. Her heart ached as she thought of her father in his Throne Room with its glittering floor of emeralds and twinkling ceiling of sapphires and diamonds. The day before her birthday she had sat in that room and heard for the first time of Kelak. Kelak, about whom she now knew far too much but also far too little.

At that thought she turned to the way of gold. A breeze danced through the trees as Adriana gazed down the path. Like the other, it turned in the near distance, preventing her from seeing anything of significance. The blue sky was offset by the shiny green of the trees, and the path itself was banked on either side by mounding flowers of yellow and white. The flowers reminded her of a particular spring afternoon from her childhood when she and Alexander had played in the fields. It was a happy memory.

Whistling for Sultan, Adriana mounted and, without a look back into the clearing or down the path she was choosing not to traverse, she turned Sultan onto the road of gleaming gold.

Adriana was forced to progress slowly, as the surface proved to be slippery. While Sultan managed fine at a walk, anything faster caused him to lose his footing. And since Adriana had no idea what she would find along this new path, and Chehalem had tempered her impetuosity, she was satisfied with the sedate pace. She had not been riding long when she saw a huge wall, thick and tall. The path continued through a massive, open archway.

Not giving much thought to her options, Adriana nudged Sultan forward to enter. But when they broke the plane of the entryway, an odd sensation spread over Adriana's entire body. It was as if they were breaking through an icy-cold spiderweb. Adriana shivered and wiped her face, thinking whatever it was had left a residue, but there was nothing there. She stopped and looked behind her. The archway was no longer an opening. The arch now held in place a solid wall of polished silver. Adriana could clearly see herself and Sultan. It was like looking in a mirror.

Adriana was shocked by her gaunt face and filthy appearance. She hardly recognized herself. The wall of silver also made her feel hemmed in and captive once again. She turned from her reflection and moved forward, deeper into this new land. Soon she began to hear noises that were more in keeping with a market or fair than a wood.

The farther she rode the louder the noises grew, but Adriana was still surprised when she rounded a bend and saw before her dozens of wagons and carriages and a myriad of people on horseback bustling up and down what had turned into a wide gold boulevard lined with ornate buildings.

As the riders and drivers approached the last of the

buildings, the ones closest to her, they turned back to go along the golden street in the opposite direction. It almost seemed like some kind of parade.

Adriana rode Sultan along the edge of the road, entering the crowd and the innumerable sounds. She tried to stay out of the way of the larger carts and carriages, pulled by robust horses of equal size to Sultan, but it was difficult, as the street was so crowded.

She took in as many of the sights as possible as she rode through the street. She occasionally passed narrow alleys that shot off in angled directions from the main road of gold, but they were dark and looked threatening, so she continued her slow progress through the throngs.

Though everyone seemed to have something to say to those riding by or standing along the side of the road, no one spoke to Adriana. Nor did they appear to even see her.

In the tidy, flowered yards of the houses, children played. The girls' dresses, ranging in color from vibrant reds and blues and yellows to the palest blush and violet and cream, were ankle-length and full, with lacy petticoats peeking out beneath the hems. The boys were dressed in leather breeches and snowy white shirts that laced at the neck. Everyone looked beautiful.

The more she took in of the people of the land, the more conspicuous Adriana felt. Yet it was as if she were invisible to those around her. Not one person looked her way. At first when she passed other riders, she nodded and smiled at them, but after passing dozens and dozens of people and receiving no response, she stopped acknowledging them. She could understand their language, but it seemed they were all saying the same thing to one another. "Hello, how are you? You look fine today. Is that a new"—and here there were differences—"dress, waistcoat, saddle, hat, or pair of gloves?" Each time, some piece of displayed finery was commented upon.

The loudest sounds and most expressive gestures occurred around a lovely young woman not much older than herself, mounted on a fine-boned dapple-gray horse. Adriana could not hear the specific exclamations, but the crowd around the attractive young woman grew ever larger as Adriana rode by on Sultan.

Though Sultan's shoulder bumped another horse's as they passed and it was difficult to weave around the people jostling to join the crowd, still no one looked in their direction. It truly was as if Adriana and Sultan were invisible.

Adriana looked down at her singed hands holding the reins on either side of Sultan's glossy neck and to her grimy breeches and tunic. Only her cloak retained some semblance of finery, but even that, with its ragged hem, was looking a bit tattered. Perhaps the people of this land were being courteous not to look her way, but still, it was odd.

Unsure what to do, Adriana kept riding. The crowds diminished, the buildings ended, and the voices gradually faded until dissipating altogether. The path, as the gold pavers ended and scattered gold nuggets took their place, continued to wind its way through the countryside before it narrowed and began ascending a hill.

As Adriana rode Sultan up the twisting trail, she noticed for the first time the shadow of a bird that seemed to be following them. Yet when she looked up to see what kind of bird and how far above them it was, she could see nothing. The shadow continued to swoop first on one side of Sultan and then on the other, but Adriana could find nothing in the sky that could be creating it. Once they crested the hill, however, Adriana was so overwhelmed by the sight that lay before her, she forgot all about the shadow.

As far as her eye could see was water, beautiful blue water with white-tipped swells that created eddies on the golden yellow beach. Once she began the descent, the water was obscured from view by the trees growing along the trail. But when the path finally ended she was right on the beach.

On the golden sand was a table, one fit for the Palace of Ayrden, under a tent draped with gossamer white linens billowing in the gentle breeze. The table was prepared for two. Beyond the table the water licked the shore, and, as last light approached, the sky began to darken. The clouds turned crimson and purple with streaks of yellow that made Adriana think of bruises.

She dismounted. As she walked closer to the table, her boots sank into the soft sand. The scent of lemons and butter filled the air.

"There you are," said a friendly male voice. "Welcome to Shahar. I've been waiting for you."

CHAPTER 17

THE SEA OF SHAHAR

Given her first encounter with Redbud, when Adriana heard the unexpected voice she anticipated seeing a figure take shape and emerge from the nearby palm trees or the undulating ocean. So she was surprised when, instead, a tall, attractive young man with a broad smile stepped out from behind one of the columns of white linen.

He was dressed similarly to the boys she had seen playing in the yards, but he was no youngster. Absent were the top hats and jackets of the men she had seen parading in the streets of the town through which she had passed. His chin was shadowed with what would have been a beard, were he not clean-shaven. Just as the stranger drew close enough that Adriana could see his eyes were deep blue and his smile friendly, a moon rose on the horizon.

Adriana gasped. The moon was beautiful, a huge orange orb rising slowly above the darkening blue sea.

The young man held out his hand. "My name is Corrigan," he said.

Adriana took a step back. "Are you my Guide? Are you sure it is all right for me to touch you?"

He laughed. "Of course it is all right for you to touch me. I am only requesting to shake your hand in greeting. As for me being your Guide—no, not exactly."

Not fully trusting his friendliness or the situation, Adriana made a small curtsy, ignoring his still-outstretched hand. "Do you know who I am?" she asked and watched as Corrigan's hand fell to his side. When she saw a puzzled look cross his face, she explained, "You said you were waiting for me."

"Oh, I see. No, I do not know who you are, but I was told one was riding over the ridge, so I anticipated your arrival. Dinner is being prepared. I was hoping you would join me."

"How gracious of you. That would be most welcome. Unfortunately"—Adriana gestured to her grimy clothes— "I am afraid I am in no condition to join you at such a lovely table."

"That can be remedied." Corrigan clapped his hands together once, and a small, dark-haired girl dressed in a plain linen shift emerged from the stand of palm trees.

"Sone, take our guest to the bath," he said to her.

Turning again to Adriana, he smiled. "Once you are done cleaning up, dinner should be ready. I will see you back at the table. Take your time."

Adriana followed Sone through the stand of palm trees that ran along the beach, Sultan trailing behind her. They soon arrived at a waterfall and pool. Water spilled from an unseen height before hitting a large, glowing red stone just above the pool. Thick steam rose off the rock and the surface of the water.

In a voice barely louder than a whisper, Sone said, "My lady, the pool is ideal for bathing." Sone bent and picked up a large bowl of flower petals and held it out to Adriana without lifting her eyes. "The bowl will float in the pool, and the petals will turn to froth in your wet hands. I will return soon with a towel."

Adriana took the outstretched bowl. "Thank you very much."

Sone stepped away and in no more than four steps had disappeared from Adriana's view. Adriana looked around, once again unsure. In the light cast from the glowing rock she would be quite visible to anyone standing unseen in the dark. But Corrigan had said he would wait for her back at the table, and she could hear nothing but the waterfall spilling onto the rock and into the pool.

The water looked irresistible. She had not bathed since Ayrden. The thought made her faintly sick. Pushing her hesitation aside, she slid out of her breeches, tunic, and underclothes and quickly slid into the pool. As her thin, tired body slipped into the water, she let out a sigh that was almost a whimper. It felt that good.

Adriana sank into the warmth and swam closer to the molten rock. She let the cascading water pour over her head and neck. The bowl Sone had given her bobbed on the surface of the water, and Adriana scooped out a handful of the flower petals. They melted into foaming soapsuds in her hands.

So thin and pale, she thought as she lathered first her arms and then her legs. She wondered once again how long she had been held captive in Kelak's cabin. Would she ever know?

She slid under the water, washing off the soapy bubbles before doing it all again. She washed her dark curls, grown so long they touched the small of her back. It felt wonderful to be clean. She cringed at the thought of pulling the soiled breeches and tunic over her just-washed body and longed for even one dress from her wardrobe in Ayrden. She surfaced for the final time and grimaced when she saw her filthy clothes piled by the side of the pool.

As she swam in that direction, Sone stepped out of the darkness, eyes still downcast, and held out a large square of white toweling. Adriana stepped out of the pool and wrapped herself in the thick softness of the cloth.

"I brought a comb for your hair, my lady," Sone said.

"Of a truth, I doubt I could work a comb through it," Adriana said with chuckle, hoping to get a smile from the demure serving maid.

"You may be surprised, my lady. Would you like me to try?"

"Thank you, Sone." Adriana sat down on one of the rocks edging the pool and closed her eyes as Sone pulled the comb through her hair with surprising ease. With her eyes closed, Adriana could almost imagine she was home in Ayrden and that it was Banah combing her hair.

At the thought of Banah, Adriana's mind returned to Kelak and his screams as she escaped from the cabin. *What was that all about?* she wondered once again, and shook her head.

"You wish for me to stop?" Sone asked behind her. "I am almost done."

"Oh, no. I'm sorry, Sone. I was thinking of something else. Please go on." Adriana sat still and silent as the comb slid through her hair.

"My lady, I brought you some fresh clothes," Sone said once she was finished.

"What? Oh thank you. I am so appreciative." Adriana turned to see white underclothes and a gorgeous dress of creamy orange and muted blue draped over Sone's arm. "The dress is lovely, and I am so relieved not to have to put my journeying clothes back on. They are as filthy as I was," Adriana said with a smile that went unseen by Sone, whose eyes remained lowered.

Sone helped Adriana into the clothes and then, after picking up Adriana's unwashed garments and boots, walked her back toward the table on the beach. As they walked, Adriana gazed out over the water. She wondered what was on the other side—more of the country of Shahar, or another land entirely? Or perhaps there was nothing but more water, endlessly undulating under the circle of orange moon.

While she walked along the water's edge, something just beneath the surface of the water caught her eye. It glowed a dull white and slowly rose to the surface. Then Adriana saw that it was a flower, fully formed and open, glowing and casting a handsbreadth of light over the surface of the water. She stopped. *How lovely*, she thought. And while she stood there, the single flower multiplied. First one more floated to the surface of the water, then two, then three, then five, then eight, and on and on until as far as her eye could see to the distant horizon, the sea was full of open, glowing flowers. It was spectacular.

Adriana could see Sone ahead, nearing the table, so she hurried along the beach, her feet bare in the warm sand. When she arrived at the table, Corrigan was standing behind one of the chairs. He gestured for her to be seated.

Before she sat, however, she first made a deep curtsy and then held out her hand to him, putting her distrust aside and expressing her gratitude. "Thank you so much for arranging the bath. I feel far more civilized now and am sure I look it, too. Sone was so kind, she even found a dress for me."

Corrigan took her hand in his and bent over it in a low bow. "My pleasure. I am most grateful you would join me for dinner . . ." He paused.

"Oh, I am sorry. I have not introduced myself. I am Adriana, from the land of Ayrden." Some instinct prompted Adriana to not fully introduce herself, deliberately omitting any reference to her standing as princess. She knew nothing of Corrigan, nor apparently did he know anything of her. *Best to be cautious and hold some information back*, she thought.

"Adriana, a lovely name for a lovely girl. Please sit down."

Adriana's mouth began to water as soon as she faced the table. Platters of food, beautiful and aromatic, provided an abundance of choices. It all looked and smelled wonderful.

Corrigan sat across from her and offered her various platters, then served himself. He picked up a utensil to begin eating and noticed that Adriana's hands rested in her lap.

"What is it?" he asked. "Are you not hungry?"

Adriana shook her head. "It is not that. Actually I am ravenous. But—would you mind very much exchanging our cups and plates of food?" Adriana asked in a rush. "I have been poisoned once before and am a bit wary of eating at the tables of strangers."

Corrigan laughed, but Adriana sensed he was not pleased by the request, perhaps resented it. "Of course we may exchange plates. How dreadful for you."

"Yes. It was," Adriana said as the switch was made. She pushed aside her discomfort at putting her host in an awkward situation. "Thank you very much, and I apologize for the request. It must seem odd."

Corrigan shrugged and began eating. Adriana tried to bring back his smile by engaging him in conversation. "I saw the flowers rise as I was coming from the pool. How gorgeous. Does that happen every night?"

A slow smile returned to Corrigan's face. "Indeed. It is amazing, isn't it? When I am here, I hardly notice their arrival each night. I am abroad on the sea quite a bit, and you cannot imagine how spellbinding the scene is from there when you are surrounded on all sides by the flowers."

With the conversation beginning to flow smoothly, Adriana ate her first bite of food. It was as delicious as what was served in the castle of Ayrden. After the pods, the varied appearance of the food was incredibly appealing.

Throughout the meal Sone and several other servers removed and added numerous platters of food. Corrigan never acknowledged the servers, and Adriana found herself beginning to ignore them as well, she was so captivated by Corrigan.

"And where do you go when you sail?" Adriana asked when there was an opening in the conversation.

"Other lands, to see other peoples. There is much beyond Shahar. And much profit to be made when I bring back what I find there," Corrigan replied.

"So you are a merchant?"

"Of a sort. And you? You seem young to be on your own with no more than a horse for company. Are you running away from someone?"

Adriana was unsure how to answer. She had not begun her Journey running away, but she had left Chehalem in exactly that situation. Although Adriana liked Corrigan, finding him both handsome and interesting, she had earned a double measure of caution in Chehalem. And if he did not already know who she was, as Redbud had, perhaps he was not meant to know. At least not right away.

"It's a bit complicated. I am on a Journey, and it was necessary for me to escape from a particular situation. But my Journey overall is more of an exploration, you might say."

"I don't mean to be rude. But you seem ill-prepared for

a journey alone," Corrigan responded. "Do you even have a weapon?"

"No, I am not traveling with a weapon. But I am not quite as ill-prepared as I look. I have been in training for the Journey for quite some time."

Turning the topic of conversation back to her host, Adriana said, "But tell me about Shahar. The town and the people were lovely, but no one spoke or, for that matter, even looked at me. I found it strange."

Corrigan smiled. "Well, they certainly had not seen you after your bath, dressed in Shahar's finery."

Adriana felt herself blush. "As filthy as I was, I would have expected them to stare all the more. And my entrance through the archway was very odd as well. Do you know what I am talking about?"

"The silver archway? Of course I know of it. But no one in Shahar would attempt to pass through it. The few people who have done so disappeared forever. We avoid the areas where the arches exist." Corrigan leaned across the table. "So you came through the silver wall? I don't know why I assumed you had come from town. I should have known there was something else at work here. Tell me again where you are from and why you are here."

Adriana paused before answering. Was he requesting the information or demanding it? There was something in Corrigan's demeanor that she found off-putting.

"I am from Ayrden. It is typical there"—*for one wishing to become King or Queen*, Adriana thought silently—"to make a Journey during one's sixteenth year." Adriana pushed aside thoughts of one of Prelechett's frequently reiterated lessons:

A half-truth is not truth at all,
but rather deception.

"We are schooled in numerous disciplines to assist us on our quest," Adriana said.

Corrigan laughed. "And for what are you questing, Adriana? A husband, perhaps? You are a lovely girl. Were there no suitors in Ayrden that would do?"

Adriana felt a slow blush creep up her neck and into her cheeks at the compliment. "No."

Corrigan pretended to look shocked. Adriana laughed. "I mean, no, I am not questing for a husband. Our Journey is more of an adventure that then leads us back home. Or not," Adriana added, thinking about Kelak and his years in the woods of Chehalem.

"So you could find something on your quest that would make it worthwhile for you to stay? Wherever that was?"

"I suppose so. I hadn't really thought about it that way. But of a truth, not all who journey forth return, so perhaps some are content with their decision to stay where their Journey takes them."

Corrigan nodded. "It grows late. Would you like to stay

in my home for the night? I have a small stable here as well, with room for your horse," he added when he saw her glance over her shoulder to where Sultan was standing.

Adriana's initial mistrust had been tempered by the food and conversation and compliments. "I would be most appreciative."

Corrigan clapped his hands together once and Sone appeared by his side. "Take our guest to the house and have Stow take her horse to the stable."

Adriana and Corrigan both stood. "Is it far?" Adriana asked, gesturing to her bare feet. "If so, I will need my boots, though they are not what I would normally wear with a dress such as this."

"It is quite near, just along the beach. You'll be fine." He gave a small bow, took her hand, and lightly kissed the back of it. "I will say good night here. We will have plenty of time to talk tomorrow. Pleasant sleep, Adriana."

Adriana gave him a small curtsy before following Sone along the beach, their way illuminated by the glowing flowers. Adriana was dazzled and thoughts of the sea, of lands unseen, and of Corrigan tumbled without order through her mind.

She rubbed a gentle finger across the back of her hand where Corrigan had kissed it. *What*, she wondered, *will tomorrow bring?*

CHAPTER 18

SONE AND STOW

Adriana woke with a start. Sone was standing beside the bed, hand outstretched, reaching toward Adriana's shoulder. Sunlight, so bright it hurt Adriana's eyes, poured into the room. Adriana sat up and Sone's hand fell to her side.

"My lady, the master has been asking for you to join him for breakfast."

Adriana pushed back the pillowed coverlet and stood up, rubbing her eyes. "I am more than happy to meet Corrigan for breakfast." She stretched and looked around the room for something to put on other than the thin cotton nightgown Sone had presented to her the night before. "Is there something for me to wear other than this? I don't see the dress I wore last night."

"Just a moment, my lady. I will go see what I can find

for you." Sone scurried out the door.

Adriana looked around the room again and headed for the corner where a clear blue glass pitcher and basin stood. She poured water into the basin and splashed it on her face, smiling to have slept in such comfort. She ran her fingers through her hair and then braided it. When Sone returned, Adriana was casting about for something to tie off the thick braid.

"My lady, the master asked for you to put these on and meet him outside." Sone laid a white shirt, thin brown leather breeches, and Adriana's own boots, clean and polished to a high sheen, on the bed. "Would you like me to find a ribbon for your hair?" Without waiting for an answer, Sone once again hurried from the room.

Adriana shook her head. How long had she slept? Sone was acting strange, rushed and harried, as if she wanted to tell Adriana to hurry. In a moment she was back again, entering without knocking. She tied off Adriana's braid with a small piece of blue ribbon and helped her into the clothing. As soon as the shirt's neck had been pulled together by the leather cord, she opened the door for Adriana and pointed across the foyer to a door. "The master is waiting for you outside," she whispered. Her eyes, as always, were lowered.

Adriana refrained from hurrying across the foyer, though she was fairly certain Sone was silently urging her to hasten. She found herself apprehensive because of Sone's odd behavior. Yet when she opened the door, Corrigan was leaning against a palm tree with a smile on his face. He was lazily flicking a riding crop against the handles of a large basket sitting by his feet.

"Good morning," he said as he pushed away from the tree. "I understand you slept quite well."

Adriana returned his smile, her anxiety melting away. "Indeed. It has been longer than I can remember since I have slept in the softness of a bed. And the sound of the sea? It was like a lullaby as I went to sleep last night."

"That pleases me. I thought perhaps we would have something to eat later, and go for a ride this morning."

"Oh. Sone said—I mean, I thought we were having breakfast. But a ride first would be fine. Should I go get Sultan ready?" Adriana realized she did not know where the stables were and felt a bit disoriented at the realization.

"No. Your horse refused to be stabled last night. Stow is saddling two of my horses for us."

Adriana felt a knot of apprehension rise in her throat. Where was Sultan? What had been happening while she had been sleeping like a queen in this stranger's bed?

Her face must have conveyed her thoughts, because Corrigan strode to her side and slid his hand down her arm. "He is fine. Come, I'll show you where he is."

Corrigan walked her along the front of the sandstone

cottage, covered in fragrant flowering vines, until they had a view of the ridge over which she and Sultan had ridden the day before. "There, see? Safely unsaddled and unbridled. Apparently, he has just been allowed to have a mind of his own."

Adriana was relieved to see Sultan grazing in a patch of grass. When she called his name he looked up, but Adriana avoided giving him a signal of any kind. No need for Corrigan to know how well-trained Sultan actually was.

Adriana noted the stable just beyond where Sultan stood. Like the cottage where she had spent the night, it was made of sandstone with a profusion of flowers climbing its walls. She saw a man who must have been Stow leading two horses toward them. One was a bay as large as Sultan and the other was a smaller chestnut mare.

Corrigan said, "All of the ladies of Shahar ride sidesaddle, but since you were riding astride yesterday, I told Stow to put your saddle on the mare."

"Sidesaddle would have been fine. I am capable of both. Thank you, though, for being so considerate."

Once Stow reached them, Corrigan instructed, "Help Adriana mount." Stow extended his clasped hands and Adriana sailed into the saddle. Odd, she thought, how small this mare seemed after riding only Sultan for so long.

Corrigan continued giving Stow directives after he mounted. "Walk with the basket to the glade. By the time you arrive, we will undoubtedly be ready to eat."

"Yes, Master," Stow said. "The blanket is behind your saddle. I placed your bow and quiver on the off side and prepared the two foils. They are in the cylinder on the near side. And as you requested, I—"

Corrigan wheeled his horse around, shielding Stow from view. Adriana heard the crack of his riding crop. At the sound, Adriana's mare leaped forward, and Adriana glimpsed Corrigan's horse rear up on its back legs and Stow stumble backward as she struggled to bring the mare under control. By the time she got the nervous horse calmed and turned back toward Corrigan, it was as if nothing had happened. Stow was picking up the basket from under the tree and Corrigan was in command on the bay.

"Sorry about that," he said cheerily. "Ready? We will be heading down the beach for a very short way and then up into the forest. There is a nice glade there, perfect for games and picnics."

Adriana followed Corrigan away from the house, looking over at Sultan and wishing she had insisted on riding him. She felt a bit dwarfed by Corrigan on the big bay and, though she was accomplished with horses, she did not have her brother Alexander's gift. Sultan could be fully trusted. But it was too late now. With a shrug she kicked the mare into a canter and drew even with Corrigan as they rode down the beach.

CHAPTER 19

A WAGER

Adriana was hungry by the time they arrived at the glade, but she imagined it would be quite some time before Stow reached them with the basket of food. The ride through the forest had been swift and arduous. The terrain was varied, the footing tricky, and the small mare had difficulty taking the bigger jumps necessitated by fallen trees. They had forded two streams, the deeper of which the mare repeatedly balked at entering. By the time they reached the other side, Corrigan was almost out of sight. Adriana wondered if he supposed the mare more able and willing than she was proving to be. But when the terrain became easier, Adriana urged the mare into a gallop and they began closing the distance. Adriana enjoyed the mare's smooth, fast gallop on the flat terrain, and they entered the glade just as Corrigan pulled up his horse. Fun as the last part of the ride had been, Adriana vowed to herself she would never ride any horse but Sultan for the remainder of her time in Shahar.

When Corrigan turned to face her, his eyebrows rose. "Did you have difficulty?" he asked.

From his expression Adriana realized she must look a mess. Her hair had pulled from its tidy braid and now, interspersed among the curls around her face and down her back, there were a few yellowed leaves and twigs from branches she had barely managed to duck. Her breeches were stained dark to the knees from the deep waters of the last stream, and her boots were waterlogged. Still, Adriana met his gaze with confidence. She was sure she had looked far worse on numerous occasions during riding lessons and hunts in Ayrden. And after all, she had completed the trek close on his heels. She might even beat him the next time, were she riding Sultan.

"None that I couldn't manage," she said evenly. "Are we stopping here?"

At Corrigan's nod Adriana dismounted in one quick motion and pulled off her boots, emptying them of water before putting them on again. She swept the twigs and leaves from her hair and, since the ribbon was gone, slipped the leather cord from the neck of her shirt and used it to pull back her hair. By the time she finished, Corrigan had dismounted and removed the various items he had instructed Stow to provide.

"Do you know how to shoot a bow and arrow?" he asked. "I told you this area was good for games. There is a target set up across the way. Would you like a bit of sport?"

"That sounds like fun. Though I imagine I will not provide you with much competition. I have not shot a bow in quite some time, and it has never been my strength."

"Perhaps I can give you a small advantage then. A pace or two to compensate," Corrigan said. He smiled down at her as they walked across the glade.

Adriana noticed again his height and good looks. She felt a pleasurable tingle travel up her spine when he briefly placed his hand in the small of her back to guide her in the direction of an archery target set up along one side of the glade. After being sequestered for such a long time in the tiny cabin in Chehalem, it felt wonderful to be outside in the sunshine, enjoying a day of fun that someone had planned with her in mind.

"Perhaps you would like to test the bow before we begin?" Corrigan asked, his voice kind and solicitous. He pulled an arrow from the quiver slung across his back and offered it to her, along with a large and finely made bow.

Adriana admired the bow as she fit the nock, the arrow's notch, into the taut sinew and tested the tension. The grip was cool, white, and elaborately carved, yet comfortable in the bow hand. Or, at least it would have been had her hand been bigger. The arrow rest was a tiny carved animal of a type she had never seen.

With a twang the arrow arced toward the target, but Adriana overshot it by several feet and the arrow disappeared into the woods.

"Here, have another try," Corrigan said, offering her a second arrow. Adriana shot again, this time just missing to the right.

"Perhaps the third time will be the charm," she said, holding out her hand to Corrigan for another. This time the arrow hit the outermost ring of the target with a convincing thwack.

"Well done," Corrigan said. "Are you ready for our little contest now?"

"Certainly." Adriana walked across to the target and pulled the arrow from it before retrieving the one that had flown right. "Should I go looking for the one I overshot?" she asked.

"Leave it for later. So what would you like to wager?"

Adriana laughed. "Wager? I am surprised you ask that. Here I am wearing your clothes, riding your horse, and shooting your bow. I have nothing with which to wager, should I lose."

"Perhaps all the more reason for you to win then. I will wager the bow against a kiss from you."

Adriana felt a hard blush hit her cheeks. "My apologies,

but I think perhaps that is not quite appropriate."

"Oh?" Corrigan's voice sounded cold.

"The bow is of obvious value," Adriana said with a playful note in her voice as she tucked a stray curl behind one ear.

Corrigan chuckled. "I offered the wager, thereby I have dictated the commensurate value. Do you accept?"

"I pledge a kiss, you the bow," Adriana agreed. "To the winner the spoils."

"Ladies first?"

"Certainly. How many arrows and how many rounds?" Adriana asked as she took up the bow once again.

Corrigan laid out the rules, three rounds with one arrow less to be shot each round, beginning with three arrows in round one. Each round would increase in value by one, the first round worth one point, the second worth two, and the third worth three. They began.

Adriana led off. Each of her first three arrows hit the target and each landed closer to the center than the one before. She was grinning broadly when she handed Corrigan back the bow.

"I am growing to like my—I mean, your bow," she teased.

Corrigan did not reply or even appear to have heard her. He fit an arrow to the bow and pulled the string taut. The arrow flew straight and true and landed in the center of the target. As did the second and the third.

"I believe that means I take round one," he said with a faint smirk.

"Obviously," Adriana said as she began walking to the target to remove her arrows. When Corrigan stood his ground and let her retrieve the arrows alone, she supposed that to be part of the game as well. The loser of the round pulled the arrows.

"The leader leads off round two?" Adriana asked when she returned with the six arrows. Corrigan nodded and chose one from her hand. It hit the target just outside the black center ring. This shot was not as close as any of his three previous ones had been.

He handed Adriana the bow, saying, "We will alternate shots in round two."

Adriana grinned. This was her chance. Two good arrows here, and the game could be hers. She chose an arrow with purple feather fletching. Taking careful aim, she closed one eye and pulled the bowstring back as far as she could.

Thwack! The arrow landed clearly inside of Corrigan's hit.

"Nice shot," Corrigan said as he fit an arrow in the bow. "You seem more than capable for this not to be your favored sport."

Adriana shrugged. Corrigan was good. But no better than she with a properly fitted bow. And he would have stood no chance against Bess, always the best of her siblings at archery. But Adriana kept all those thoughts to herself. She was relishing the sunshine and the pleasure of the game. It felt more like home than anything she had done since her Journey began.

Corrigan's second shot landed just inside the edge of the black center. Adriana knew if she could best him by just a bit, she could win with her last shot in the final round. Choosing a yellow fletched arrow from his hand, she let fly a perfect shot that landed dead center in the target. She had won round two.

With a broad smile she turned to Corrigan and waited, assuming he would retrieve the arrows as she had done previously, but he did not move forward. Instead, he was replacing the arrows in the quiver. He looked up.

"What?"

"Are you not going to retrieve the arrows? I assumed the round's loser did that, as I fetched them last round."

"What?" he repeated, sounding confused. Then he hastily said, "Oh, of course. I am not used to being the loser of a round, I suppose." Adriana watched his fair hair catch the light as he strode forward. She glanced up. It was almost high light, she judged, which reminded her she had not eaten breakfast. She hoped Stow would be here soon. She was hungry.

Corrigan returned and placed all the arrows in the

quiver. "Last round. The winner of this takes what was pledged. One to two, the leader leads," he said, nodding to Adriana.

She took her stance, planting her feet firmly, and turned for an arrow. Corrigan pulled one from the quiver and presented it to her. As she fit the arrow to the bow, the striped feathers of the fletch just below her chin, she noticed once again the little animal carving on the arrow rest. She pulled the sinew tight, holding it for a brief moment before releasing it and watching it sail toward the target. *Yes!* The aim was perfect. But then, just before the arrow reached the target, it began to descend. *No,* she thought with a groan, *too soon, too soon.* She watched as the arrow landed just in front of the target, missing it altogether.

"Ah, a very good shot. Just short," Corrigan said, sounding sympathetic. He took the bow from her hand and slid the purple fletched arrow from the quiver into it. It arced gracefully toward the target, where it landed well within the innermost circle of black.

With a grin he turned to Adriana. "Game over, four to two. And I retain possession of the bow." He stroked the upper curve of the bow with a finger as he looked at her. "Remind me. What was it that you pledged, should you lose?"

Adriana felt a pulse begin to beat in the hollow of her

throat. "At your suggestion," she said, stressing the last word, "I believe I pledged a kiss."

"Ah, right. Now I remember," Corrigan teased as he stepped forward. His head blocked out the sun as Adriana tipped her head back to look up at him. He put both hands on her hips, pulling her closer than Adriana thought appropriate, and bent his head toward her.

Just then there was the sound of someone crashing through the bushes at the end of the glade. "Master," Stow called out, "I have arrived with the basket of food."

Adriana turned her head just in time to see Stow emerge from the woods, making more noise than seemed necessary. Corrigan's kiss landed on her cheek. She felt the faint stubble on his chin graze her face as he looked up, anger etching his face.

Adriana gave a laugh, a mixture of relief and disappointment filling her at Stow's arrival, and stepped away from Corrigan.

"You would renege on your pledge?" Corrigan asked her.

Adriana was a bit shocked at his accusation, particularly in front of Stow, who was now busying himself at arranging lunch on the blanket he had unfurled in a shady spot in the grass. She said lightly, "The pledge was for a kiss. Be it hand or cheek or lips, we did not specify. I consider the pledge paid."

Corrigan bowed slightly in her direction. But his mouth was tight and his smile gone, and Adriana wondered if perhaps his good humor for the day was gone with it.

CHAPTER 20

CASTLE AND SWORD

Corrigan was quiet during lunch. But not unpleasant. His anger seemed directed at Stow, whom he commanded to pack up the remains of lunch once they had finished. He then ordered Stow to return with haste to the beach cottage.

While Stow was repacking the basket, Corrigan invited Adriana to walk to the far end of the glade. After a few paces he said, "You seem unusually skilled for a girl your age. Is that typical in the land from which you hail? Ayrden, I believe you said?"

"As I mentioned last evening, I have been in training for quite some time. I am pleased you found me to be proficient in archery."

"Not just that," Corrigan replied. "Your horsemanship must be excellent as well. I checked your progress as we rode, and I did not slow my own in spite of the smaller mare you were riding. You seemed comfortable enough with any difficulties you encountered. What other skills did you learn in Ayrden?"

"Fencing, hand-to-hand, philosophy, charting, and of course how to read and write."

"Active skills for the most part. Did you take lessons in beauty?"

"Beauty?" Adriana was not at all sure what Corrigan meant.

"Things of beauty, acts of beauty, such as art or singing or—"

Adriana interrupted with a laugh. "Ah, I am afraid you have found my weakness. Of a certainty, I enjoy beauty of all kinds, artistic and musical, but I was not graced with much ability in that regard. And of a truth, the beauty of the natural world, like your flowers of light and flaming orange moon, are more to my liking than a canvas or a never-changing piece of stone."

"Then you will enjoy the view from the edge of the glade more than most," Corrigan said. "It is one of the most spectacular sights in all of Shahar."

As they reached the end of the glade, the smooth footing of green grass fell away in a steep hill that ended at the edge of a large lake. A path of gold encircled the lake, and flowering trees of yellow and white grew in perfectly spaced splendor along each side. Rising up all around were more green hills like the one on which they stood. Across the lake, on the crest of the far hill, stood a partially erected castle of white stone, inlaid with shining gold.

"How lovely," Adriana said. And it was. But it did not overwhelm her with its beauty as she imagined Corrigan had anticipated. Instead, she thought it looked too arranged, too planned, too perfect. It made her miss Ayrden and the multicolored vistas of mountains and streams visible from every window of her father's castle.

"Do you like it? I am having it built for my bride."

"Your bride?" Adriana spun on her heel to face him. "You are soon to be married?" She flushed as she thought of her earlier flirtation with him over the kiss.

Corrigan took a step toward her, his blue eyes crinkling at the corners as he smiled down at her. "I am fairly certain I have found the one I am intended to marry." He appeared to be enjoying himself. "As I asked you before, do you like it?"

Adriana's heart raced. Was he speaking of her? What was he implying? She was attracted to Corrigan, was confident that he was attracted to her as well, but to marry? Or was that even what he meant? She barely knew him, and he knew even less about her. In the moment that she paused before answering, he reached up and brushed her pink cheek with one finger before tucking a curl of her hair behind one ear. His finger traced the line of her ear and then her neck to the hollow of her throat where a pulse had begun to beat rapidly. "Do you like it?" he repeated, his mouth soft and upturned.

"It is lovely." Adriana stepped back to look once again at the lake and the castle. "It looks as if it required a great deal of planning. Have you been working on it for a long time?"

"Quite some time. I knew the fates would eventually bring the right girl to me."

Adriana was increasingly uncomfortable with the turn this conversation had taken, with Corrigan's proximity, and with the isolation of the glade. Stow had long since left the clearing, and though the castle was clearly under construction, there was no indication that anyone was across the way working on it. They were very much alone.

And there was something else. Something about Corrigan put her off kilter. There was a subtle mismatch between what he said and how he actually behaved. Like the whip, the way he treated Stow. So while her heart was racing from the pleasure of his touch, her mind was sounding alarm bells of caution. She chose to listen to the peals of warning for now.

"Thank you for showing me the castle," Adriana said as she turned to begin walking back the way they had come. "I am sure it will be magnificent when it is finished. Should we be leaving? I am not really sure how long it took us to ride here."

Corrigan followed, ambling by her side. "No need for haste. You did say you learned fencing in Ayrden? Perhaps we could have a bit of sport again? I brought a pair of foils. I will try not to draw blood," he added with a chuckle.

"I did learn to fence. In fact, my fencing instructor was both renowned and one of my favorites. I imagine he would be quite disappointed in me if I let you draw blood," Adriana jested.

"Ah, now that is beginning to sound like a challenge. Are you interested in another wager?"

Adriana laughed. "I think one wager for this day is aplenty. Plus, you have me in height by a good deal, and in strength as well, no doubt. I will make every effort for a good showing, but I think it best not to wager this go-round."

"So you are judicious as well as courageous."

"Courageous?"

"Courageous to duel with me at all."

Adriana tilted her head a bit in puzzlement, watching Corrigan withdraw two foils from the long cylinder. "You did say we were merely taking sport with the swords, correct? In Ayrden we practice with the foils sharpened only when we are clothed in light mail. I assumed the blades were unsharpened, nigh then impossible to draw blood with at all."

Corrigan presented the sword, hilt first, to Adriana. "Correct, the blades are not sharpened," he replied. Then, as she took the sword in her hand, testing its weight, he added, "Only the very point is rapier-sharp and able to cut. But I am sure you will be careful. As I will be. Five touches, anywhere on the body. Ready?"

Before Adriana had time to process how she might deal with the sharp points on the foils, Corrigan took a fencing stance and feinted toward her. With a quick motion she brought the sword up. She grinned at him when she realized he meant only to make her react and take her stance. "Ready," she said.

They circled each other for several seconds, Adriana watching Corrigan's body as Emaht had taught her. She was learning the subtleties of his posture and the positioning of his sword. Just before he took a first lunge, she stepped aside and flicked his back with the edge of her sword. He had given his intention away with a noticeable transfer of weight. He thrust again and Adriana parried. His height was a significant advantage, but Adriana had agility on her side. And something else now.

The touch on his back must have provoked him to anger, because his attacks grew in intensity and lost any tactical elegance, becoming brutish. Yet Adriana was able to deflect or dance away from each of them. His moves were impulsive, giving Adriana a distinct advantage. At strategic moments, she lunged or attacked and was able to strike him three more times with the edge of her sword.

Eventually Corrigan withdrew a bit. Swords raised, they circled each other, both of them flushed and winded.

Focus, Adriana thought, *only one more touch for the win*. Then she saw it, the perfect opportunity for a lunging thrust. She made the move in one fluid motion and felt the point of her sword touch Corrigan's chest. She withdrew the sword instantly, hoping not to have drawn blood. However, at Corrigan's sharp intake of breath, she assumed she had not succeeded.

Adriana swept her foil in a large arc in front of her, the thin blade whistling as it sliced through the air, laid it flat against her right leg, and bent from the waist in a bow of thanks for the duel. This concluding pleasantry was part of the fencing tradition of Ayrden, serving to give the loser a chance to collect himself unseen by the bowing victor.

When Adriana righted herself, the first thing she saw was one tiny point of red blood seeping into the pristine white of Corrigan's shirt. The first thing she felt was the point of Corrigan's blade at the base of her throat.

CHAPTER 21

CORRIGAN'S WIN

"Did you think you had won?" Corrigan asked. The tip of his blade remained at Adriana's throat. She could feel the cold steel point of Corrigan's sword but also knew he had not, as yet, drawn blood. Adriana considered her options.

Corrigan's eyes were calm, his face impassive. His stance was such that he could run her through in an instant, thus making the sword by her side useless. She stood her ground and looked him squarely in the face. "Yes. Did I misunderstand the rules?"

"Obviously, you misunderstand a great deal," Corrigan said as he withdrew the sword and brought it to his side. "You drew first blood, but that was not our goal. You should feel fortunate that I did not repay the honor. The contact you made with the edge of your sword counted for naught. To garner a score, all touches must be made with the point."

"But how, then, were we to duel without drawing blood?" Adriana argued, shocked at having misunderstood the rules to such a degree and more shocked still to discover what the rules had supposedly been.

Corrigan raised his eyebrows, widening his blue eyes as he surveyed Adriana from her head to her toes. "I drew no blood. And I had the opportunity for a fatal pierce. As I think you are much aware."

"Yes. But only because I had put my sword down. I am mystified as to how we could have dueled without bloodshed—if only touches with the point were to count. Of a truth, I was trying *not* to draw blood with my final attack."

"It seems you should have asked more questions," Corrigan said. He reached out a hand for Adriana's foil. She hardly had time to lift it toward him before he had removed it from her hand. "It is well for you that we did not place a wager on that game. You would have had to pay up twice." Corrigan walked over to his horse and began preparing to leave.

"You still think you won?" Adriana asked in disbelief.

"No," Corrigan said. "I know I won. I always win." He looked over his shoulder at her. "But you made a very good showing, quite excellent, in fact. Best to mount up.

We will take a shortcut back to the cottage, but it is still a fair distance to ride before moonrise."

The trail they took back to the cottage was well traversed, heavily shaded, and cool. The path was also narrow enough that Adriana was forced to follow Corrigan once again.

As they rode, she replayed the sword fight and their conversation beforehand in her mind. She wondered whether she had been mistaken about the rules or Corrigan was misleading her because he resented being beaten. He had made that comment about courage—perhaps she should have understood that the danger of the duel was in scoring points with the honed tips of the swords. She gave a frustrated shake of her head as she looked at his tall figure on the horse in front of her.

And what about before the duel? When they stood on the grassy bluff above the lake and the partially completed castle. What had Corrigan meant about the fates having brought the girl he was to marry to him? Did he mean her? He had certainly seemed to. But Adriana thought again of the point of his sword pushing against the hollow of her throat. That had seemed unduly dangerous and threatening.

However, she had to acknowledge that other than the dispute over the duel, the day had been lovely. She thought back to their wager and Stow bursting into the glade just before Corrigan kissed her. The memory brought a smile to her face. There was no doubt, Corrigan was very attractive and he made her feel—what, exactly? *Beautiful*, Adriana decided. He made her feel beautiful. And she liked that.

The narrow path opened up, and Adriana could see the darkening sky over the water in the near distance. She nudged the mare forward and drew even with Corrigan. "It appears we will make it back before moonrise," she said.

Corrigan turned toward her. "We should. I have been thinking of how well you performed today, with both the bow and the sword. Would you be interested in going hunting tomorrow? Did you grow up doing that in Ayrden?"

"I did. And thank you, I would enjoy that. For what will we be hunting?"

"Whatever we find, most likely deer. Though one never knows what will cross one's path in the hunting grounds. As for tonight, I have need to go into the city, so I will not be joining you for dinner."

Adriana was disappointed and it must have registered on her face, because Corrigan reached across and laid a gentle hand on her arm. "My apologies. I have received word that two of my ships are soon to come into port. Arrangements need to be made in town. It cannot be helped, or I would stay and enjoy another seaside dinner with you. I will instruct Sone to prepare something for you at the cottage. Is there anything special you would like?"

"Whatever Sone prepares will be lovely, I am sure."

When they arrived at the stable, Corrigan ordered Stow to ready a horse and carriage for the trip into the city. Another two servants dealt with the horses, and Corrigan sent yet a third to the cottage with a message for Sone regarding dinner.

"You need to go back to the cottage now, before darkness descends," Corrigan said to Adriana. With a courtly bow he took her hand in his and pressed a kiss to her palm. Continuing to hold her hand, he said, "Make my home your own. Enjoy another bath in the pool if you wish. I will see you in the morning for our hunt."

With a small curtsy, Adriana said good night and walked toward the cottage alone. She was pleased to see Sultan grazing nearby. *Tomorrow's ride ought to prove a great deal more fun than today's,* she thought.

CHAPTER 22

WOOD'S WOLF

My lady, wake up. It is past dawn already."

Adriana woke with a start to find Sone once again standing over her bed, an anxious look on her face. "Thank you, Sone," Adriana said sleepily. "Do I have clothes to wear for the hunt? I failed to ask you that last evening."

"You do, my lady. The master sent these." Sone lifted up a long linen shift and loose trousers.

"I am to wear those for the hunt?" Adriana asked. "I have never seen such loose riding pants. I think I might prefer—"

"These were specifically sent by the master, my lady. And I have your boots, clean and polished from yesterday."

Adriana gave a shrug. "If you are sure. Is Corrigan

waiting for me again today? I would like to saddle Sultan before he has one of his own horses brought for me."

"No, my lady. He has not yet come out of his bedchamber."

"Excellent. Do you think you could find me a piece of fruit or something for breakfast, Sone? Just in case Corrigan wants to leave as soon as I return with Sultan?"

Sone scurried from the room without answering, and Adriana dressed in the simple clothes, then pulled on her boots. Sone met her in the foyer and pressed a ripe apple and a piece of fresh brown bread into her hands. "I think you should hurry. When the master calls for you, it would be best if you were here."

Adriana slipped out the door and gave a single snap of her fingers as she walked toward the barn. At the sound Sultan trotted over, then walked alongside her toward the stable.

Adriana ate a bite or two of apple before giving Sultan the remainder. "Did you miss me yesterday?" Adriana asked as she fed him. "I certainly missed you."

When the pair arrived at the stable, Stow had the small mare from yesterday readied for Adriana, but he transferred the saddle and bridled Sultan without comment at her request.

"How far is the ride to the hunting grounds?" Adriana asked as she pulled Sultan's forelock through the bridle's browband and smoothed a hand down his face.

"Not a great distance, miss. Close enough that no one need ride out with you. If a kill is made, the master will sound the horn and a group of us will then go meet you to prepare the animal."

"Corrigan said there was a variety of game on the hunting grounds?"

"Indeed. One can never anticipate what one might find there. I mean no offense, but are you sure you are up for it, miss?" Stow asked as he fussed with the saddle on Corrigan's big bay. "As I said, you and the master will be riding out alone."

Adriana tilted her head and looked quizzically at him. "I am not at all sure what you mean, Stow. Because I am riding Sultan? He is quite exceptional, for all that he proved difficult for you at my arrival. I assure you I will come to no harm upon him. We have covered more than a little ground together at this point."

"No, miss. What I mean is—"

Before Stow could finish, a breathless servant ran into the barn. "Hurry, Stow! The master is calling for the horses! Oh, I am sorry, miss. He was asking where you were as well."

"Why don't I mount up here, Stow? I can even take Corrigan's horse to him, if you like."

Stow looked aghast. "Oh, no, miss. It would be much

better if you hastened to meet the master on foot. He would not be pleased at you bringing the horses. I will wait a moment or two and bring them up. And, miss, go through the back of the cottage, so as not to raise suspicion you were down here talking to me."

Adriana was perplexed as to why Stow would be concerned about Corrigan knowing they had been talking, but, regardless, she did as he suggested. When she slipped into the cottage through the door that led to the kitchen, Sone looked relieved to see her and immediately took her to Corrigan, who was already seated and eating breakfast. He looked delighted to see her, and they were having a pleasant conversation about the hunting grounds when Stow appeared with Corrigan's big bay and Sultan.

"Who told you to saddle the stallion for her?" Corrigan asked, anger evident in his voice.

"No one, Master," Stow replied. "The horse wandered into the stable on his own and looked as if he could use a bit of exercise. Do you wish for me to change the saddle over to the mare of yesterday?"

Adriana was shocked. Why in all of Ayrden was Stow lying about how Sultan came to be readied for her? And why was he suggesting he saddle the small mare for her? She had no intention of riding any horse but Sultan. She was about to say so when Corrigan replied.

"No. Leave it. We have wasted enough of the light as it

is. Adriana, my dear, do you mind riding your own horse?" Corrigan asked, turning to her with a pleasant smile.

"Not at all," Adriana replied, walking over to mount.

As Stow put his hands together to boost her into the saddle, he said in a voice so low only Adriana could hear him, "Thank you. Be careful."

Corrigan wheeled his horse around and Adriana saw strapped to his horse the bow and quiver from the day before, a sheathed knife, and an ornately carved horn. "Do you have a bow for me? You did say we would both be hunting, did you not?" she asked.

"Stow! Did you forget to put a bow and knife on Adriana's saddle? Your ineptitude is wearing upon me," Corrigan said. But something in his voice seemed off to Adriana. The words themselves were harsh, yet Corrigan seemed almost jovial. "So sorry, Adriana. We will share the bow I suppose. We do need to be on our way. Stow, be prepared to bring a contingent when you hear the horn. I plan on our having a feast tonight."

As Adriana and Corrigan rode out along the beach path once again, she was conflicted. She was off to go hunting without a weapon, which made no sense to her whatsoever. Perhaps that was what Stow was thinking about when he told her to be careful. But she was riding Sultan, both a comfort and an improvement over yesterday. However, as she suspected, the loose-flowing linen of the trousers was going to be a problem. They were already chafing the insides of her thighs. She sighed and tried to pull the material tight with one hand as she rode with the other. Oh, well. It was a lovely day for hunting, she was with a most handsome escort, and apparently she had a feast to look forward to tonight.

Corrigan was in an excellent mood. And once they turned onto the wooded trail, he began talking of various attributes of Shahar.

"And the name? Shahar—does it have any special meaning?" Adriana asked as they rode through the thickening forest.

Corrigan turned a bit in his saddle to look at her. "Yes. It refers to the breaking of our day, the dawn. It is even more spectacular than the evening flowers of light. But you haven't been awake that early yet, have you?"

"No." She felt as if she were being scolded, though Corrigan's expression was pleasant when she checked his face. Still, she felt the need to explain herself. "As I mentioned to you before, this is the first time I have slept in a bed for quite some time. Perhaps an entire year, I am not sure. It was kind of you to send Sone to wake me both mornings."

Corrigan shrugged and turned his horse down a barely discernible path. "You proved to be an excellent shot yesterday with the bow. Let's see if we can find dinner.

Perhaps you will be able to earn your day's keep."

Adriana was unsure how to take his comment. Was he implying that she was in his debt? He had invited her to stay, after all. Yesterday evening he had even told her to make his home her own. Had that been mere courtesy? She thought back to his attentions the day before. Smiling at her own thoughts, she decided she was most definitely a welcome guest.

They rode farther than Adriana expected before Corrigan pulled up and dismounted. "We'll leave the horses here and approach the meadow on foot. Deer are easily startled, so it is best to keep silence." Corrigan tied his horse to a tree branch and began removing the bow and knife from the saddle.

Adriana dismounted and gave Sultan a signal to stay.

"Are you not tying him up?" Corrigan asked.

"No need, he will be here when I return."

"So you say. But if he is not, do not expect me to spend the day looking for him." Corrigan had slung the horn across his chest and the quiver across his back. He held the bow in one hand and a skin flask in the other. "It is still a fair distance to walk. Would you like a sip of water before we head out?"

At Adriana's nod he lifted the flask and squeezed water into her mouth before doing the same for himself. Once more he did the same, this time missing her mouth just a bit. Quickly bending his head, he kissed away the water at the edge of her lips. "Ah, a kiss with no wager. What will the rest of today bring?" he joked as he capped the flask and flung it over his shoulder.

Adriana flushed with pleasure, though his action had startled her. When he stretched out his hand to her, she laced her fingers through his and they began their silent walk to the meadow.

It was not long before the lush meadow opened before them. Brilliant green grass rolled across the open space until it reached a large pond, where the trampled grass gave way to yellow mud. The pond was obviously well used. They were standing in a strategic downwind location midway along the long side of the meadow.

Corrigan squatted back on his heels and leaned his back against a tree, motioning for Adriana to do the same. He held the bow loosely in one hand and an arrow at the ready in the other, waiting. The dark forest behind them and the bright meadow in front of them were still and silent.

Adriana's eyes swept the meadow. It appeared empty of animals, so she looked for more subtle signs: swaying grass that might indicate wild boar or turkey, or movement at the edge of the forest that might reveal larger game.

Then, as she remembered them so often doing in Ayrden, a herd of deer seemed to materialize out of thin air along the line of trees on the far side of the meadow. Two large does sniffed the air while three small fawns grazed on the deep grass. Several more deer appeared, some skittish, others nonchalant as they moved with unhurried grace in the general direction of the pond.

She reached across the space to Corrigan and touched his arm, pointing with her other hand, her eyes never leaving the herd of deer. She felt Corrigan move and heard the soft sounds of an arrow being threaded into the bow, though the animals were still too far away for the shot.

As the deer continued their sporadic parade across the meadow, Corrigan gradually stood and took his stance, moving several paces ahead of where Adriana still crouched. She was so focused on the herd it took a moment for the sound behind her to register. When it did she had a sinking feeling in her stomach. It was a growl. And it was near.

She slowly turned her head.

A wolf, darker and larger than any Adriana had ever seen, was no more than two stallion strides from her. He was in a stalking stance, his eyes large and yellow, his teeth bared and menacing. He moved slowly and deliberately toward her, as focused on her as she had been on the deer.

"Corrigan!" Adriana called out as she spun around and faced the wolf, blood thundering in her ears. She scrambled to remember anything from her training in Ayrden that might help. She had already locked eyes with the wolf. If that was the wrong thing to do, it was too late. She had no weapon, and there was no cover offered by the meadow—she would be easy prey there. The wolf was on the path, and the trees and brush alongside her were too dense to provide a way of escape.

But relief flooded her as she thought of Corrigan behind her, bow at the ready, arrow already nocked. She took a low hand-to-hand stance, knees bent and hands at the ready, not knowing what else to do as she waited for Corrigan to take the shot. The wolf continued to advance, one slow step and then another.

"Corrigan! Take the shot!" When nothing happened Adriana dared to turn her face away from the wolf for just a moment to look behind her. Corrigan was midway across the meadow, his quiver of arrows bouncing against his back as he ran. The deer scattered into the woods in front of him as he beat a path of cowardice away from the wolf, leaving Adriana to defend herself alone.

Sultan! Adriana gave two sharp whistles and hoped Sultan was within earshot. The wolf stopped progressing toward Adriana, and a moment later she could hear the pounding of Sultan's galloping hooves.

The wolf continued to eye Adriana but was no longer growling. Sultan came into sight and whinnied before skidding to a halt just behind the wolf. Adriana, hoping to frighten the wolf away, gave a double snap of her fingers and Sultan reared up, pawing the air. The wolf did not run but did turn to look at Sultan. Back on all fours, Sultan blew loudly and shook his head before stretching out his neck and lowering his nose to the wolf.

Adriana's heart sank. Sultan's neck was completely vulnerable. If the wolf latched on, he could tear Sultan's throat out and he would be dead in a moment. Adriana again gave two snaps of her fingers, hoping to save Sultan from harm. But Sultan ignored the command.

"Sultan!" Adriana again gave two snaps of her fingers. But the horse and the wolf continued to stand nose-to-nose for another two ticks. Then, with one bound, the wolf leaped over the thick brush alongside the path and disappeared into the forest.

CHAPTER 23

THE HEART'S CORNER

Adriana was weak with relief. She mounted Sultan but was unsure what to do next. Corrigan was nowhere to be seen. She rode to the edge of the meadow and called out his name, but there was no answer. She did not like the thought of leaving him but liked the idea of staying in the forest where the wolf might return even less. She rode Sultan to where Corrigan had left his horse, which was still tied to the tree.

Adriana considered this new dilemma. Her inclination was to leave the horse for Corrigan. Otherwise, he would have to make his way back to the cottage on foot. However, the wolf had obviously been stalking prey and the bay, though large, would make an easy target tethered as he was.

Adriana finally decided to take Corrigan's horse back with her. Perhaps Stow could return for Corrigan. *Or perhaps*, Adriana thought, *there is a logical reason for Corrigan's having run across the meadow.* Maybe he had gone for help, thinking an arrow was inadequate to fend off the wolf. She considered riding back to the meadow and looking for him, but the encounter with the wolf had made it clear to her how little she knew of Shahar. She settled on riding back to the cottage with all speed.

When she arrived at the stable she explained the situation to Stow, who nodded and said, "I am sure the master will blow the horn when he is ready for us to come to him. Are you all right, miss?"

"Yes. Thank you, Stow. A bit shaken, but I am fine."

Adriana felt somewhat foolish that she had forgotten Corrigan had the horn. She left Sultan with Stow and walked toward the cottage, her thoughts confused. Why had Corrigan left her like that? He must have had a clean shot at the wolf. Surely he could have mortally wounded it with the arrow he had in hand. Why hadn't he?

Adriana stopped on the beach and gazed out over the water. The day was growing overcast, and Adriana saw what looked to be a sailing ship on the horizon. As the water lapped the golden shore, Adriana scuffed her boot in the sand and wondered what she should do.

Her father had told her the Journey was all about the decisions she would choose to make. She had chosen to stay here with Corrigan these past two nights, but should she continue to stay? If so, for how long? She needed to talk to him. Where was he? And why, she wondered again, had he left her? She made a frustrated sound in her throat.

"You should be leaving Shahar now."

The voice jerked Adriana out of her thoughts, and she looked with surprise at Sone, who had silently appeared beside her.

"What? Why?"

"This will be your only chance," Sone said.

"I don't understand what you mean." How could Sone be so sure of what she needed to do? Did she know what had happened on the hunt?

"You think he cares for you," Sone said in her soft voice, eyes downcast as always. "But he is not who you think he is and he does not."

"What do you mean? Because he left me when the wolf was attacking?" She wondered how Sone already knew of the situation, but she assumed Stow had relayed the tale to her.

There was no question that Adriana was disappointed in Corrigan. She badly wished he had stood his ground with her against the wolf. Doing battle together was an indispensable ethos of Ayrden. But was that really enough to call his feelings for her into question? She needed to see Corrigan himself. Talk to him. Let him explain. And who was Sone to be passing judgment?

"No," Sone said, "because he is a slave merchant. You did not know that, did you? He is not being kind to you. He is planning on enslaving and selling you. He is a merchant of slaves. He captures girls from across the sea and sells them here in Shahar."

Adriana looked at Sone, her face doubtful. "Are you sure?"

Sone looked Adriana in the eyes, the first time she had ever done so. Her gray eyes were clouded with anger, and her gaze hit Adriana like a fist in the face, but the handmaiden's voice stayed as soft as ever. "Do you think I could ever forget the man who ripped me from my mother's arms and ran my father through with a sword? Do you really think I am not sure? He has been testing you to see what skills you have, in order to determine how much you might bring in the marketplace. Or he might choose to keep you for himself, but certainly as a slave. Not as an equal, and certainly not as a bride. I assure you, his sole intention is to make you a slave. As I am."

It was Adriana's turn to look down. She was embarrassed that she had questioned the docile serving maid, who was actually Corrigan's slave.

"I am so sorry," Adriana whispered. "Of a truth, I did not know. But . . . I am not sure you are right about me. I am not from across the sea. And—Corrigan said some things that led me to believe he thinks of me differently."

Still Adriana kept her eyes down, noting for the first time that she and Sone were both dressed in the same slim shift of thin white linen and full trousers. Corrigan had chosen her attire. He had dressed her today as a slave, and she had not even noticed.

"You do not know that he is betrothed to another, do you?" Sone asked, and Adriana detected a hint of pity in her voice.

"Betrothed? Are you sure? To whom?"

"Lady Katerina from town. He gave her a betrothal bracelet the evening before you arrived. I am surprised you did not hear it talked about as you passed through."

With a sinking feeling Adriana remembered the crowds streaming to exclaim over something the beautiful girl mounted on the dapple gray was wearing. "She rides a gray? A girl not much older than myself?"

"Yes, that would be her. I imagine it caused quite a stir, and that she would have been hard to miss as you passed through."

Adriana nodded. "Sone, if what you say is true, why don't you fight for your freedom? I can stay and talk to Corrigan, convince him to free you. Perhaps the culture of Shahar has not advanced to the place of understanding the evils of slavery. I can help you."

"My lady, who do you think you are? I appreciate your offer, but you do not understand the one whose hospitality you have been enjoying. The feast he mentioned as you left earlier? It is to be a feast for his marauders. They are returning across the sea now with his fresh cargo, his newest slaves. He went into town last evening to prepare for them. Please, my lady. I suppose you find this hard to believe, but it will be very bad for you if you stay."

"Don't you want me to help you?" Adriana asked Sone. "I can help you escape from him."

"No. What I want is to return home, across the sea. If I escape Corrigan but stay in Shahar . . ." Sone shrugged one shoulder. "I would just be captured by someone in the town and be further from realizing my dream of returning home. At least here I am near the sea, that much closer to a chance of that. But you—if you dare to exit through the silver wall, you can still escape. It is not too late. Once Corrigan returns, now that you have seen him for the coward he is . . . He will not be kind to you on his return, my lady. Please, leave while you can."

Adriana looked around, wondering what to do. She could not deny the logic of Sone's words, but she also felt a pull to see Corrigan once more, to verify what Sone was saying. A horn blew in the distance.

"That is the hunting horn. Stow and the others will ride out to find him. The master will soon be back."

At the words Adriana felt fear clutch her throat. Her body told her what her mind did not want to acknowledge.

Corrigan had betrayed her. She was in danger from him.

"Sone, I believe you. I am sorry I doubted you. But please, let me stay and fight for you. I will go into hiding and devise a plan for us both."

"No. You need to go. Please, my lady. Get your horse, but stop here before you leave, and I will tell you how to reach the closest silver archway."

Adriana was frustrated by the sense of hurry she felt. She could see Stow and several others preparing to leave on horseback. She had to make a decision, and soon.

She took off at a run toward the stable. Sultan was nibbling on some hay when she reached the barn and she hurriedly saddled and bridled him. When she returned to the cottage, Sone was there with her journeying clothes.

"The master told me to burn them. But I washed and kept them for you," Sone said as she helped Adriana change. Sone's previous urgency seemed to have abated now that Adriana had made her decision to leave.

"They appear to be new. Thank you for mending the hem," Adriana said as Sone hooked the clasp of the soft velvet cloak around her throat.

"May I ask you a question about that?"

"Of course."

"Why were you so taken with the master when you already had a love at home?" Sone asked.

"I don't understand. I have family, but I am not

betrothed, nor do I 'have a love at home,' as you say. Why would you think so?"

"The hem, my lady. The heart's corner was torn and empty. I supposed there to have been a love note in it."

Adriana examined the neatly mended hem of the cloak. It was the corner that had ripped open in Kelak's hand when she had escaped from the cabin in Chehalem. "This is the heart's corner?"

"Yes," Sone said, a gentle smile crossing her face. She moved Adriana's hand, still holding the corner of the cloak across her chest, so that it lay comfortably over her heart. "The heart's corner. So the words of one's love might be close at hand and close to heart. It is a long-standing tradition of Veritrias, my homeland. And yours as well?"

"No, I do not believe so. The note in the hem was not for me. It must have been intended for another." Adriana thought of Kelak wailing about Banah as she walked with Sultan away from his cabin in Chehalem. Had Banah put a note in the hem of Adriana's cloak? For Kelak?

With a shake of her head, Adriana returned her attention to Sone and the present situation. "I suppose I must go now, Sone. Which way will most quickly lead me to a silver archway?"

Sone pointed to a narrow path that ran away from the cottage along the beach. But before Adriana rode off, Sone pressed a sword and scabbard into her hands. "It is a two-edged sword, my lady. Take it for your protection. The marauders are nearing shore. You should reach the archway before they land, but in case you do not . . ."

"Thank you, Sone. For everything."

Adriana had ridden only a short distance along the beach path when the wind began blowing. This was not the gentle breeze of the past few days, but an increasingly loud and blustery gale.

Seawater soon swamped the sandy path, making the way almost impassable, and torrents of rain blew in diagonal sheets that drenched her through. Though it was near high light, the day grew darker and darker, and the trees on either side of the trail bent in the wind, several times almost blocking her way.

Just when Adriana decided she would have to stop and seek shelter, Sultan's head, and then his neck, disappeared. She screamed. But somehow she kept moving. Then she felt it. The shivery, shimmery sucking of the silver wall pulled her and Sultan through the mirrored archway of Shahar.

CHAPTER 24

A TALISMAN AND A BOX

The stillness after the howling wind and slashing rain was a relief to Adriana, but the suddenness was disorienting. She stopped close to the silver archway. From this side it looked like nothing more than a large open doorway through which she could see the storm still raging. She looked about her. She was back in the original clearing. All was calm and green.

She sat on Sultan and continued to gaze at the storm, waiting for the way to snap closed as it had when she had departed Chehalem. But nothing happened. She was not afraid, nor did she feel it necessary to hurry any longer. Corrigan had been clear that the inhabitants of Shahar avoided the silver archways. And she was confident that from the Shahar side, this archway, like the one she had entered through days before, would only cast back a silvered reflection. She could see into Shahar without being seen.

She was, however, curious. Why was the land of Shahar still open to her? Was she meant to return? She thought about that for several moments. Freeing Sone would be rewarding, and restoring her to her family would be cause for great joy. But Adriana knew the true appeal of entering Shahar again was seeing Corrigan, feeling his lips on her hand or cheek, perhaps even her lips. Despite everything she now knew about him, he was like a magnet pulling her back toward him.

Corrigan did not deserve her fidelity, Adriana reminded herself. Though she wished she could disregard all that Sone had told her, in her heart she knew it was the truth. But still, Adriana wondered how accessible Shahar would be should she change her mind. She dismounted and approached the archway on foot. Breaking the plane of the arch with her hand, her fingers immediately felt clothed in spidery, cold wetness.

She pulled her hand back and walked toward Sultan, who stood watching her. That was when she saw something shiny glinting in the grass. Bending to retrieve it, she was astounded to be holding the thin, round disk of her own crest. The last time she had seen it was in her room in Ayrden, the night before she left on her Journey. She had pressed it into the warm indigo wax she'd used to seal the letters to her parents and siblings. It was the seal she had used for all but Alexander's letter.

She had written to him last and slipped the sterling crest into his envelope, sealing it with unmarked wax. She had left him the disk as a sort of talisman, a token of her belief in him and a thank-you for his gift of Sultan.

Banah was to deliver all of the letters at breakfast the day Adriana left on her Journey. So what was her crested seal doing here?

Adriana looked around the clearing and then back through the archway. Had Banah not delivered the envelope as asked? Even if she had not, how had the disk gotten here? Adriana's heart sank at her next thought. Had so much time elapsed that Alexander had gone on his Journey and left it here in the clearing for her to find? Or was it not actually hers at all? Perhaps it was not unique, as she had always supposed, and this was another with the same crest and seal.

She turned the disk over in the palm of her hand. It was just as she remembered it. One side was flat and smooth, while the other was engraved with a circle of ivy garland, broken by three standing lions and two full baskets of bread. In the center was a deep etching of the castle of Ayrden. It was as familiar to her as the weight of her hair in her hands. Surely this was her seal.

Adriana cast about for somewhere to put it. She had no

pockets and no saddlebag—she supposed it was hanging somewhere in the stable of Shahar. The scabbard Sone had pressed into her hands was strapped to her chest, but there was no place within or without to put the small disk. She picked up the edge of her cloak, remembering the heart's corner that Sone had described, and found that the stitches could be spread just enough to drop the crest into the corner of the hem. *Not exactly a love note*, Adriana thought, *but a special token all the same.*

She looked across the clearing to the only path she had not yet traversed. The jewel tones of the road and the flowers banking it gleamed in sunny contrast to the torrential rain she could still see through the archway to Shahar. Fingering the round disk through the corner of her cloak, she wondered once again if Alexander had ridden through this clearing. Might he have been in Shahar? Or could he already be in the color-drenched land through which she was about to embark? Surely not either, for that would mean she had been gone over a year, or even two, and that did not seem possible. Dropping the edge of her cloak, Adriana remounted and nudged Sultan onto the path of gemstones, which was lined on either side with mounds of flowers and trees tinkling like wind chimes in the light breeze.

After some time, the path's stones turned to jewel-colored flowers growing low to the ground. Every time

A TALISMAN AND A BOX

Adriana paused, the smell of the just-crushed flowers beneath Sultan's hooves wafted to her. The fragrance was pleasant and familiar, though Adriana could not quite remember what scent from Ayrden was so similar. There was the occasional spring, and the musical trees had given way to ordinary fruit trees growing in small orchards along one side of the path, so she was unconcerned about going hungry and wasted no time foraging for food. She simply stopped occasionally and picked a piece of fruit and drank from a spring.

Along the other side of the path ran a deep ravine with the most spectacular river Adriana had ever seen at the bottom. The water was deep sapphire blue. Yet it was so clear and slow she could see the gemstone riverbed beneath. The walls of the ravine were green stone, and bright violet and amethyst flowers spilled down the steep embankments until they touched the water.

The path eventually cut away from the ravine, and the terrain along both sides of the path became rocky. Outcroppings of rough green stone stretched well above her head, and as the shadows lengthened, Adriana began to wonder where she was going to find shelter for the night. Just as last light arrived, the path grew wider, and she spied what looked to be an entrance to a cave ahead. Darkness descending, she hurried Sultan to the spot and jumped off him, pulling her sword as she did so. It was a cave, but who knew what she might find inside?

She paused at the entrance. When Sultan pawed the ground she quickly looked around, memories of the wolf making her skittish, but she saw nothing. The cave was small, far too low for Sultan to enter, and very dark. There was just enough light remaining that she could see to the back of the tiny space, where there appeared to be nothing but walls sloping to a point and a hard rock floor. At least it would provide some shelter.

Adriana hurried to unsaddle and unbridle Sultan before the light faded completely. She had just succeeded as darkness pressed in on all sides. Feeling her way to the opening with one hand and gripping the sword with the other, she ducked her head and entered the cave. The walls were warm, from the sun she supposed. She was surprised it had grown so dark. Was there no moon tonight? She could see nothing—not Sultan, not the sword she held, not even her hand, no matter how closely she held it to her face.

She murmured, "One step," and heard a single fall of Sultan's hoof. She might not be able to see him, but he was there. She waited a hundred counts of her heart and quietly sheathed her sword. As it was too dark for her to see anything, she presumed it was too dark for anyone or anything to see her. Taking the heart's corner of her cloak in her right hand, she found the seal embossed with her crest through the thickness. Pressing it between her finger and thumb, she rested her head against the warm and oddly soft side of the cave and closed her eyes.

Adriana awoke with a start. The weak early light allowed her to see Sultan's hooves and legs through the small opening of the cave. Suddenly the walls began to vibrate and move, contracting and then expanding. Adriana ran to the entrance of the cave, now wide enough that Sultan could have walked in without even bending his head. Then one wall of the cave rose over her head and hung in midair. Sultan gave a frantic neigh but stood like a sentry waiting for her.

When she turned to look back, a green scaled and feathered creature, which she had mistaken in last light to be part of the rocks, rose into the pale morning sky. Adriana had not spent the night in a cave. She had sheltered under the wing of a creature as large as one of the small foaling barns of Ayrden. Where the creature had been, where Adriana herself had just been, was in fact a craggy precipice at least twenty trees high.

The creature flew higher, its wings undulating, into the milky sky before banking around to soar over the rocky ledge. As Adriana took in the sight, she noticed something sparkling on the very edge of the cliff.

She approached it with caution, still a bit shaken to have so misjudged the situation the night before. The creature continued to fly away from her over the vast wasteland that she could now see stretching out below the sheer drop. On the very edge of the precipice was a tiny, colorful box, sparkling so brightly that it almost seemed to be moving.

Careful not to draw any closer to the edge than necessary, Adriana picked up the box and hurried back to Sultan. It was surprisingly weighty to be so small, she thought, turning the odd-shaped box over in her hands. It was made of dark purple stone. Its four sides flared away from a small square top, rimmed in the brightest gold, to a wider center before cutting inward again and ending in a tiny square of black onyx upon which the box had been resting. All over the top and sides of the tiny box were squares made of smaller squares of sapphires and rubies and triangles made of tinier triangles of alternating gold and emeralds. Diamonds of every shape were randomly scattered across its entire surface. And at the top, on what would be the lid of the box, were two interlocking gold rings.

Though she turned it over numerous times in her hands, admiring the workmanship and wondering at its purpose, the box remained firmly sealed. Adriana wondered if it opened at all. She pulled gently on the intertwined rings, but nothing happened.

The box fit easily in her hand. She wondered whether she should take it with her or leave it. Had the creature deliberately left the box for her? Had it been left behind by mistake? Would she be hunted down for it if she took it with her? Or perhaps the creature had no knowledge of the box at all.

Adriana looked around her. There was no one to be seen and no dwellings were in sight. The path of colorful flowers continued on into a wooded section, leaving behind the high green bluffs through which she had ridden late the day before. It did not seem to make sense to leave the box, so she decided to take it with her.

As it was too large to fit in the heart's corner of her cloak, Adriana settled for riding one-handed and cradling the small jeweled box in her left hand. Perhaps she would soon encounter someone who could speak to her of its rightful owner—and explain the creature that had given her shelter. She cantered Sultan along the path, eager to meet someone, anyone, in this land of conundrums.

CHAPTER 25

THE MUSIC OF BERYLLIOS

It was the sound of drums that Adriana first heard. She slowed Sultan to a walk in order to more easily hear the fast, syncopated rhythm coming from farther down the path. Next, a jangle of wind chimes glided from discordant notes to a tinkling melody that kept time with the drums. When a stringed instrument joined the melody, Adriana stopped Sultan to listen.

As the music swirled louder and faster, it evoked a vivid memory for Adriana. She was twirling in the heat of an Ayrden summer with Bess. Their lightweight blue dresses floated around them as they spun and laughed until they collapsed, dizzy, in the grass of the meadow. That had been years ago, a memory she had all but forgotten. It had come to her mind because the music was like that moment:

youthful, carefree, joyous.

She smiled and walked Sultan forward, following the sound. Adriana saw movement in the clearing ahead. It was a dancer, spinning and leaping, wild with exuberance.

Just then the dancer saw her as well. With a jangle of wind chimes and cymbals, the girl turned and began to run from the clearing.

"Oh, don't run! Please, wait!" Adriana called out.

The dancer stopped and turned. Wisps of fair hair floated around her pale face, and her clothing was unlike anything Adriana had ever seen. From the girl's toes to the top of her head, she was clothed in a multicolored one-piece garment that was somehow both formfitting and flowing at the same time. It looked, Adriana thought, like a stained-glass window turned to silk and fashioned to make its wearer into an earthbound human butterfly.

The girl reached up a silken-covered hand and pushed back the tight-fitting hood of the garment. Adriana heard a tinkling sound at that moment and looked around for the musicians, but she saw no one other than the girl. Her blond hair floated free of the hood, making a halo around her face before it settled against the jewel colors of her collar.

"I am so very sorry I startled you," Adriana said. "In truth, I mean you no harm. Was that you making the music? It was quite gorgeous."

The girl gave a silent nod.

Adriana rode Sultan closer. "I am Princess Adriana of Ayrden." Though she had kept her identity veiled in Shahar, something about this girl elicited Adriana's trust.

"It is nice to meet you, Adriana. I am Elissa of Beryllios." The girl's voice was unexpectedly mature and her brown eyes warm and friendly. "Did you say you were from—"

But before Elissa could finish her question, a tall, dark-headed young man burst into the clearing from Adriana's right. "Elissa!" he hissed. "You know you may not dance. Stop before—"

Believing he posed a threat to Elissa, Adriana jumped from Sultan's back and pulled her sword in one fluid motion. Standing between the two and pointing her sword with a steady hand at the intruder, she uttered her own command: "Stop! You may not threaten her."

His face changed from shocked confusion to amusement. Giving first a smile and then a quiet laugh, he raised both hands. "I surrender. I will do her no harm."

Sultan fell to the ground and it was Adriana's turn to look confused. "Sultan," she called across to him, concerned. Then, noticing the young man's raised hands, she commanded, "Sultan, up!"

Sultan leaped to his feet. Why in all of Ayrden had Alexander taught him that trick? And why would Sultan be taking signals from this stranger?

"Oh, Adriana, it is fine, truly. This is Theodore, my brother. And he is right. I should not be dancing here," Elissa said, rushing over to put a hand on Adriana's arm. Her movements gave rise to several drumbeats and a cascade of flute notes. She made a frustrated sound. "I am sorry, Theo. Adriana, would you put your sword down and help me out of my chimanga? If I remove it myself, I will only make all the more noise."

With reluctance, Adriana lowered her sword and sheathed it. Elissa stood still and gave instructions. "If you will untie the neck and unbutton the back, then pull the collar over— Oh, wait. Before you do that, there are tiny buttons along my wrists."

Adriana waited for Elissa to raise her hands, but the girl remained still. "You will need to move my arms for me, to prevent the chimanga from sounding," Elissa said. Adriana lifted the girl's wrists one at a time, opening the sleeves almost to the elbow, and then slid Elissa's hands free of the silken material before returning her arms down to her sides. No music sounded.

"Now pull the collar up over my head"—Elissa bent from the waist, sounding two short violin notes—"and smooth it down to my feet and hold the toes. I should be able to step out of it. . . . Perfect!" Elissa said with satisfaction as she made a silent exit from the garment. Elissa picked it up in both hands and held it out to Theodore. Despite the

197

movement, the raiment made no sound. "Do you want to keep it?" she asked him.

"No, of course not. But what made you think to bring it out today?" Theo asked.

"I saw Zimley fly out toward Eremia, and I thought it would be all right."

An expression of concern spread across Theodore's face as he looked up into the sky. "Did he see you?"

"Of course not! I was camouflaged in the lookout."

Adriana felt every bit the intruder she was. The brother and sister were very comfortable with each other, and there was no animosity in Theo's voice and no shame in Elissa's. Her voice conveyed genuine sorrow for—what? For dancing? For making noise? Did the costume, which Adriana surmised was the source of the glorious music, not belong to Elissa? And who was Zimley? And what of Eremia? Was that actually where Adriana was at this moment? Or was she in Beryllios, the land Elissa had identified when she introduced herself?

Perhaps she should continue on her Journey. Adriana moved toward Sultan, thinking to remount and proceed along the path. Without question her curiosity was piqued. She would have much preferred to stay and discover the answers to her many questions, but her mother's training came to mind:

Never presume upon another's hospitality—

THE MUSIC OF BERYLLIOS

better to spend time alone than with a host
made awkward by your presumption.

She saw a sparkle glinting by Sultan's hoof and realized she must have dropped the gem-encrusted box when she dismounted. As she bent to retrieve it, both Elissa and Theo spoke.

"Oh, Adriana, our apologies—" began Elissa.

"We are not usually so rude—" began Theo.

"Please stay," they spoke in unison.

The three of them laughed as Adriana turned with the small box in her hand. "Thank you. I—" she began, but before she could finish Theo interrupted, pointing at the box.

"Where did you get that?"

Adriana held the box out in the flat of her palm. "Do you know to whom it belongs?"

"Perhaps. But where did you get it?" Theo asked again, reaching out a hand toward it.

Without hesitation Adriana placed the small bejeweled item in his palm. After all, it did not belong to her, and she had brought it in hopes of returning it to its rightful owner if he or she could be found. "On the precipice of the cliff. I spent the night there and saw it in the morning light. There was a creature that left it behind. I think. Or perhaps it was there already and it was merely uncovered when the creature rose into the sky and flew off."

Theodore turned the box over in his hand, and Elissa drew near to look at it as well. "Theo, could that be—"

Theo spoke before she could finish the question. "What creature?"

"The creature that gave me shelter through the night. It appeared to be a dragon perhaps. Beyond that, I have no idea what it was. I know nothing of this land. I entered it only yesterday, and past high light at that."

"And who are you exactly?" Theo asked, looking at her with an unwavering gaze as he handed the box back to her.

"Princess Adriana of Ayrden. I am on the Journey of my sixteenth year. When I heard music and saw your sister, I stopped. We had just begun talking when you burst into the clearing. Is this Beryllios?"

Theodore looked to Elissa, who shrugged her shoulders, lifting both palms up in a gesture Adriana did not quite understand.

"It is. What do you mean, the creature gave you shelter?" Theo asked.

Before Adriana could answer, a soft, rapid whistle came from overhead. Elissa touched her brother's arm. "We have to go, Theo. Adriana, do you want to come with us? I am so very sorry—to interrupt and hurry us along—but we must take cover. You are welcome to join us if you wish."

Elissa did not wait for Adriana's response. She ran into the woods with Theo close behind. Adriana was left standing by Sultan, once more unsure what to do.

Grabbing Sultan's reins, Adriana ran after them. She found an easily followed footpath that ended in a mossy embankment. She looked around in confusion.

Where were they? No sooner had she thought the question than the moss bank opened wide. It was a hidden door. And there stood Elissa and Theo, waving her inside.

CHAPTER 26

THE INNER SANCTUM

Adriana followed Theo and Elissa down a long, sloping tunnel, Sultan trailing along behind her. The tunnel was high and very wide, enough so for a dozen men to walk abreast, Adriana judged. In front of them, by the light of the torches that lined both sides of the passageway, she could see others walking. From behind her, she could hear the soft thud of the door as others entered the tunnel.

After some time they arrived in a large, round, vaulted room with twelve archways. Overhead a mosaic of beveled jewels depicted a bright blue sky with white clouds. People were gathered in small groups talking, but when they saw Adriana they fell silent. Except for Theo and Elissa, everyone, it seemed, was staring at her. Their expressions were difficult to read, but they did not appear unfriendly.

Unlike in Shahar, her clothing did not make her feel conspicuous, and not merely because it was clean and repaired. Many of the inhabitants of Beryllios were dressed in clothing similar to hers. Both men and women were wearing breeches, though most of the women's were brightly colored. And though neither Elissa nor Theo was wearing a cape, most of those standing in the room were. And their cloaks bore a striking resemblance to Adriana's, though, again, they were in an array of colors or were festooned with colorful embroidery and embellishments. Only Elissa, in tight-fitting black leggings and a snug white vest, was dressed differently. Adriana supposed that was because she had been wearing her chimanga.

Sounds were muffled in the underground tunnel so Adriana had not been able to hear what Elissa and Theo were discussing as they walked. But once the three stopped in the vaulted room, it became obvious.

"Adriana," Elissa began, "Theo and I have decided I should take you to be introduced to the Elders while he takes care of your horse. Unfortunately, Theo and I alone cannot make the decision that you may stay. And since you raised your sword to Theodore—strictly in my defense, I know," Elissa said reassuringly as Adriana began to interject in her own defense, "we thought it best that I answer the questions of the Elders alone. Does that meet with your approval?"

Adriana gave a slow nod but asked, "And where will

Sultan be? I quite prefer to look after him myself."

"I totally understand," Theo answered. He pointed down one of the tunnels leading out of the round room. "Down that tunnel is the area for animals. We have only a handful of horses at the moment, so he will have a large stall all to himself. Once the Elders approve your visit, I will show you exactly where he is."

After her dealings with Kelak and Corrigan, Adriana was amazed that she was prepared to trust this latest stranger. But there was something about Theodore that made Adriana believe him trustworthy. It was apparent Elissa thought him so. And Sultan clearly trusted him as well.

After Sultan left willingly with Theo, the two girls walked down another of the tunnels, this one narrower but far brighter. The walls were covered in gemstones, and the farther they walked, the clearer and more reflective the stones became. The tunnel finally ended in a wall covered in cut diamonds. The brightness glinting off the many facets caused Adriana to lower her eyes. When she did so she saw a glove, made of a material similar to Elissa's chimanga, lying off to one side on a low table.

Before Adriana could ask why it was there, Elissa picked it up and slid it onto her right hand. As she swept her hand in a circle from left to right and then waved it about in front of her, music poured forth from the glove. It was not the melody Adriana had heard in the clearing when Elissa had been dancing, but it was reminiscent of that. With a final flourish, Elissa soundlessly slid the glove off and returned it to the low table.

The two girls stood in silence for several moments and then the wall slid open before them.

"Greetings, Elissa," said the man on the other side of the door. He bowed in welcome and Adriana and Elissa stepped across the threshold. "The Elders are gathering. They have agreed to see you and have you introduce your guest. It will only be a few moments." He stepped out of the room and closed the door behind him, leaving them alone.

Like the large room with the twelve tunnels, this one was round with a domed ceiling, but it was quite a bit smaller. There were twelve narrow, arched doors on the far side of the room. In front of each door was a high-backed chair, and in front of the twelve chairs was one long semicircular table. In the center of the room, several feet below the table and twelve chairs, was a small table inlaid with multicolored stones. And on the table was a pitcher made of amethyst, along with two matching cups.

The walls of the room depicted scenes and symbols in mosaics of gemstones. Rising from the floor were dozens of torches that encircled the room. Their flickering light upon the mosaics made the scenes appear to move. Adriana recognized the gemstone path upon which she had entered

Beryllios and the sapphire blue river cutting through the green-walled ravine with its profusion of flowers. But most of the mosaics were indecipherable kaleidoscopes of color to her.

"I do not know if the Elders will ask you questions or not," Elissa said in a soft voice. "If they do, it is very important that you answer with truth. They will have me speak first, so just follow my lead."

The twelve doors opened simultaneously, and a symphony of music emerged with the twelve figures. Each was wearing a distinct chimanga of different colors and patterns, and each was creating a portion of the music. Only the Elders' faces were visible, and Adriana had difficulty determining if they were male or female from where she stood. As they settled into their chairs, the music subsided and silence once again filled the small chamber.

Then the Elder on the far right spoke in a deep, rumbling voice. "Elissa, please take your place at the Veritas Mensula."

Elissa stepped away from Adriana and down twelve shallow steps to the table.

A light, feminine voice came from the Elder seated on the far left. "Elissa, please give us the name of your guest."

"Princess Adriana of Ayrden," Elissa said in a calm, clear voice.

Adriana saw several of the Elders raise their eyebrows

and glance at one another.

"Has she threatened you?"

Adriana was not sure which of the Elders had asked the question, but she was taken aback. It seemed an odd thing to ask. Why would they assume she had threatened Elissa? She was suddenly quite aware that she still had the sword slung across her body. Should she have left the sword with Theo, as Elissa had left her chimanga?

"No, she has not threatened me," Elissa answered, her voice still calm and unconcerned.

"Thank you. Please have a sip of the flotande, Elissa," requested another of the Elders in a pleasant voice.

Adriana watched as Elissa poured a small amount of thick liquid out of the pitcher into one of the amethyst cups and drank. Adriana could not see Elissa's face from where she stood, but each of the twelve Elders leaned forward in their chairs, tinkling music sounding in unison as they did so, to scrutinize Elissa's face.

After a few moments each of them nodded, and the sound of soft drums filled the air. They seemed satisfied. With what Adriana was unsure, but they all leaned back in their chairs to the sound of cascading harps.

All except one.

One of the two center Elders still sat forward, elbows on the table, chimanga-clothed fingers steepled in front of his or her face. "Elissa, one more question, please," the

Elder asked, in what Adriana determined to be a female voice. "Why did you invite your visitor to stay? Please provide us with all of your reasons."

There was a pause before Elissa spoke. "She was most pleasant when we met and seemed concerned regarding my welfare. When I heard the warning whistle, I thought my invitation to her would be a return of that sentiment."

Elissa paused then said, "And also, she said she was from Ayrden. And in addition"—here there was a longer pause, as if Elissa were presenting this as the grand finale—"she carried a small bejeweled box of ten sides."

The sudden movements of the Elders were as discordant as the music that erupted in the small domed chamber. Two of the Elders leaped to their feet and turned toward the doors behind their chairs as if to flee. Another three began to hurry toward Adriana across the room. Unsure of their intentions, she stepped back and almost immediately felt the closed door at her back. The others remained seated, but there was urgent talking among them.

"Halt!" commanded the Elder seated beside the one who had asked the question. His voice resonated in the small chamber. "Listen to yourselves! There is no harmony among us. Please, everyone sit back down. Elissa, thank you. I am confident that was an honest reply. But to satisfy any possible question in that regard, please have another drink of the flotande."

THE INNER SANCTUM

Elissa again drank from the amethyst cup. Again the Elders leaned forward and looked closely at her.

One of the Elders who had not yet spoken said, "Thank you, Elissa. Elders of Beryllios, do you have any more questions for Elissa before we call her guest forward?"

Adriana's heart sank. Drumbeats, created by the Elders as they shook their heads, sounded, and twelve pairs of eyes turned to her in focused attention. It was as if she were onstage in a leading role with no idea of the script or even if the play was to be a comedy or a tragedy. Elissa turned and walked back to where Adriana stood. She gave Adriana an encouraging smile as she joined her at the top of the steps.

"Guest of Elissa, welcome to the Inner Sanctum of Beryllios. Please take your place at the Veritas Mensula," said the Elder who had called for the Twelve to return to their chairs.

Adriana moved forward, holding the heart's corner of her cloak in one hand and tightly squeezing the bejeweled box that had caused such consternation in the other. As she descended the wide shallow steps to the table in front of the Elders she rubbed the seal through the fabric, thinking of Ayrden, thinking of her gifts. She could face this panel with courage, of that she had little doubt. But kindness? When three of the Elders had looked prepared to charge her and perhaps take her by force? Improbable.

And her true fidelity lay not with Elissa but with Ayrden, which she felt was somehow under siege in this room. She had no understanding of why the name of her kingdom would cause such quizzical expressions and elicit such odd questions from these Elders. She was on the defensive. And what meaning did the jeweled box hold? It meant nothing to her, though their reaction when Elissa mentioned it greatly elevated its importance in Adriana's mind.

Head held high, she stopped in front of the table and looked up into the twelve faces peering down at her, her eyes sweeping from left to right.

"Before you begin asking me questions," Adriana said, "might I have the privilege of knowing who it is I am facing? By what name should I address you?"

Several faces revealed shocked expressions, due, Adriana supposed, to her boldness in speaking first. But the two center Elders appeared to be suppressing smiles. "You may," one of them said. "We are the Twelve Elders of Beryllios, the current judges and rulers of this kingdom. You may call us Elders or Twelve, whichever you prefer. We, the Twelve, thank you for appearing before us."

Then the Elder on the far right said in his deep voice, "Tell us your name, please."

"Elders of Beryllios, I am Princess Adriana of Ayrden."

"Please pour a fresh cup of flotande from the pitcher, Princess Adriana, and take a single sip," said one of the other Elders.

Adriana wondered if it was a request or an order, but she nonetheless reached for the pitcher. She could see through the amethyst stone that the liquid inside was flecked with something. Was it seeds? Were the flecks moving? Were they tadpoles? What was this? And why were she and Elissa required to drink it? She was glad Elissa had drunk before her and appeared to suffer no ill effects.

She lifted the pitcher and carefully poured a small amount of the viscous fluid into the empty cup. Wondering what was in the liquid and dreading how it was going to taste, Adriana lifted the cup to her lips and took a small sip. She gagged. The taste was not unpleasant, but the texture was almost unbearable. Thick and gelatinous, it made Adriana close her eyes in disgust and involuntarily open her mouth and expose her tongue, the tip firmly lodged behind her bottom teeth, as she tried to keep the liquid from coming back up. She could hear wind chimes ringing, and when she opened her eyes she could see all twelve of the Elders leaning forward and scrutinizing her tongue.

They must have been satisfied with whatever it revealed because several of them nodded and the center Elders leaned back in their chairs.

"Elders Eleven, I will take over the questioning," said one of the two centermost Elders in a deep voice. Adriana looked directly into his face, which revealed nothing of his thoughts.

"Princess Adriana of Ayrden, why have you come to Beryllios?" he began.

Adriana explained the statute of Ayrden that required its heirs to go on a Journey in their sixteenth year and briefly described having been in Chehalem and Shahar. She omitted all details of her time in both lands. The Elder's face remained inscrutable.

"That explains how you have come to be in Beryllios, but *why* are you here?" he asked. "What are your intentions?"

Adriana was at a loss as to what to say. What were her intentions? What had been her intention in any of the lands? To survive, yes. But surely that could not be the extent of what she was to learn on this Journey. She spoke from her heart, "I have no specific intentions for my time here in Beryllios. I was gifted at my birth with courage and kindness and fidelity. In different ways the honing of those gifts has happened in each of the lands through which I have journeyed."

As the words rolled from her lips, she realized they were true. So far that was exactly what her Journey had accomplished. "I assume the same will happen here, if I am allowed to stay," she concluded.

The Elder's gaze dropped to the amethyst cup on the table, and Adriana dreaded the command to drink again. But instead the Elder nodded, a gentle drumbeat sounding

212

as he did so.

"Princess Adriana, please place the ten-sided box Elissa mentioned on the table."

Adriana uncurled her fingers and placed the tiny box on the table. Jangles of wind chimes, erratic beats of drums, and slivers of other musical sounds erupted, along with several loud expletives when the Elders saw the box.

"Silence!" the questioning Elder said with a frown. "Princess Adriana, one final question: To what or to whom does your fidelity belong?"

"I am a princess of Ayrden. My fidelity belongs to Ayrden alone." Though Adriana wondered if that would be a reason to expel her from Beryllios, she was comfortable with the truth of her statement.

"Another sip of the flotande, please, Princess."

Gagging before the amethyst cup even reached her lips, Adriana nonetheless took a sip of the disgusting liquid. Unbidden, her mouth opened and her tongue exposed itself to the gaze of the Elders once again.

"You are showing yourself to be gifted with honesty as well, Princess." Adriana thought she detected approval in the Elder's deep, rumbling voice. "You may stay in Beryllios as Elissa's guest, Princess Adriana of Ayrden. You may also keep the box. It belongs to you as much as to any other."

The room erupted in discordant music and heated discussion. Ignoring both, Adriana picked up the box and began ascending the stairs to where Elissa waited. Then, from behind Adriana, a female voice called out above the noise, "Elissa?"

Adriana turned back in time to see one of the two center Elders push back the hood of her chimanga to reveal blond hair that floated around her face before falling to her shoulders.

"Please bring your guest to dinner at the Residence this evening," the Elder continued.

With a nonchalant wave of her hand, Elissa said, "Thank you, Mother. We'll see you tonight."

Of course Elissa was the daughter of one of the Elders, Adriana thought. It explained her ease in front of the august body.

As Adriana continued up the stairs, something captured her attention that made her pause midstep. There, in mosaic gems above Elissa's head, was a perfect depiction of the castle of Ayrden. It was exactly as Adriana remembered the palace that she still considered home—with one exception. On the uppermost parapet of the castle's keep perched a dragon. Its huge green wings were unfurled and its mouth, filled with flames, spewed glittering red fire at a smoldering pile of gemstones as chimanga-clad people fled from their destroyed kingdom.

CHAPTER 27

RIDDLES

So your mother is an Elder?" Adriana asked Elissa as they walked back through the glistening tunnel.

"Not exactly. She is Queen of Beryllios and my father is King. It was he who was questioning you. They will both be at dinner tonight. But they will be far less overwhelming, I promise you," Elissa said.

Adriana's mind was teeming with questions, and the image of the Palace of Ayrden crowned by the dragon initiating destruction did not leave her mind. Why would Beryllios depict that in its mosaics? There was no literal dragon of Ayrden, of that Adriana was sure. The dragon was of Beryllios. She had seen that for herself. The depiction was wrong. It had to be. Didn't it?

Still she held her tongue. She would wait and see how the day and the evening unfolded and what information was offered without her asking.

Once the girls found Theo, they walked the length of another tunnel to where Sultan was stabled. He was munching hay in his stall, looking comfortable and unperturbed.

"There are groomsmen to feed, water, and walk him," Theo said to Adriana, "so you needn't worry about him while you are here."

She noticed for the first time that his eyes were the same warm brown as his sister's. "I appreciate your tending to him, and I appreciate even more being invited to stay."

"We are happy you were granted permission to do so. Would you like a tour of the tunnels? To get your bearings?"

The underground habitat of Beryllios was extensive. The animal tunnel, which lay to one side of the wide entrance that led outside, held half a dozen horses and a dozen cows, as well as a small flock of sheep and a herd of goats. But it was large enough to have easily held thrice the number of each.

On the other side of the entrance was an armory tunnel. Small rooms were filled from the floor to the low ceiling with bows, arrows, swords, catapults, torches, and other necessities of battle. Beside the armory was the lookout tunnel. It ended in a ladder, of which only four rungs were visible. As the three approached it, Theo touched Adriana's arm and put a finger to his lips, indicating she should be silent. Then Theo ducked low and began climbing the ladder. Elissa motioned Adriana to follow him.

It was very dark inside the shaft, and it took a dozen rungs before Adriana could see they were inside a hollowed tree. Above and below various branches were tiny eyeholes through which she could see outside. The farther they ascended, the brighter it became. Right before they reached the top, there was a tiny platform that had just enough room for the three of them to stand tightly together. From Adriana's vantage point, she could see the cliff where she had spent the night and into the desert wasteland beyond. This must be the lookout that Elissa had mentioned when they were in the clearing.

Above them, the ladder rose another few rungs, and Adriana could see a pair of shoes dangling over the shaft. A watchman lay prostrate on a limb above them. But the person was so well disguised as he or she lay along the large branch covered with foliage that although Adriana knew someone was there, her eyes kept losing their focus and seeing only leaves.

The three soundlessly descended the ladder and exited along the lookout tunnel. "We have an assigned sentry on guard day and night," Elissa volunteered, speaking quietly, "but everyone in Beryllios has access to the lookout."

"The whistle, the one that caused you to flee to the tunnels. That is from whence it came?" Adriana asked.

"Yes," Theo answered. "We are, and have been for a long time, at war with the dragon and his minions. Bringing the wilderness that is called Eremia with them, they draw ever closer, so we are forced inside the tunnels all the more often."

"The dragon is Zimley?"

"Yes," answered Elissa. "But of course you know of him from Ayrden. Do you not?"

"No, not at all. Is that his depiction on the back wall of the Inner Sanctum? Atop the castle of Ayrden?"

"It is," Elissa said.

Adriana nodded and walked on in silence between the two siblings. No need to tell them that though she had not known of Zimley previously, she was, in her own way, intimately acquainted with him. Just as she had recognized Ayrden in the mosaic, so she had also recognized the dragon. Zimley was the creature that had given her shelter on the cliff.

They emerged from the lookout tunnel into the large central room. "This room is called the Vault. It is a type of crossroads for Beryllios. And there"—Elissa pointed to the left of the lookout tunnel—"is the hospital. Unfortunately, it is quite busy at the moment. Zimley's most recent attack occurred a mere three days ago. He invaded with more minions than ever. Several of our warriors were killed and even more were wounded. Are you squeamish? If not, you might be interested. The Healers are working through sunrise and moonset."

At Adriana's assent the three began walking the length of the hospital tunnel. The air was warm and moist, and Adriana soon realized why. In each room was a hot, glowing fire over which hung a steaming alabaster cauldron. As every room was doorless, the steam rolled out of the rooms and into the tunnel. Adriana could feel the loose tendrils of her hair begin to curl around her face and stick to her temples, and her eyes and nose stung from the pungent smell of the steam. Each room held one or more patients. Most were sitting up looking very fit, but a few lay motionless with bloody, oozing wounds that were quite visible from the tunnel. At the first room where a Healer stood over one of those patients, the three stopped.

A man lay prone on the bed, numerous bloody cuts in various stages of healing across his trunk. A small child, his face solemn and pinched, cupped his hands atop the man's chest, and a woman Adriana supposed to be a Healer worked her hands in small rapid movements upon the child's. "What are they doing?" Adriana asked in a hushed voice.

Theo replied, "The wounded warrior is Garret, and that is his youngest child. A Healing Stone is cupped in the child's hands over his father's breastbone. The Healer is rubbing her hands over the child's."

As Adriana watched, one of the almost healed gashes disappeared completely. Then the largest, deepest cut slowly ceased bleeding and the gaping edges of the wound turned bright red. After a few more moments, the Healer ceased moving her hands and simply placed them over the child's.

The child looked from his father's face up into the Healer's. Adriana could just hear his soft voice ask, "Will he be better now?"

"We shall see. But we know your gift of yourself has begun his healing. See?" the Healer said. She pointed to the clean, scarless skin where the cut had healed. "And he is not bleeding any longer. We will have you back tonight if you are willing. Yes?"

The child nodded and gave his father a kiss on the cheek before jumping off the small stool on which he stood. When he passed by on his way out of the tunnel, Theo ruffled his hair and gave him a smile. The little boy stopped and gave Theo's leg a hug before running down the tunnel toward the Vault.

The three finished walking the length of the tunnel where a dozen more Healers worked over various men and women.

Once they emerged Elissa continued as if what Adriana had just witnessed was the most normal thing in all of Beryllios. "And beside this is the men's tunnel, where the single men of marrying age live. Theo lives there."

"Wait!" Adriana said, stopping. "Explain to me what we just saw in the hospital tunnel."

"What do you mean?" Elissa asked, cocking her head to one side with a puzzled look on her face.

"I saw no potions being given, no incantations, no poultices being applied. Yet so many of those patients looked fully recovered. And you said the battle was a mere three days ago. How does the Healing Stone work?"

"You still use potions as your primary form of healing in Ayrden?" Theo asked.

"We do."

"Interesting. That is our healing of last resort, as it is slow and often ineffective. We use that only if a person has no blood relation. It is not just the Healing Stone and it is not just the Healer. We are not sure exactly how it happens, but the three together, as you just saw: blood relative—the younger the better; Healer; and Healing Stone. It takes all three, but it works. Recovery is certainly not instantaneous, but it is rapid and progressive. The method was discovered a generation or so ago."

"How very wonderful," Adriana said, still in awe of what she had seen.

Elissa said, "Ready for the rest of the tunnels? To the left of the men's tunnel is one of the tunnels of family abodes. And of course you recognize the tunnel to the Inner Sanctum." Elissa continued with her hand outstretched as she slowly turned in a circle describing each tunnel's purpose. "And beside that is the second tunnel of family abodes, and then the women's tunnel. That is where you will be staying with me. And then we have my two favorites, the practice tunnel and the booths. Let's do the booths first."

As the three walked across the Vault, Adriana could feel the eyes of those in the room following her. Word of her interchange with the Elders must have spread, Adriana thought. Many of their expressions were now unfriendly, and she could hear murmuring as she passed the various clusters of people.

If the mosaics in the Inner Sanctum were some kind of history of Beryllios, she could understand why these people were hostile. Surely being from Ayrden meant she was considered their enemy. But if that was true, why, then, were Elissa and Theo treating her as a friend, an ally even? They not only showed her the lookout, they trusted her to go up in it with them. For that matter, why had the Twelve allowed her to stay? It had been obvious that some of them considered her less than benign. Yet the Queen had even asked Elissa to bring her to dinner.

Adriana was so deep in thought trying to puzzle out the situation that she was taken aback upon entering the tunnel of booths. It was a busy marketplace. Market booths lined both sides of the tunnel, and overhead torches and open brick ovens produced black soot that hung low in the air. There was a pleasant buzz as sellers attempted to lure buyers to their stands.

"Ah, Elissa! I have your favorite curried vegetables today," called a small, wizened woman from one of the booths.

"Theo," called another, "your sweetmeats sold out just moments ago! You should have been here earlier!"

The three threaded their way through the busy marketplace. Theo bought a loaf of bread and some figs, and Elissa bought a goodly portion of the curried vegetables and a flask of some beverage.

"Let's duck through here and eat in a practice room," Elissa suggested midway through the tunnel. She pushed open a rough-planked door and Adriana followed, entering yet another tunnel, this one dark and damp. She pulled her cloak closer, shivering a bit.

Theo put an arm about her and gave her a quick hug. "No worries, it is a short tunnel and only a connector. We will be to the other end in three blinks."

Adriana relaxed at his comforting touch and words. And indeed, almost immediately there was another door, this one exiting into a well-lit tunnel where music of all kinds seeped from behind thick closed doors. Like the Inner Sanctum, the walls were bright with gemstone mosaics.

Depictions of chimanga-clothed dancers seemed to lead toward the Vault, which Adriana could see to the right.

"This way," Elissa said cheerily as she practically danced across the smooth amethyst floor down the brightly colored tunnel.

"My sister is the enthusiastic sort," Theo said as they followed at a more sedate pace. "What do you think of our underground kingdom?"

"It is amazing, and very different from what I am accustomed to. As I met both you and Elissa aboveground, I suppose you do not spend all of your time in the tunnels?"

"Not at all. We sleep and eat down here, and we are supposed to only wear our chimangas down here as well. But we hunt and fish and gather food above virtually every day."

"So that is why you were upset at Elissa?"

"Upset at Elissa?" Theo looked confused. "Oh, you mean in the clearing. I was not upset at her. I was concerned for her safety. The sound of a chimanga is like a clarion call to battle for Zimley. Elissa can be impetuous. And never having witnessed an attack by the dragon firsthand . . ." Theo shrugged. "She takes liberties with her safety."

"Do your women not go to battle alongside the men?"

"They do. But not until they have had their seventeens Festival of Twelve."

Before Adriana could ask what that was, they reached

Elissa, who was standing with her ear pressed hard against a door. "I hear nothing," she whispered. "This room should be free." She slowly turned the handle and opened the door wide to reveal a perfectly square room four strides by four strides. The room was empty of any furniture and totally white. The floor was marble and the walls were mother-of-pearl with just the faintest iridescent sheen.

"I hope you don't mind sitting on the floor, Adriana," Elissa said with a smile. "I thought it might be best for just the three of us to have luncheon together today. Normally I would eat in the women's tunnel and Theo in the men's, but you would have to field so many questions from the other girls, I thought this might be more pleasant."

"This is lovely," Adriana replied. "Would you like to use my cloak as a blanket for us to sit upon? I wouldn't mind."

At Elissa's positive reply, Adriana pulled the cloak from about her shoulders and spread it across the marble. The thick green velvet covered the entire center of the room.

"Can you see why I wanted to practice wearing my chimanga outside, Theo?" Elissa said as she spread out the food. "Our practice rooms are so tiny, I cannot create what needs to be sounded by me."

Adriana was not exactly sure what Elissa meant. But remembering the exuberant leaps and wild movements of her dance, Adriana could easily imagine that a chimanga-clad Elissa would feel cramped within this small space.

"Better to make a portion of your true sound than to have your sound cut short permanently," Theo said cryptically.

The bread was fresh, with a crisp crust, and the figs were sweet and juicy. And when Adriana took a bite of the curried vegetables she made a delighted sound. "Oh, these are delicious! I don't believe I have had curry since I was a tiny child. It tastes exactly like I remember."

As they ate, Elissa entertained Adriana and Theo with tales of her chimanga practices in the small rooms. She had both of them laughing as she told of bruised elbows and toes and even a crash resulting in a black eye, and it was as pleasant a lunch as Adriana could recall ever having.

After Adriana finished eating, she licked her fingers, savoring the distinctive taste of curry. "Thank you for sharing such a delightful lunch with me. Am I keeping either of you from things you need to be doing? I am well able to amuse myself, I assure you."

"Actually, given all those fiascoes, I do need to practice, albeit in one of these small spaces. Theo, did you put my chimanga back in my room?" Elissa asked.

"I did. There are things I need to go check on myself. Adriana, why don't you go with Elissa and wait for the dressing bell in her room? Meanwhile, she will find you something to wear for dinner. There are books all along the walls of the living quarters. You can help yourself to any that you like. And I will see you at the Residence for dinner."

"Oh, good! You're going to be there too?" Elissa said. "That is a wonderful plan, Theo. You go on ahead. I will take care of Adriana."

With that they parted.

And that was how Adriana soon found herself alone, snuggled into Elissa's bed and reading about the bizarre intersection of Berylliosian and Ayrdenish history. The tome Adriana had chosen to flip through was a beautiful book that told of the history of Beryllios in stylized lettering and pictures. Early in the volume there was a gorgeous rendering of a bejeweled castle centered in an open circular courtyard, with twelve spokes leading to twelve elaborate structures. The path to each ornate building was adorned with gardens and statuary. Adriana could easily see the similarities in the layouts of the flourishing aboveground castle pictured and the underground network of tunnels where she was now hidden. After spending some time skipping about the text, reading about the weapons of warfare and the products mined, grown, or produced in Beryllios for trade, Adriana saw a familiar word in an unfamiliar context and began reading more closely:

After centuries of friendly trade between Beryllios and Ayrden across the seasonal natural bridge, Ayrden sent the deceiver Naicon, the eldest heir of the King of Ayrden, to Thebazeli, the beautiful daughter of the King and Queen of Beryllios. Though he courted Thebazeli with happy tales of their jointly ruling the two kingdoms, Naicon's true desire was to add Beryllios to the Kingdom of Ayrden and to rule them both with an iron fist. Before Thebazeli could decline Naicon's offer to join the kingdoms through marriage, Naicon's brother, Lebar, came from Ayrden.

After no more than a moon cycle, Naicon lured his brother into Eremia, though historians are unclear of his motive. Even more of a puzzlement is why the beautiful Thebazeli rode out with Lebar to meet Naicon. But once there, Naicon and Zimley, the dragon of destruction, struck them both dead.

Zimley labored alongside Naicon and waged war against Beryllios. The first siege on the castle lasted from one dawn to the next. Once the sun rose over the fair Beryllios and its inhabitants, the dust of the ground so shook in sorrow at the death and destruction that the morning star disappeared from the sky and the seasonal land bridge to Ayrden was severed for all time.

The deceiver Naicon was killed through the bravery of the Elders of Beryllios, but Zimley flew free and continues to wage war on all the true inhabitants of Beryllios. For each battle won by Zimley and his minions, more land is converted from the lush Beryllios of the past to the dry and arid Eremia that continues to encroach upon us to this day.

Adriana had never heard of any of this. Never heard of these two brothers, Naicon and Lebar. Never heard of Ayrden trading with a kingdom called Beryllios. Never heard of anyone in Ayrden combining forces with a dragon of any sort, much less one of such evil intent. Curious as to when these events were supposed to have occurred, Adriana flipped through the pages searching for dates, but she found none.

Picking up the tiny, ten-sided box from the table beside the bed, she lay back against the pillows and absently turned the bejeweled trinket in her hands as she mulled over what she had just read. Mentally scrolling through her ancestral history, she tried to determine where these two brothers might fit into her own family tree. She eventually recalled there had been a King of Ayrden in the distant past whose only two children, both sons, mysteriously disappeared and never returned. Perhaps, Adriana thought, those two sons had been Naicon and Lebar. Upon the King's death, Ayrden had passed to his sister and then on through her heirs, of whose histories Adriana was better informed. But as to how Zimley the dragon fit into the story, Adriana was clueless. Though she continued to flip through the book for some time, she could find no mention of the dragon before the incident with the brothers in Eremia.

The book made Adriana even more uncertain as to why the Elders should have allowed her to stay. And why Elissa and Theo should be treating her as a friend, not a foe. Was their welcome genuine or a mere ruse? Perhaps dinner at the Residence this evening would give her some insight, and also an opportunity to redeem her homeland in their eyes. She wanted to portray Ayrden and her people as she knew them to be. Ayrden was a beautiful land of freedom and benevolent rulers. Its inhabitants were interested in peace, not instigating war and destruction. As long as she was here she would defend Ayrden and its rulers, past and present. Soon enough, she believed, the truth of Ayrden's relationship to Beryllios would be clear.

In truth, as Adriana would discover, it would require more than a little time in Beryllios for the situation to become clear. And once Adriana understood the role she herself played in the future of Beryllios, it would be too late for her to return to Ayrden unscathed.

CHAPTER 28

THE IMAGO

Elissa returned with clothes for Adriana. There were breeches and tunics, much like her journeying clothes, but in both soft and vibrant colors with embroidery and trim, and several floor-length dresses with a slim silhouette. These, Elissa explained, were to be worn for dinner.

"I hope it is all right that you share my room," Elissa said as she placed the garments alongside her own in a wardrobe. "We are a bit short of rooms in the women's tunnel at the moment. There will not be one free until the next wedding. And actually," Elissa said, cocking her head to one side, "I hear the next bride approaching." At Adriana's questioning look, Elissa continued. "Hear the finger bells coming down the tunnel? It's our reminder that it is time to dress for dinner. They are rung by the next bride of Beryllios."

As Adriana listened she could hear the bells approaching and growing more distinct. They rang in a little cascade of five rings, pause, five rings, pause. Adriana smiled. "That seems like a nice tradition."

"I suppose," Elissa replied with a shrug. "Unfortunately, it is a tradition that in no way is as grand as the one it replaced." She pointed to the tiny bejeweled box on the table by the bed. "That box you found? It is the last betrothal box ever made in Beryllios. It disappeared the same day the war began."

"Then why did your father say for me to keep it? I don't understand."

"Quite frankly, neither do I. There are numerous mysteries regarding the days surrounding Zimley's initial attack. But the betrothal box and its design are well known. It was made by the Master Artisan for the eldest heir of Beryllios, Thebazeli, twelve generations ago. Our custom was for a box of ten sides to be given by the bride-to-be to her chosen as a token of betrothal. The ten sides, plus the two individuals, make twelve, the number of completion," Elissa explained. "But when Thebazeli died, the box disappeared, and Zimley appeared. The King at that time ordered the custom changed for as long as Beryllios was at war with Zimley. So the little ritual of ten finger bells being played by the betrothed replaced it. It is still ten plus the bride and groom to equal twelve, just in not nearly as beautiful and romantic a way."

By the time Elissa finished explaining about the box, the two girls were dressed and ready to leave for the Residence. They walked out of the women's tunnel, through the Vault, and to the end of one of the family abode tunnels. Adriana tried to piece together this information with what she had read earlier. So to whom had Thebazeli intended to give the betrothal box? Was the history she had read earlier wrong? Had Thebazeli in truth returned Naicon's feelings? Or had she chosen to marry someone from among her own people for whom the box was intended?

Greeting the Queen and the King and meeting the guests invited for the evening pushed the questions from Adriana's mind. The food was plentiful and conversation around the table centered on activities in Beryllios. No one asked her to further explain her presence, and she enjoyed being among a family again. It made her miss Ayrden, her parents, and her siblings. *Perhaps*, she thought, *I should leave tomorrow and continue my Journey*. But, though the thought was intriguing, Adriana had a distinct sense there was a purpose for her here. There were too many unanswered questions for which she seemed to have partial clues. She would work at showing the best of Ayrden to this kingdom and wait a bit, confident she would know when the time was right to continue on her Journey.

A CLEARING IN THE FOREST

After that first of many dinners at the royal table of Beryllios, the days fell into a pleasant rhythm for Adriana. Each morning she would climb the lookout and check for any sign or news of Zimley. If the area was clear of his presence, she would saddle Sultan and ride out for the morning. Afterward she often spent the day with Elissa or Theo and one or more of their friends. Together they fished in the clear water of the ravine and gathered berries from the purple flowers spilling down the walls. Adriana proved to be a nimble and fearless climber. And as loose gemstones were prized for their trading value at the booths, she was a sought-after partner for gem hunting. However, they never ventured out of earshot of the sentry.

They always returned for the midday meal, or at any time the warning whistle of the sentry was heard. In the afternoons Adriana typically read in Elissa's room, attempting to fill in missing pieces of information about Beryllios and its ties to Ayrden. Each evening she and Elissa ate at the Residence with Elissa's parents or at one of various other homes. Most often Theo was there as well.

One morning as Adriana cantered Sultan round and round the clearing where she first met Elissa, trying to keep him suitably exercised while at the same time keeping them both safe should Zimley put in an appearance, memories of home intruded into her thoughts. It had been a long time since she had ridden circles in so small a space. It reminded her of Beecher teaching her to ride, his instructions called across the small bullring in his always jovial voice.

"Princess, keep yer heels down.

"Settle into the saddle, hands up a bit, relax—relax.

"Give the pony a little heel and ask her to canter."

Adriana remembered her frustration at not being able to make Squirt, the little pony that was her first mount, do anything more than walk faster. And then Alex, so small his head barely came above the bottom rail of fencing, had said "Canter" in his eager little-boy voice, and the pony set off at a canter so immediately Adriana was almost unseated.

Thoughts of home suddenly overwhelmed her. To distract herself, she left the clearing and turned Sultan toward the bluff where she had sheltered her first night in Beryllios. She was surprised to find Theo standing there, looking out over Eremia.

Adriana was unsure whether to approach or to return to the underground tunnels when Theo turned and saw her.

"Good morning," he said, motioning for her to continue approaching. His dark hair curled above his high forehead and his eyes were bright. "So Elissa let you out of her sight?" he teased. A dimple creased along one side of his mouth.

"She did. I thought Sultan could use a bit of exercise, and she had planned on gem hunting this morning. Do you ride?" Adriana asked. It occurred to her that she had not seen anyone ride anywhere since she'd arrived.

"I do, though not so often anymore. We are down to no more than a half dozen horses. The last battle with Zimley and his minions resulted in many being slaughtered or running away."

"I'm sorry," Adriana said as she slipped off Sultan and joined Theo at the edge of the precipice. "Are you searching for something?"

"Not exactly. I was looking for any visible changes in the wilderness of Eremia."

"Do you expect changes?"

"No, I have no reason to expect there to be any change, at least no change for the better. I remember when one could see Eremia only in the distance. There were flowers and trees and streams of water far across the flat."

"I'm sure you and your people will find a way to rescue Beryllios and return it to glory."

"I hope so." He turned to look down at her with a small smile. "You are optimistic, aren't you? Thank you. I needed that bit of encouragement today."

Theo turned and the two walked back toward the entrance tunnel in companionable silence. From that day on, Adriana's interest in reuniting Ayrden and Beryllios began to grow. It was difficult to imagine a life without these two siblings who were becoming such dear friends.

Throughout all her time as the guest of the royal family, Adriana felt free to leave and continue on her Journey. But she also felt welcome to remain in Beryllios as long as she pleased, and the longer she stayed, the friendlier all of its inhabitants became toward her. But no one was more pleasant to her than the Queen herself.

Still, everyone was surprised when, one evening over dinner at the Residence, she asked, "Adriana, would you care for us to have a chimanga made for you?"

Elissa gave a gasp and Theo choked on his water and started coughing.

Adriana smiled at the Queen. "I would be so excited to have my own chimanga. We have nothing like it in Ayrden, though, so my music might sound quite terrible. Do you not train for a very long time?"

The Queen gave a nod. "We do. Traditionally our young adults receive their chimangas as twelves. But the art of the chimanga is more a refinement of the sound one makes than a learning of how to make sound. The music itself is part of the warp and weave of each individual; the chimanga merely gives it voice."

"It is most generous of you to offer. If it's not too much trouble, I would love to have my own," Adriana said.

"Will it be ready for the Festival of Twelve?" Elissa asked.

"That would be my intention," the Queen answered before turning back to Adriana. "How old are you, my dear?"

Surprised by the question, Adriana replied, "Oddly enough, I am not sure. Sixteen, I suppose. I left for my Journey the day after my sixteenth birthday, but I have no inkling how long ago that was. Why do you ask?"

Before the Queen had a chance to respond, Elissa interjected, "We receive our chimangas as twelves. But we may do no more than practice in them until we are seventeen. Then, on the twelfth day of the twelfth month at the twelfth hour, all who are seventeen come forward publicly for the first time. It is the Festival of Twelve. This will be my first year to participate."

Elissa continued, her voice conveying her ever-growing excitement. "The first dance is solely for those of us who are seventeen. The next dance includes all those who are eighteen, the next those who are nineteen. So the first nine dances are reserved for the seventeen to twenty-fives. After that, all who are chimanga-clad are welcome to dance. Last year I was able to attend and watch. Not in my chimanga, of course. But this year I will be able to dance."

Adriana felt disappointment well up within her. She much preferred the idea of participating and not merely observing. "I am not sure what to say. I would wish to be seventeen, of course, but I have no way of knowing with certainty whether I am."

The King, who rarely spoke at table but whose word seemed to always be final, said, "I think a trifecta of the Twelve could make that determination. But it would require you to again drink the flotande, Adriana. Are you willing?"

Adriana felt herself beginning to gag at the thought of drinking the disgusting liquid. But the idea of a chimanga of her own was too much of an enticement to decline the offer. "I am willing."

"Tomorrow, then. Come to the Inner Sanctum immediately following breakfast," the King said.

Elissa began babbling about how chimangas were designed and the requisite visit to an Imago before the Weavers began their work. Adriana listened with interest as the Queen gave an enigmatic smile to her husband and glanced from Adriana to a grim-looking Theo.

The next morning found Adriana standing alone at the Veritas Mensula. Above her, seated at the semicircular table, were the King and the Queen and a third member of the Twelve. Adriana thought she perhaps recognized him from her first visit to the chamber. But with only the oval of his face visible in his chimanga, it was difficult to be certain. On the table before her sat the same amethyst pitcher and a single cup.

The member of the trifecta unknown to Adriana began, "Princess Adriana of Ayrden, please pour a small amount of flotande into the cup."

Adriana picked up the pitcher and watched as the thick, flecked liquid slid from one amethyst vessel into the other.

"Adriana," the King said, "you said last night you were sixteen when you left on your Journey. We are going to determine, with the help of the flotande, how old you are currently. Please be aware that if you answer falsely, the truth seeds that remain on your tongue will be obvious to us and uncomfortable for you." Adriana's heart sank. *How uncomfortable?* "However, in this particular circumstance we are not holding you accountable for any lies you might utter, as we understand you do not know the correct answer. Please answer only with a simple yes or no to each of our questions in order to determine your age. Do you understand?"

"I do."

"Very well. Princess Adriana, are you sixteen years of age?"

Adriana struggled to decide what to say. She assumed

she was. But it seemed like much more than a year since her birthday ball. Could she really be only sixteen? "No," Adriana finally said with decisiveness.

The King's eyebrows rose, but he motioned with his hand for her to drink. She steeled herself for possible pain as she took a sip of the liquid. As before, her eyes involuntarily closed and her mouth opened, exposing her tongue. She felt no pain. In fact, she felt nothing unusual at all as the thick liquid slid down her throat.

When she opened her eyes the King and Queen were barely nodding to a soft slow cadence of what sounded like finger bells.

"Are you seventeen?" the Queen asked, leaning forward to the sound of a harpsichord glissando.

If she were no longer sixteen, Adriana thought, she must certainly be seventeen, mustn't she? Surely she had not been gone more than two years. But perhaps the flotande did not work on her at all, as she was not of Beryllios. Fairly certain the answer she was about to give was a lie, but willing to test the flotande all the same, Adriana said, "No, I am not seventeen." How uncomfortable could it be, after all? She took a sip of the flotande.

Instantly her tongue felt as if it were being pierced with a myriad of tiny, fiery needles. Tears began streaming from the outside corners of her eyes. If she had been able, she would most certainly have screamed.

"Oh, my dear!" she heard the Queen exclaim. Adriana could hear the sounds of gentle drums, cymbals, and a lyrical flute melody advancing toward her. "Here is some water. Do wash the seeds away and off your tongue. It is quite safe for you to swallow them," the Queen said as she pressed a cold metal mug into Adriana's hand and helped her lift it to her mouth.

In moments the pain disappeared, leaving behind only the tiniest of numb spots scattered all across her tongue. When Adriana opened her eyes, the Queen was standing so close to her she could see flecks of gold in the irises of her brown eyes.

"So. You are seventeen," she said softly. "You will be able to dance at the Festival of Twelve. I believe we should take you to the Imago right away."

Adriana merely nodded.

By the time the Queen and Adriana arrived at the door of the Imago, Adriana knew only that they remained underground. They had exited the Inner Sanctum through a very small round opening centered between the arched doorways of the Queen and the King. The monarchs had each put a hand on either side of a mosaic butterfly, and the seal of the doorway had opened on invisible hinges with the sound of breaking glass. The Queen had entered first, bending low and carefully stepping over the rounded ledge a foot or more above the ground. She held a torch, and by its light Adriana could see they were in a tight, round tunnel. It gradually grew wider the longer they walked. The way seemed circuitous to Adriana, bending back upon itself time and again, descending down numerous steps before rising again. The music from the Queen's chimanga was almost like a lullaby, rhythmic and calming.

The Queen stopped and so did the music. She and Adriana stood in front of another round door, this one much larger and as obvious as the first was hidden. It was mirrored, with clearly visible hinges and a sparkling, multifaceted doorknob.

Adriana was surprised to see her reflection, which she had not clearly seen since she had looked into the silvered archway of Shahar at her arrival in that other land. Her cheeks were pink and her green eyes bright. Gone was the emaciated waif who had left Chehalem. She looked healthy and confident. She turned away, not wishing to appear vain, but she was pleased.

"You must knock," the Queen said.

Adriana raised her hand and gave three soft knocks. She pulled her hand away and saw her mirrored image withdraw as the door swung open.

"Yes, what do you seek?"

Adriana took a step back. Though she was not at all sure what she had been expecting, it was certainly not this.

She was no longer standing in front of the mirror, but she might as well have been. For the person asking Adriana the question appeared to be Adriana herself, speaking in Adriana's own voice—albeit an Adriana dressed in the simple chimanga undergarments of tight black pants and white vest who was already inside the room.

"I repeat, what do you seek?" Adriana heard and saw this identical twin self ask.

"A chimanga," Adriana whispered.

"Then enter," the Imago said and stepped aside.

Adriana stepped across the threshold and turned back toward the Queen.

"I will wait here. The Imago will tell you what to do," the Queen said. Her face was impassive, confusing Adriana all the more. Was there some treachery afoot here? Was this a snare of some sort? How was it possible that this Imago would look and sound just like Adriana herself?

The Imago closed the large round door with one slim hand, and Adriana noticed a fading crisscross of scars on the Imago's wrist. Adriana ran a single finger across her own wrist, feeling the bumpy roughness of the scars she still carried from her time in Kelak's bonds. Her heart picked up pace and she could hear the pounding of each beat as she attempted to assess the situation.

THE IMAGO

The room was round with a high, flat ceiling. Spaced all around the ceiling's edge were pinholes through which tiny beams of light shone, creating a single small circle of light on the sandy floor. In the center of the room was a shallow pit, no more than a handsbreadth deep and an arm's length wide, with sand in the bottom. There was a decorative dressing screen, from which hung a long length of white fabric. Otherwise, the only thing in the chamber was an assortment of pitchers, of every color imaginable, sitting in notches in the smooth curved wall. Some were translucent, others opaque. All appeared filled with water.

"If you would step behind the screen, undress, and wrap yourself in the white, we will begin," the Imago said in what Adriana recognized as her own gentling voice. It was the voice she used with the twins when they were inconsolable because of some imagined fright.

A shiver ran up Adriana's spine. It was unnerving to be addressed in your own voice, to hear yourself speak, but to not be the speaker. Yet, at the same time she found it oddly reassuring, as if she could surmise the Imago's sentiments.

Adriana slipped behind the screen and disrobed, then wrapped the long length of white fabric under her arms, twisting and tying the ends securely. When she stepped out, the Imago was waiting on the other side of the shallow pit. The small circle of light had moved across the floor, drawing closer to the pit.

"The timing should work perfectly," the Imago said as she motioned toward the circle of light. "You need to listen carefully to my instructions. First, choose one of these, please."

The Imago held out a dozen sticks in varied colors. Each was the length of Adriana's forearm and no bigger around than the circumference of her little finger.

Adriana approached and chose a hyacinth blue stick flecked with gold.

"Excellent choice. I like that one very much," the Imago said in the voice Adriana reserved for a handful of her favorite things. "Now, toss it into the center of the pit."

Adriana did so. As the stick hit the sand the color of the stick intensified, even as the color bled from it all across the sand. *Amazing*, Adriana thought, *but what does this have to do with creating a chimanga?* What was even happening, anyway?

When the Imago made a soft sound at the color transference, Adriana recognized it as the sound of pleasure that she sometimes made in her own throat. The color was pretty, but why should it bring the Imago pleasure? *This whole situation is bizarre*, she thought.

"And now, we need to step into the pit. You will do it like so." The Imago laid a single white stick down in front of her and put one foot on either side, toes pointing in toward the stick just at its middle. "Do you understand what we must do?"

Adriana raised her eyebrows. "What *we* must do? Don't you mean what I must do?"

"If you wish to phrase it that way. Do you understand the instructions?"

"Yes, I think so." Adriana stepped carefully into the pit. The sand was oddly warm in the cool room. Her toes pointed in awkwardly toward the stick.

"Just right," the Imago said reassuringly as she moved away from the pit's edge. "Now, look at all of the pitchers and choose four."

Adriana cast a quick glance over them all. It seemed so obvious to her, the emerald green and the cobalt blue, the poppy orange and the pink fuchsia. As she pointed out each translucent pitcher, the Imago pulled it from a shelf and placed it by the edge of the pit.

"And now, before you place your hands, I need you to choose another four pitchers," the Imago said, casting a quick glance at the circle of light that was creeping ever closer to the sandy pit.

Adriana looked around the walls again. "The gold, the pearl, the onyx, and . . ." Here she paused. "Is this my last pitcher or are there more to choose?" Adriana asked the Imago as the onyx pitcher was placed alongside the others.

The Imago merely lifted one slim shoulder in a shrug and gave Adriana a slight smile. Adriana knew that look.

Knew what was behind it. She had given that look dozens of times to Alex, to Bess, to Ty, and to the twins. It was the look of: *I know the answer, but unfortunately you will have to discover it for yourself.*

It irritated her beyond measure. But she still wanted to make the correct choice. Or was such a thing possible? Was there a correct choice or just a preference? Out of the corner of her eye Adriana could see the circle of light moving closer. It was nearing the edge of the pit. She refused to be hurried.

"The ruby pitcher in the very center," she finally said.

The Imago's face grew somber. "Your final choice is the red pitcher then. Before I retrieve the pitcher, I need you to spread your hands so." The Imago spread wide the fingers of each hand and placed the heels of her palms close, but not touching. "Without moving your feet, place your hands on either side of the stick, above your toes. And remain still until I tell you to move."

Adriana bent and placed her hands as instructed, squatting in the hyacinth sand and watching as the Imago walked across to the wall and retrieved the last pitcher.

The circle of light crept over the edge of the pit. At the very moment the entire circle appeared in the blue sand, the Imago held the emerald pitcher over Adriana's head and began to pour. The water, if that's what it was, was neither hot nor cold. It was almost impossible to feel, it was so much the same temperature as Adriana's skin. The scent was pure and heavenly. Adriana dropped her head and closed her eyes against the deluge. The pitcher seemed to hold an amazing amount of liquid.

The Imago poured the contents of each pitcher in a slow stream over the crouching Adriana, the pit gradually filling as the circle of light crept across it. Each pitcher's liquid had a slightly different scent, though none were recognizable to Adriana. The last drop from the ruby pitcher touched the crown of her head just as the circle of light began its ascent up the side of the pit.

"You may stand up now, Princess Adriana of Ayrden," said a clear, strong voice Adriana did not recognize.

Adriana's eyes flew open and she leaped from the pit. The being she now faced was like nothing she had ever seen. The Imago was robed in a chimanga that seemed made out of light itself and stood so tall the Imago's head almost touched the ceiling. Her or his, Adriana could not be sure, face and eyes seemed to be no color at all, but mere translucence.

"Do not be afraid. You chose well and truly. The Queen waits for you just outside the door."

CHAPTER 29

VISIT TO EREMITE EMUN

The days that Adriana spent waiting for her chimanga to be delivered seemed to pass more slowly than any she had known before. Perhaps it was because she did not want to talk about her experience of meeting the Imago. It felt too personal, too intimate, to discuss with anyone. And yet it seemed to be all she could think about. Her mind kept wandering back to the her-who-was-not-her who had opened the mirrored door and the final, transformed figure of the Imago.

She had asked the Queen about it as they walked the length of the tunnel back to the Inner Sanctum. "You were not surprised by the appearance of the Imago? That it looked like me?"

"Not really," the Queen replied. "I was pleased that the Imago was able to greet you as yourself. As you are not of Beryllios, I was unsure. The Imago's method promotes the genuineness of the experience. Taking instruction and direction from oneself prevents undue outside influence, creating a purer chimanga design. Of course, usually there is enough difference between the twelve- and the seventeen-year-old selves that when the children of Beryllios meet the Imago they are often unaware it is actually themselves as they will be. And we do not broadcast the fact. But still, it seems to work well."

That had been almost an entire moon cycle ago. Elissa spent more and more time in the practice tunnel, as did all of the seventeens. So Adriana and Theo began to spend long segments of each day alone together, often sent on expeditions by the King or the Queen to check on one of the Eremites, citizens of Beryllios who lived as hermits in various caves in the walls of the ravine. They sometimes had valuable information regarding Zimley to pass along.

Adriana and Theo most often went on foot, as the ravine walls were far too steep for horses to climb, and to leave the animals could expose them to an attack by Zimley. They tried to stay hidden as much as possible, since all of the Eremites lived out of hearing of the sentry, and Zimley was unpredictable in his descents upon Beryllios.

It was on one of these excursions that Adriana began to regard Theo as more than just Elissa's older brother and the heir apparent of Beryllios. After walking from early light to past high light, they had arrived at the spot where they needed to drop over the ledge of the ravine to visit Eremite Emun. His cave was located near the bottom of the ravine.

Theo shifted his sword to his back before lowering himself over the ledge. Adriana did the same. But her head had no more than dropped below the ledge of the cliff when she felt Theo grab her by the waist and pull her hard against his chest. The ledge on which he stood was so narrow that Adriana's feet dangled over the edge.

Her back to his chest, he whispered urgently in her ear, "Don't make a sound!"

In truth, Adriana thought of screaming, though she was aware there were precious few to hear her. She was in a dangerous situation, and Theo had put her there. She stood not a chance of fighting him off without sending them both plummeting to the bottom of the ravine.

But the days spent with Theo had built her trust in him, so although she could not imagine what he was doing, she remained quiet and still, while her heart beat a heavy tattoo in her ears.

When Adriana saw the shadow of a blunt head followed by a thin neck and wide, gargantuan wings, she understood. He had seen Zimley. He had pulled her with him to safety, precarious safety, but safety nonetheless. A thin overhang shadowed them from Zimley's view as he flew over them.

The dragon circled within the confines of the ravine, flying in ever-shrinking circuits until he landed far below the two on a rocky promontory. Adriana remained motionless. But when she felt Theo's arms begin to tremble from the strain of holding her, she wondered what she should do.

As if he could read her thoughts, he spoke again in her ear, this time in a voice no louder than a breath. "I have you. I will not let you go."

They remained as they were until Zimley finally lifted his wings and flew down the river and out of sight.

Theo turned and placed Adriana's feet on the narrow ledge beside him. She grasped the wall with one hand for additional purchase, but still he did not remove his arms from around her.

"Theo, you can release me now. I am secure," Adriana said, turning to look at him over her shoulder.

His face was ashen, but his smile was amused. "I would, but it will take awhile for my arms to relax. Can you wait as you are for a moment?"

She laughed softly. "I think I can bear to wait."

Standing there pressed against him as he flexed first his fingers, then his wrists, Adriana realized how much she had come to trust him and how much she was enjoying his arms about her.

They resumed their climb down the ravine walls, but Adriana was aware of Theo in a way she had not been before. Their quiet chatter about the better footholds and handholds was soothing, but the occasions when their hands touched or their arms and legs brushed Adriana found anything but calming. She was somewhat astounded to realize she was falling in love with Theo.

It put her flirtation with Corrigan, whom she had not thought of in many days, in perspective. He had made her feel attractive and desirable. Theo made her feel like her best self, free and joyful, as well as attractive.

But was she desirable to him? How did he feel about her? Adriana was still mulling over these thoughts when they arrived at the Eremite's cave.

That night, only family and Adriana supped at the royal table. The King asked for a retelling of the visit with Eremite Emun. Though Theo told of seeing Zimley, he did not mention the length of time they hovered over the ravine on the ledge. But he did tell the King in detail what they had learned that day from the Eremite.

"Eremite Emun said Zimley has been unusually active the past several days," Theo began before elaborating on the activity the hermit had witnessed. "He concluded by saying that only in the days before the Great Assault has he seen the dragon this active. Emun believes Zimley is preparing for a massive invasion and that he is fervently searching for the way into underground Beryllios. Eremite Emun also asked me to remind you that we are in the time of the twelfth generation."

"As if we could forget," muttered the Queen.

"Thank you, Theo," the King said, casting a warning glance toward the Queen. "Adriana, what are your thoughts about the Eremites?"

"I have found them interesting, and oddly familiar. In Ayrden we have the Wise Ones. They are much like your Eremites it seems. They assess the past and bring perspective to the future." Adriana paused. This royal family had shown her consistent kindness and inclusion, in spite of the fact that many, if not all, of their histories laid the blame for their current situation on her Kingdom of Ayrden. She did not want to be a harbinger of unwanted news, but her lessons in philosophy, logic, and strategic defensive warfare, combined with her visits with Theo to the Eremites, had convinced her that there was an attack of momentous impact coming.

"I also believe Zimley is preparing a massive attack, and quite soon. During our trips to the Eremites it seems the reports have escalated. I believe Zimley already knows where the underground kingdom lies and is honing his

strategy. I believe he intends this to be a final, fatal assault."
When Adriana finished speaking there was silence as each
of the four stared at her.

"Well," Elissa finally said with a determined edge to her
voice, "I hope Zimley holds off until after the Festival of
Twelve. If we have to go to battle, I would at least like to
have had a chance to show my splendid skills at chimanga."

The next day Theo and Adriana once again found
themselves alone. They had spent the morning scaling
down the ravine walls gathering gemstones. When they
reached the bottom Theo took off his boots and waded
into the river. He hopped from one rock to another until
he stood in the center of the course of water. A deep, lilac-
colored pool eddied in front of him, and he smiled back at
Adriana and motioned for her to join him.

Adriana slid off her boots and rolled up the legs of her
breeches. Today she wore a pair in soft sage green with an
embroidered tunic of creamy yellow and pale violet. The
water felt pleasantly cool to her feet as she waded to the
nearest rock. She hopped from one smooth amber rock to
another before reaching the pale blue sapphire rock where
Theo was sprawled, taking up most of the surface. She
playfully nudged him in the ribs with her wet foot. "Best to

move before I step on you," she said.

He grabbed her ankle. But the quick flick of pleasure she felt at his touch was immediately followed by alarm as she lost her balance and felt herself toppling backward. Theo quickly grabbed her hand and held her steadfast on the rock.

"Two saves in two days. You seem to be making a habit of coming to my rescue," Adriana said lightly as she stepped to his other side and sat down beside him.

He continued to hold her hand and touched her wrist with a single finger, tracing the red welt of the scar that encircled her wrist.

Adriana was tempted to pull away or pull the tunic sleeve over her wrist. The scar was ugly, uneven and rough. But Theo's touch was kind and intimate. "Does it hurt?" he asked.

"No." Adriana appreciated that he did not ask how she had received it and wondered if that would be his next question. She hoped not.

But as they sat there, something about the water cascading around the rock on which they sat made her feel cocooned. And something in Theo's demeanor made her feel safe. So she continued. "It's from a leather thong with which my uncle bound me—for a long time. I encountered him in Chehalem, the first land I traversed. Do you know of it?"

He shook his head but did not break his silence.

"He kept me captive in his cabin. I thought kindness toward him would enable me to win him over and gain my freedom. But eventually I had to use other means to escape. And you?" Adriana asked, looking over at him. "Do you have any scars?"

"Yes. But none that are visible. When will your Journey end?"

Adriana was surprised by the question. Both because it seemed an abrupt change of subject and because she realized it had been many days since she had thought about her Journey at all. "When I arrive back home in Ayrden, I suppose." It was a shock for Adriana to realize how little she had thought of home in recent days.

"And what will you do when you find yourself back home?"

Adriana laid her arm across her knees and her head on her arm. She was close enough to see the gold flecks in his brown eyes. "In truth, I do not know. Would you like to go with me?"

The question hung in the air between them. Adriana herself was stunned that she had given voice to the question. The words and the thought had occurred simultaneously.

Theo looked away, gazing down the river. "Adriana, I cannot. You are right about Zimley and the impending attack. You well discerned the collective message of the

Eremites. But I am of the twelfth generation. No one understands what that means. Or at least almost no one. I cannot leave with you."

Blushing, at both her impetuous question and his rejection, Adriana hopped lightly to her feet. "That makes perfect sense. You are to be King. How would you go with me anyway? It is my Journey. And Beryllios and Ayrden are no longer joined in any practical realm."

Theo glanced up at Adriana with an inscrutable look. "How? Through the means of love. But I cannot—"

Adriana did not wait for him to finish the thought. Giving a light laugh, she leaped gracefully over the rocks until she reached the shore. Pulling on her boots, she looked at Theo, who still sat on the rock looking down the river.

"If you don't hurry, I will beat you to the top," Adriana called out to him, returning to her earlier, teasing voice. She pretended she had not heard the last of his sentence. But as she climbed the sheer wall, her face was grim as she acknowledged to herself what she had heard. "But I cannot love you," was exactly what Adriana had heard him say. And she assumed it was exactly what he had meant.

CHAPTER 30

THE FESTIVAL OF TWELVE

Even when Adriana reached the room she continued to share with Elissa, Theo's words were still resounding in her head and her heart stung. Falling in love with Theo had well and truly complicated her Journey.

She was not sure one was supposed to have fun on one's Journey, but being in Beryllios had been fun. Elissa had become a dear friend, and the royal family had been unerringly gracious. Additionally, the time spent speaking with the Eremites had given her days meaningful purpose. And Theo—Adriana realized she had been weaving her life about his, planning, without realizing it, a possible future together with him. But that would never be. Theo's comment had made that clear. *It is time for me to plan my departure*, she thought as she entered the room.

Then she saw it.

In the center of the bed lay a brightly colored silk pouch with a small card atop it that read "Adriana" in an elaborate, multicolored script. Heart thumping, Adriana hurried to the bed and picked up the silk pouch. She turned it over in her hands, looking for a clasp hidden among the bright cobalt- and poppy-colored swirls. She hoped this was her chimanga but dared not think too much about the possibility. She knew if it was something else, her disappointment would be keen. And the day had held enough of that already.

Just as she found the vibrant pink toggle that would give her access, the door opened and Elissa swept into the room. She gave an immediate cry of delight when she saw what Adriana was holding.

"Your chimanga! It has arrived! Have you looked at it yet?"

Adriana shook her head and smiled. "No, but I was hoping that was what the pouch held." She unhooked the silk toggle and gently pulled out the chimanga.

The fabric was cold to the touch and felt like the thinnest of silk. But the garment was surprisingly heavy as she lifted it and held it in front of her.

Elissa drew close and ran a finger along one sleeve's outer edge. "I've never seen one with jewels," she said as her finger ran the entire length of the garment and sent the row of pear-shaped aquamarines silently swinging.

"It's gorgeous," Adriana said in a voice filled with awe. "I think it is the most beautiful garment I have ever seen."

Elissa grinned at Adriana, her eyes dancing. "Then the Imago did a good job. Or perhaps I should say, you did a good job. That's the response everyone has to the truest chimangas. I certainly felt that way about mine. And still do, even after almost five years. Do you want to try it on?"

"Can I?" Adriana asked.

"Of course. If you wish. Did Mother send the underdressings?" Elissa asked as she opened the wardrobe. "Ah, here. Put these on and I will help you into the chimanga."

Once Adriana was dressed in the tight, sleeveless white vest and black leggings, Elissa held out the oddly shaped chimanga. The first such garment Adriana had seen, on Elissa herself, had reminded Adriana of a stained-glass window that had been softened, thinned out, woven. But this, her chimanga, seemed more reminiscent of a kaleidoscope. The pattern seemed circular, yet the circles were made of triangles and lines and angles. And the colors! While Elissa's chimanga was made of bright primary colors, Adriana's was full of vibrant colors bleeding to pearly pastels before growing vibrant again. Circles and swirls of fuchsia and orange and cobalt met gold and lilac and a blue-green that was neither teal nor aquamarine but a color all its own. And then there was red, sprinkled in tiny drops with no apparent order, almost invisible until one saw them. Then the tiny crimson circles and triangles created their own pattern, as if all the other colors were a mere backdrop.

The fabric was icy as Adriana slid her foot inside the slipperlike portion of the chimanga. Yet as soon as her foot was encased in the material, the cold dissipated. It was like wearing her own skin, obviously present but impossible to feel apart from an outside touch. When Adriana moved to put her chimanga-clad foot on the floor, the tiniest tinkle sounded.

Adriana gasped. "Oh, Elissa," she said, looking up with delight. "It works! I mean, it works for me!"

Elissa finished helping Adriana into the chimanga by tucking her hair into the hood, buttoning the tiny aquamarine buttons along the sleeves, and finally tying the cobalt blue and gold ribbons that crisscrossed the back.

Adriana was so excited she could not help but laugh. At her slightest movement there was a sporadic percussive sound. "So what do I do? How do I begin?"

"Take a walk around the room first, and then take a few twirls, or whatever feels natural to you," Elissa advised.

Adriana walked about the small room, entranced at the sound the chimanga made. She began dancing, taking spins and pirouettes and small leaps in the crowded space, testing each for the sound it would make.

She finally stopped and turned to Elissa, who sat cross-legged on the bed watching the entire performance with a smile. "It will be interesting to see if you have a pair," Elissa said.

"A pair of what?"

Elissa laughed, rolled off the bed, and began unbuttoning and untying Adriana's chimanga. "Not a pair of anything, silly. A pair, a mate, an other. What do you call it in Ayrden?"

"You mean a partner?" Adriana still wasn't sure she understood.

"Yes. But not exactly. Sometimes two chimangas will actually create a melody when they move together. Of course, when everyone is wearing chimangas there is a collective melody, but this is different. It's as if the two chimangas, and the two people wearing them, create a perfect new melody, though each of their individual melodies sounds beautiful and complete independent of the other. It's called point against point or point-counterpoint. It's rare, but it is what we all hope for—and dread at the same time."

"Dread? Why?" Adriana asked as she looked over her shoulder at Elissa.

"Because one has no control, it just happens. And it's obvious to all that the two people are meant to be together as a pair, partnered, as you would say. But what if you detest your point-counterpoint? Point against point is not necessary for betrothal. If it were, we would be extinct, it's that rare. But it is taken for granted that when it occurs the pair should move toward marriage. It has led to some interesting turbulence in the past."

Adriana carefully folded her now-silent chimanga and placed it back in its silk pouch. Her heart hammered in her chest. What if Theo was her pair? He would deny her. She would be humiliated. She pushed the thought away. She was not even of Beryllios. The thought was ludicrous. Another thought intruded. What if she had a pair and it was some other young man, one she did not even know?

Adriana gave a shake of her head. *No need to borrow worry*, she thought. Elissa said it was rare. But a tiny fissure of anxiety had tarnished the purity of her excitement.

After lunch Adriana had her first session in the practice tunnel. Elissa stayed long enough to show how she herself practiced, but assured Adriana that there was no right or wrong way, barring pretense. Movements that borrowed from another and were not genuine to the wearer caused a horrible racket, perhaps worth trying for amusement's sake, but otherwise a waste.

A CLEARING IN THE FOREST

In no time at all it seemed, Adriana was alone in the practice room. The white marble floor was slick beneath her chimanga-clad feet, and she spent the first few moments simply sliding across the floor. As she did so the chimanga sounded a harp glissando. She laughed. As she had told Corrigan, she had not excelled in any of the arts taught by the Teachers of Ayrden. She could paint, but she was always unsatisfied with her finished canvases. She could sing, but her range was not as wide as that of Bess, who had a lovely voice. She could dance, but the strict structure of the dances of Ayrden always left her feeling as if something were missing, freedom, perhaps. She had always much more enjoyed those endeavors that required constant strategy and adjustments to changing situations such as fencing, horseback riding, and her favorite, hand-to-hand.

But this was different. Adriana felt incredible freedom as she danced in her chimanga, though to produce the sounds she liked best did require concentration. She discovered that the music changed with both her movements and her thoughts. She was pretending to hold a foil in her hand and dancing about as if she were parrying with an opponent when she thought of Corrigan and the debacle of the sword fight in Shahar. The tone of the music grew somber and ominous. Surprised, she tried to turn her mind to something happier. One of her last fencing lessons with Emaht came to mind. He had not been coaching her as much as providing her with practice in the many techniques he had taught her throughout the years. Adriana began to replay the match in her mind and with her body, feinting and thrusting as she danced around the room. The music swelled into a joyous collision of strings and wind instruments. Adriana finally stopped and laughed in delight.

That afternoon, and every morning and afternoon that followed over the next ten days, Adriana practiced alone in one of the rooms. She grew more and more comfortable with the way the chimanga sounded and the melody it produced. The music became more consistent the longer she practiced, and every morning her body ached from the intense physical exertion. But it occupied her time in a legitimate fashion, so that she saw Theo only at dinner each night at the Residence.

On the night before the Festival of Twelve, while at table with the royal family, the Queen asked, "Adriana, do you feel you will be ready to come forward in your chimanga tomorrow?"

Adriana had been so busy practicing she had not given much thought to the actual festival. She felt her heart skip a beat. "I suppose. Does someone need to watch me dance first to make sure I am doing it correctly?"

The King gave a chuckle and the Queen laughed

outright. "My dear, there is no correct way, other than that which is correct for you. Elissa tells me you have been in the practice tunnel every day, both morning and afternoon. You should be fine. I only wondered how you *felt* about it."

"Oh, I actually feel quite wonderful about the sound. It's beautiful." Adriana could feel a blush rise to her cheeks. "I am sorry. That sounded prideful. . . ."

"No, no, my dear," the Queen said, giving a quick glance at the silent Theo. "The chimanga *should* make a beautiful sound. And though you are quite lovely, the music is not a reflection of your externalities but of your life force, your essence. That always begins as beautiful, so it is good you are pleased. Preparations will begin at eight o'clock tomorrow morning. So I suggest you two retire after dinner," the Queen said, looking at Adriana and Elissa.

When they departed for the evening, the Queen stopped Elissa and kissed her cheek before pulling her close. Adriana felt a pang of loneliness, wishing in that instant for her own mother.

"You have waited a long time for your turn to dance at the festival," the Queen said to Elissa. "I am glad it has finally arrived without interruption. Sweet dreams, my love. I am looking forward to tomorrow."

Moments before twelve the next day, Adriana stood behind Elissa in the women's tunnel waiting for the signal to enter the Vault. She was surprised at how vulnerable she felt. Her chimanga was less like a covering for her body and more like an uncovering that revealed her true self. It left her feeling awkward. She desired the approval of those who watched, yet she knew that the only way to create truly gorgeous music was to be as authentically herself as she had ever been.

She stood shoulder to shoulder with a girl dressed in a chimanga of marbled orange and cream swirls. She bumped gently against Adriana's shoulder like a slow-moving metronome. Every time she did so, a soft guitar chord sounded. There were another four girls behind each of them, for a total of eleven to make their entrance as seventeens.

Adriana had never heard so much music. It came from every direction as the Vault in front of her filled with all of Beryllios dressed in their chimangas. Every tone and pitch and instrument she had ever encountered or imagined presented itself. Yet there was an underlying harmony to it all.

Though Adriana could not see into the Vault, she began to hear the music dying down until there was silence. Even the girl beside her stilled.

Then she heard the King's voice. "Welcome to the

Festival of Twelve. At this twelfth hour on this twelfth day of this twelfth month, I invite all seventeens to make their entrance and lead off the dancing."

Elissa leaped forward, and Adriana was momentarily confused. She had thought they would perhaps walk out or gracefully run, but Elissa had center stage in the Vault all alone for the moment. Her movements were explosive and wild and perfectly appropriate for Elissa.

But not for Adriana, nor apparently for the girl beside her in the orange and cream chimanga, who stepped off in a smooth walk accompanied by a guitar and piano melody. It was odd. Adriana was accustomed to Ayrden, where the music started and then the dancing began. This was exactly the opposite. She had to force herself to dance out of the tunnel and into the Vault, and when she did so the music, her music, began. She smiled and twirled on one foot, her chimanga flowing around her first in one direction and then the other. Her nervousness began to subside as she heard the music she was making. The citizens of Beryllios stood four-deep along the walls of the Vault, but Adriana did not try to find anyone particular in the crowd, allowing their faces to blur as she danced and spun past them in the center of the domed room.

Twenty-one seventeens danced—eleven girls and ten young men. The chimangas were varied in color and pattern, and the music from each was distinct, yet harmonious.

Adriana realized her own music sounded better when she danced near particular people. She was pleased to realize that her music blended well with that of Elissa, which was exciting and verged on feverish. Adriana thought her own sound was magnificent, gloriously melodious, full and rich, creating a balance for Elissa's, which she found very pleasing. There was also a young man who danced in their vicinity in a cobalt blue and red chimanga patterned in geometric shapes. His music added an additional melody, and Adriana's enjoyment began to increase.

When the King, standing on a raised platform in front of the tunnel to the Inner Sanctum, called a halt to the dance of the seventeens, Adriana followed Elissa's lead and moved with her and the others into the center. As she did so, she saw Theo for the first time. Their gazes locked for a moment before Adriana looked away, seeking someone—anyone—else.

The King called for the eighteens to come forward, and Adriana silently watched as they began dancing. After only a few moments Elissa joined the dance, and the rest of the seventeens followed her.

There were new sounds being created all around Adriana, and she could feel herself relax. She grew bolder in her movements and cast aside any self-consciousness, closing her eyes in order to let her sense of hearing take over. When she eventually heard the music around her moderating and quieting, she slowed her movements and finally stopped. When she opened her eyes she was pleased to find herself once again near Elissa, who smiled broadly at her. The seventeen in the bold cobalt and red geometric chimanga was once again nearby, as well as two girls Adriana could not identify by sight but whom she instantly recognized by their music as the dancers moved once again to the center of the Vault.

When the King called for the nineteens to move onto the floor, Adriana became acutely aware of Theo's presence. She could hear his music distinctly, though it was no louder than the others'. She could feel herself stiffen as she wondered whether he would avoid her. She felt a pang as she saw Elissa bound off in his direction, giving a joyous leap through the air that appeared fueled by excitement alone.

Adriana danced off in the opposite direction. She forced herself to wipe her mind clear of any thoughts of Theo and scrambled to think of some adequately distracting memory. She closed her eyes and thought back to her entrance into the forest, her desperate attempt to enter this Journey she now seemed unable to exit. She closed her eyes and her dancing picked up pace as she remembered galloping Sultan toward the closed wood and the way opening before them just before she thought she must certainly pull him to a stop. She remembered the way closing behind them, the trees snatching and pulling at the edges of her cloak as the branches hypnotically opened in front of her and closed behind. She was brought out of her reverie by the sound of a new melody.

Was it someone else's? Or was it her own? Her melody was definitely still sounding, but there was another that was combining with hers, creating a different song. It was a lush, rich melody full of ecstasy. She still danced with her eyes closed, but she drew closer to the other half of the song, reveling in the new, distinct melody. Then she realized what she was experiencing. Point against point.

Her eyes flew open.

She found herself looking directly into Theo's brown eyes. Of course it was Theo. Somewhere in the recesses of her heart and mind she had known it would be Theo. The two continued to dance, circling each other, Theo's face impassive, Adriana working hard to guard her own. She tried to prevent herself from revealing her true emotions, her love and desire for him alone.

The other music in the Vault grew quieter as all the other dancers gradually began to still, until it was just Adriana and Theo dancing in the center of the room. She could hear tiny ripples of sound, voices and musical fragments from the onlookers, as she circled Theo and then he her. They drew close to each other before withdrawing, the music still sounding and playing its unique, never-before-heard melody. Adriana could feel the crescendo of the piece nearing, and when Theo took her hand she melted into his rhythm, his leading.

When the music finished Adriana was wrapped in Theo's embrace, their arms woven together in front of her. She saw that it was not only their music that created a single unified whole, but their chimangas as well. She could not tell where hers ended and his began. She was breathless and her heart tripped in her chest. *What now?* she wondered.

The citizens of Beryllios began an enthusiastic round of applause, accompanied by the sounds of drums, cymbals, bells, and tambourines, which echoed off the walls of the Vault. Theo's arms dropped with a discordant jangle that only Adriana was close enough to hear. She turned to look at him, not sure what to expect, but his expression did not change, remaining flat, without emotion.

He gave a courtly bow and walked away.

CHAPTER 31

POINT-COUNTERPOINT

driana was devastated, Elissa euphoric, both for the same reason. It was obvious to all that Theo was Adriana's point-counterpoint.

As soon as the two reached the tunnel for the scheduled respite before the twenties were called to join the dance, Elissa grabbed Adriana about the waist and spun her around so rapidly Adriana's feet lifted off the ground. Elissa's excitement was palpable. "Adriana! It happened! For you and Theo. Oh, my, this is the grandest of news! Can you believe it?" Only Elissa was creating music, as Adriana remained perfectly still.

When Elissa stopped twirling she grabbed Adriana's hands and looked into her face. "What? What's wrong?"

Adriana cleared her throat, unsure how much to tell Elissa. How was she supposed to answer that question?

What was wrong? Everything. Nothing. Adriana opted for as superficial an answer as she could muster. "The point-counterpoint—it was quite a surprise. I have never had an experience like that. Of a truth, I feel a bit undone."

Elissa's expression shifted from anticipation to puzzlement and she dropped Adriana's hands. "But it's Theo. Surely you are excited that it's Theo."

"Of course!" Adriana said, giving vehement voice to the truth her heart held. She was thrilled it was Theo. It validated all she had been thinking and feeling these many days in Beryllios. But Theo had been clear. And the look on his face as they had finished their dance only underscored the truth he had spoken in the ravine. His heart was as closed to her as the way back to Chehalem or Ayrden.

Adriana felt her heart sink. *Home.* Would she ever find herself back home? She did not want to face Theo's rejection yet again. She needed to leave Beryllios. Now.

She smiled at Elissa, forcing her face to reflect all the happiness their friendship had brought her. "Sweet friend, you know me well. I am excited. But a little overwhelmed all the same. Would it be a terrible thing if I went back to our room for just a bit?"

"Of course you *may*, if you feel you must. But you do realize it will be evident to all that you are absent? Everyone has heard the new point-counterpoint melody, and they

will be waiting to hear it, and to see you and Theo, again."
Elissa's eyebrows drew together in disapproval. "It borders
on rudeness, Adriana. Are you positive that is what you
want to do?"

"I am. I will return as quickly as possible."

Adriana fled down the women's tunnel toward Elissa's
room. Her now-familiar melody sporadically changed
keys like a young horse repeatedly switching leads. When
Adriana arrived at the room, she took a deep breath and
slowly exhaled before pushing open the door.

Focus, she thought. First, what did she need in order to
leave? Her journeying clothes, the sword Sone had given
her. She looked down at her chimanga. Were she to walk
through the Vault dressed in her journeying clothes and
cloak, there was no way she would escape notice. There
were two connector tunnels on this side of the Vault,
between here and the practice tunnel and between that
and the booths. She knew what she would do. It was not
a perfect plan, but she thought it would work, particularly
once the festival dancing included all of Beryllios.

Adriana grabbed her cloak and wrapped it around the
sheathed sword. She paused at the bedside table where
the tiny ten-sided box twinkled, even in the dim light.

Grabbing a quill, she jotted a dozen words on a piece of Elissa's heavy parchment paper, placed it beneath the box, and slipped out of the room.

She could hear the music just beginning again as she passed through the door into the connector tunnel. Music poured from her chimanga. It no longer changed key, but the melody had taken on the rhythmic sound of a march, constant and resolute. She passed through the practice tunnel and into the connecting tunnel to the booths, remembering Theo slipping his arm around her the first time she had entered the dank hallway. Her melody gave a trip and for just a moment flowed into a waltzlike rhythm. Once among the deserted booths, the music from the dancers in the Vault bounced around the emptiness, oddly amplified. Adriana stopped at the booth closest to the mouth of the tunnel, where she was not quite visible to anyone standing in the Vault, and placed her bundle out of sight behind some pottery jugs.

Trying to decide how to reenter unnoticed, Adriana recalled a tactic from Prelechett's philosophy class on infiltrating behind enemy lines:

Act as if you belong,
and others will assume you do.

Adriana gracefully danced into the room and through the crowds at the mouth of the tunnel. She held her head high, her arms sweeping in full and graceful motions. With less surprise than she anticipated, the onlookers made way for the errant dancer who had appeared behind them. And they began smiling when they once again heard the point-counterpoint melody that grew louder and more distinct the closer Adriana drew to the center of the Vault.

The vast Vault floor was not yet crowded, but as each year was added to the dancing throng, it was easier for Adriana to dance near, but not with, Theo. After the second set of three songs, there was another break. As soon as it began, Adriana slipped down the animal tunnel to saddle and bridle Sultan.

The animal tunnel too was deserted. Only the lookout tunnel across the way showed any activity. A different sentry rotated each and every song, so no one missed any more than necessary of the festival.

Adriana was just approaching Sultan when it occurred to her that he might be startled by her appearance, dressed in her chimanga.

But such was not the case.

Before he even saw her she could hear his hoof pawing at the door, and when she pushed it open he stretched out his nose toward her cheek in his typical greeting. Adriana gave her first genuine smile since the third song had revealed her point-to-point pairing.

Her plan was to wait until the next break in the dancing to remove her chimanga and don her cloak. After that, once all of Beryllios had begun dancing and there were no spectators, she would slip from the booths to the animal tunnel and retrieve Sultan. Though they would have to briefly skirt the wall of the Vault, she would have both surprise and a head start in her favor. If anyone cared to follow her at all.

As Adriana walked alone back toward the dancing, she acknowledged to herself that she was running away. It did not make her proud—in truth, she was disgusted with herself at the realization. But the thought of even one day of walking the tightrope between the royal family's expectations and Theo's coldness left Adriana numb to any other solution.

She danced the next two dances, sometimes close to Theo and sometimes with him. Still he did not smile. In fact, the more their new melody developed in intensity and beauty, the grimmer his face grew. Adriana's resolve to leave strengthened, and she waited with increasing eagerness for the final break before all of Beryllios joined the dancing throngs.

During what Adriana knew to be her last dance, she allowed herself to throw aside all thoughts of anything but her true being and her true feelings for Theo. She could instantly hear the difference in the music. It was both more liberated and more intense. Perhaps Theo had the same thought, for the melody they were creating together grew

280

increasingly climactic until once again everyone stopped dancing but the two of them.

The music they were making initially rose and fell together. Then it separated to reach into the highest octaves and the lowest at the same time before coming back together and weaving into a lush singular melody. A multitude of instruments sounded. Strings, from harps and guitars to violins and cellos, combined with wind instruments, flutes and piccolos and tubas, while there was a sometimes-syncopated rhythm of percussion that undergirded the entire piece.

This time when they finished, Theo was holding her in his arms and her face was pressed against his chest. She was so sad to be leaving she was surprised she had no tears. But anger at his refusal to admit what was so evident to everyone else offset her sadness. She gave a deep curtsy to Theo before turning and heading toward the tunnel of booths. Theo did not follow her.

Adriana retrieved her cloak and sword from the tunnel of booths and attempted to hide the bundle in the folds of her chimanga. Then she skirted the edge of the Vault before slipping down the animal tunnel to Sultan. With all the citizens of Beryllios preparing to dance, she felt she had reached her destination without attracting undue notice.

Disrobing took longer than she'd anticipated because of the laces down the back of her chimanga. When she finally stood in just the black pants and white vest, she lifted her sword into place across her chest and pulled her green cloak about her shoulders. Feeling the tiny bit of heaviness in the heart's corner, she fingered her Ayrden seal for just a moment and thought of home, wondering if this time a way would open for her to return.

She picked up her chimanga and laid it across the bottom half of the stall door, gently fingering it one last time as she did so. Then she led Sultan toward the Vault, listening to the disjointed music as everyone milled about. Just before she reached the mouth of the tunnel she heard the open dancing begin. The music sounded like the beginning of a symphony. She knew this was her best chance to escape unseen.

Mounting Sultan, she walked him out of the animal tunnel and along the wall. The chimanga-clad dancers were moving toward the center of the Vault to dance. No one seemed to notice her at all. Once in the wide entrance tunnel, Adriana nudged Sultan into a canter. After wearing her chimanga for the many dances, it seemed strange to be moving without making any sound, strange and sad.

CHAPTER 32

FIDELITY

When Adriana reached the cliff where she had spent her first night in Beryllios, she heard the warning whistle of the sentry. Habit made her stop and begin turning back toward underground Beryllios. But then she hesitated. If she was indeed leaving, should she not continue? Was it right for her to seek shelter from the citizens of Beryllios when she had already departed? In truth, the dragon had not harmed her the first time she had encountered him; rather, he had given her shelter. Perhaps she herself had nothing to fear from Zimley at all. She stayed on the path and continued on her way.

Then she heard it. It was a battle cry. The warning whistle had given way to a call to arms.

The Festival of Twelve and all those gathered

underground would be under assault. She turned Sultan back toward Beryllios and kicked him into a gallop.

Overhead she saw Zimley, approaching underground Beryllios from the opposite direction, followed by a flying hoard of creatures. Some appeared to be dragons, others were almost human in appearance. Zimley descended, but where he landed Adriana was unsure—somewhere in front of her. His minions flew past him. Then she saw the smaller of the flying creatures descend one by one down the lookout tower. Just before the trees blocked her view, she saw the watchman fall from his precarious perch far above the ground.

Soon a cacophony of noise erupted from the vicinity of the underground entrance tunnel. Adriana could not yet see what was happening, but she could hear distant screams and animal-like screeches mingled with fragments of music and the metallic ring of clashing swords. When Adriana reached the clearing where she had first seen Elissa, she jerked Sultan to a stop and leaped from his back.

Zimley waited in the center of the clearing.

Though Adriana had seen the dragon that first morning in Beryllios, and again the day she and Theo had gone to visit Eremite Emun, she was still stunned at Zimley's size. He towered over her. Long, sharp talons glinted on his feet and clawlike hands. His long, sinewy neck, bright green near his head before growing darker like the rest of his body, arched down toward her. Like a venomous snake, he appeared ready to strike. His eyes were red, the black pupils vertical slivers. When his mouth opened Adriana fully expected flames.

Instead a voice rumbled from him. "Prepare to die. Or surrender and serve me."

In a voice of resolute courage, Adriana said, "I will not surrender. Nor will I serve you."

She grappled with her options for fighting him. But not in her choice to defy him. This creature had reigned over these kind people of Beryllios for twelve generations—long enough. If this was to be the end of her Journey, then she wanted to be proud of her courage in helping to defend them. Adriana continued to hear the clamor of battle. But no one entered the clearing. With a sick feeling she thought of Elissa and Theo. Were they doing battle inside the tunnels? Had they been killed? What was happening to those she had grown to love?

"What are these people to you?" the dragon rumbled. "They are not your people. You are of Ayrden. It was your ancestor that brought me into being, your ancestor that started this war. If you wish to be true to Ayrden, you should desire to join me."

All the while Zimley spoke, Adriana watched him closely. Both his talons and his razor-sharp teeth appeared quite capable of tearing her to shreds, but she focused not on his strengths, but on possible vulnerabilities.

"Be that as it may, I will not," Adriana called back in a strong voice.

Then several things happened at once. The dragon's neck arched in fury and flames spewed from his mouth. The grass caught fire. And she found a vulnerability she could exploit. Where the darker green scales began, halfway along his neck, there was a thin ribbon of unscaled, and therefore unprotected, flesh. She drew her sword. That was when Theo stepped up behind her and spoke softly in her ear. "This will end it."

Relief flooded Adriana. He was alive.

She assumed he had a bow and arrow or some other means of vanquishing the dragon from the distance at which they stood. But when Theo stepped in front of her she realized with horror he was completely unarmed. He stood totally defenseless in the black and white clothes that he had been wearing under his chimanga. He spread his arms wide, shielding her with his body.

A contemptuous laugh erupted from Zimley, and with a rapid strike the dragon's head lunged forward and his teeth plunged into Theo's chest, ripping it open. Theo stood for one brief moment before collapsing at Adriana's feet.

In that instant, Zimley's vulnerability was perfectly exposed. Adriana slashed the middle of Zimley's throat with her sword.

With a roar the dragon's neck swung up, his head pointed skyward, and his front feet landed with a thud a short distance from where Adriana stood. Before he had opportunity to seek her out with his eyes, she jumped over Theo, ran through the smoldering grass, and rolled underneath the dragon.

She stood up, sword drawn. But she was undecided as to how best to attack. She had a momentary flash of memory: Paktos towering over her in Chehalem, asking, "What is a heart for?" A fatal thrust to the dragon's heart. That would end it. *Exactly what Theo said*, Adriana thought as she beat back thoughts of what had just happened. *Focus! My sole intent is to destroy Zimley.*

Adriana saw Zimley's head swing to one side, searching for her. As he did so, his body twisted so low that Adriana had to crouch to avoid being grazed by his massive chest.

He twisted up in the opposite direction, and as he did so she lifted the two-edged sword, the one Sone had given her, with both hands and held it low and ready. She crouched, coiled and waiting. Adriana focused on a tiny space between scales the size of small shields, which she assumed covered his heart. She hoped he would repeat the same motion as before.

He did.

A Clearing in the Forest

As Zimley's heavy body swung rapidly toward the ground, Adriana thrust the sword with all the power she could muster toward his heart. The sword slipped into his chest as though sliding into a scabbard. With a roar the dragon reared up on his back legs. Adriana held tight to the sword's hilt. She was jerked off her feet and dangled above the ground for several long moments before the bloody sword slipped from the dragon's chest.

She tumbled to the ground but scrambled immediately to her feet, sword once again at the ready. The dragon staggered back and fell to the grass before rising unsteadily. He unfurled his wings and flew in an erratic pattern toward the ravine.

Adriana ran back to Theo. She dropped her sword to the ground and fell to her knees beside him. She cradled his dear head in one arm and pressed the gaping wound in his chest with her cape. She could feel the hot warmth of his blood seeping through the thick velvet, into her hand.

She looked around frantically for Elissa, for a Healer, for help of any kind. She could still hear the ring of swords clashing as the battle raged, but the swordsmen remained out of sight. She and Theo were alone, in the clearing where she had first seen him.

"Theo! Theo!" Adriana cried.

His eyes opened. "I knew it had to be this way," Theo labored to say. "You are safe now. Beryllios is safe. We saved them." His voice grew faint. "Your courage and my ..." Theo's eyes closed and he drew in a shuddering breath.

"Don't die. Oh, please, don't die! Theo, I love you, please, Theo." She put her face against the warmth of his cheek, not wanting to watch the pain etched across his face. She could feel each ragged breath as if it were her own, and when he stilled she pressed her lips to his, tears streaming down her face.

The earth began to shake beneath her. The wind began to blow. Clouds, so dark they blocked out the light of the sun, rolled across the sky like an unfurling scroll. Everything suddenly grew still and quiet. For a moment there was no sound at all. Then an explosion of thunderous sound came from the direction of the ravine.

"I love you, Theo. I will always love you." Adriana sobbed as she rocked back and forth, holding him in her arms.

CHAPTER 33

EVER AFTER

Three days later Adriana was still struggling with the realization that Theo was gone, grappling even more to believe that he was gone forever. She lingered in the room she had shared with Elissa, absently fastening and unfastening the clasp of her cloak. The green velvet felt uncomfortably heavy, more from what it signified—that she was leaving—than its actual weight. Saying good-bye to Elissa was proving to be difficult as well as painful. She was leaving both a dear friend and her closest connection with Theo.

"Are you positive you are meant to leave?" Elissa asked. Since Theo's death her voice had become soft and melancholy. The sadness it conveyed was a sentiment Adriana understood far too well.

"No, not really," Adriana replied. "But I don't feel I

should tarry any longer. If I wait for something to prompt my leaving, I may never resume my Journey at all."

"Wouldn't you like to stay?" Elissa asked, her tone unsure and wistful. Adriana gave her a hug and the two friends held each other, their heads resting on one another's shoulders, one fair, the other dark.

"Ah, friend. You know I would. But Theo's loss makes me long to let my family know that I am alive. And your life is here. I would ask you to go with me, but your parents would never forgive me if I were the catalyst for both of their children disappearing."

Elissa pulled back and looked Adriana in the face. Her eyes were red-rimmed from crying, and her face had the boneless look of grief that Adriana felt but could not see in herself. "Oh, Adriana. You blame yourself for Theo's death?"

"Yes. No, not really. I don't know." Adriana gave a sad smile. "I would hope to see you again, Elissa, but if not, please know I will never, ever forget you. You are the dearest friend I have ever had—will ever have."

With one last hug Adriana left Elissa behind in her room, as they had earlier agreed upon. She retrieved Sultan from the mouth of the animal tunnel where a silent groom held him ready. Sultan, laden with two quivers of arrows and a bow, a sword, and a saddlebag of provisions, was prepared for their departure.

A CLEARING IN THE FOREST

Adriana led Sultan out of underground Beryllios to the edge of the ravine, where she stopped. She thought of Theo. "Did he love me? Did he know I loved him? Did he hear me say it before he died?" she whispered to herself.

She thought back to the day they had talked on the rocks, water eddying around them as it coursed into the pool. He had said, "I cannot love you." But what had he meant? That he was not able to love *her*? Because he found her lacking in some essential way? Because he loved another? Or did he mean he could not *allow* himself to love her? Because he knew what was to happen? Because he knew he would leave her alone and grief-stricken?

Adriana prepared to step away from the edge of the ravine, but not before she looked one last time at a very specific point downriver. It was where the steep walls bent hard to the right. Where anything that traveled down the clear water between the high walls and cascading purple flowers disappeared from view. Where she had last seen Theo, or at least Theo's body.

The body his mother and sister and she had prepared. They had allowed her to participate in this most intimate of family acts, acknowledging what Theo would not. That she loved him. That she was made for him, uniquely designed as his point and counterpoint.

The three had bathed him, gently washing away all the blood that had spilled down his chest and around to his back, wiping his face and feet, and brushing his hair away from his face. Then they had dressed him in his now forever silent chimanga, as the three of them, clothed in their own musical raiment to prepare his body, sounded a symphony of minor key mourning. The men of Beryllios had lowered his body, strapped to a bed of fresh-hewn wood, down into the ravine, and the King had carefully set it adrift down the river.

Behind her, Adriana heard someone give a soft cough.

"Adriana," the Queen said softly. "Can we talk before you depart?"

"Of course."

The two women walked away from the river toward the green cliffs that looked out over Eremia, by unspoken agreement taking a path that would avoid the clearing where Theo had died. Sultan trailed behind Adriana. "I want to apologize," the Queen began.

Adriana was surprised and her face showed it. "What possible apology could you make to me? You have lost your only son and a dozen citizens as well. Your heartbreak is my own. You owe me no apology."

They stopped in the gap between the cliff walls and looked out over Eremia. The wilderness had begun its transformation, surrendering its barrenness to a slow onslaught of gemstone-colored flowers, now that Beryllios was free of the dragon's tyranny.

The Queen continued, looking not at Adriana, but far into the distance, where the wasteland still held nothing but stark barrenness. "I sought to circumvent prophecy. And I made you my key tool. I read what I hoped was a caveat to what had been foretold, but I was mistaken."

"I don't understand," Adriana said. She was confused. She did not feel used by the Queen. And to hear that she had been gave rise to a subtle mistrust of this royal who had been so kind to her.

"As the seated King and Queen, we have access to scrolls of hidden prophecy and history. We came into power—what little power we have had during our reign—in the eleventh generation of the dragon. We are a land of twelves, a number we take to mean completion. So we suspected our children would play a critical role, even before we assumed the thrones of the Inner Sanctum and read the scrolls.

"Elissa told me of your interest in the intersection of our histories with the brothers of Ayrden and Thebazeli of Beryllios. So let me explain that first. Do you have any suspicions regarding what might have happened?"

Adriana nodded. "It seems to me the ten-sided box of betrothal must have played a key role. Though none of the histories say so, I have wondered if Thebazeli had the box prepared for Lebar. Perhaps she rode out with him, to tell

Naicon she had chosen to wed his brother?"

The Queen smiled. "Well deduced, my dear. That is exactly what happened. You know of Naicon's courtship of Thebazeli and the historians' assumption that he intended evil for our kingdom, and in fact Ayrden as well. But the question left unanswered is what happened in the then tiny wilderness of Eremia. The untold fragment of history that you sought reads thus:

> Before Lebar arrived at the castle of Beryllios, he encountered the fair Thebazeli by the Pools of Lilac. Their courtship was intense, mutual, and secret. Thebazeli had the Master Artisan prepare the ten-sided box of betrothal to give to Lebar. But their romance was not as well concealed as they believed. While spying on Thebazeli, Naicon discovered her intentions and was furious. He devised a plan to kill Lebar in the wilderness, lie about the circumstances, and ultimately win Thebazeli over by being her nearest comforter. However, Lebar arrived with both the box of betrothal and Thebazeli herself. The plan was foiled. Naicon killed them both, and the dust of the wilderness mixed with the blood of innocents and rose up as the dragon, Zimley.

"Thus began the encroachment of the wilderness and our continual battles with Zimley and his minions. All of our citizens who surrendered to him became his cohorts, the humanlike creatures you saw descending into the lookout tunnel. Each murder and act of violence over the generations gave rise to another, lesser dragon."

"And the disappearance of the enemy creatures at Zimley's death?" Adriana asked. "So many citizens bore witness to me that those they were battling collapsed and dissolved into dust at the very moment they heard the crash from the ravine."

The Queen nodded. "Prophecy is always unclear, so no one anticipated the instantaneous demise of the dragon's minions at his own death. But we assume that is what happened. That you played a role, however . . ." The Queen turned to face Adriana and reached out to take hold of both her hands. "I was hopeful of that from the time I entered the Inner Sanctum and saw you clutching Thebazeli's betrothal box. The penultimate prophecy of Beryllios is this:

> *A daughter of the dragon will appear*
> *to threaten the heir with a sword.*
> *She will approach,*
> *a token of Beryllios in one hand,*
> *a talisman of Ayrden in the other.*
> *She will bring courage,*
> *the heir sacrifice,*
> *and the two kingdoms will be one.*
> *Or, as love untied so love will unite.*

"You seemed to fulfill only half of the prophecy. The watchman saw you dart from beneath the dragon's wings that first morning you were in Beryllios. Easy enough to see, that could make you a daughter of the dragon. But you did not threaten my child with your sword and you carried no talisman of Ayrden, only the glittering box and your cape. I so badly wanted to spare Theo as the saving sacrifice. So I convinced myself the last line was an alternative method of bringing the kingdoms together, instead of the synopsis of the prophecy before it. I wanted the two of you to love each other and resolve our plight in that manner, and you did. But still it required Theo's sacrifice and your courage." The Queen's eyes shimmered with unshed tears, and her face was inscrutable to Adriana.

Did she wish Adriana had never appeared? Did she consider the freedom of Beryllios worth the cost of her only son? Adriana sighed. "But I did fulfill the prophecy. The wrong question was asked, and there was something you could not see. I pulled my sword on Theo when he first appeared in the clearing, believing he meant harm to Elissa. And the talisman of Ayrden was hidden in the heart's corner of my cloak."

Adriana gently pulled her hands away from the Queen's and drew the sterling seal of Ayrden from the corner hem of the green velvet mantle. "It appears Theo and I fulfilled all the requirements of the prophecy. But Ayrden and

Beryllios are still not united, so perhaps Theo did not love me, and that is where the failing lies."

"Adriana, I knew my son. He loved you. He must only have wanted to spare you pain. I am sure that is why he kept his feelings for you hidden. I watched how he looked at you, how he gazed at you as you danced." The Queen shook her head. "I have no doubt he loved you.

"Thank you for telling me of the talisman. I suppose the uniting of our kingdoms is for another generation. He was not supposed to know of the prophecy, not yet. But his last words to you make me wonder. I suppose it is not for us to know all. There seems to always be a little mystery left, yes?"

Before Adriana mounted Sultan, she pulled the pouch holding her chimanga from the saddlebag. "We wrapped Theo in his chimanga, and I thank you yet again for letting me place the betrothal box in his hands for his burial. But I would like for you to have this, if you would wish. I know it is not Theo's, but it could be a visual reminder of my half of our full point-counterpoint melody."

The Queen accepted the silken pouch from Adriana and cradled it in her hands. "Thank you. Safe travels, Adriana. May your next path take you to the place you most long to go."

As Adriana rode Sultan between the high rock walls, she considered her choice to leave Beryllios the way she had entered. She most longed to be with Theo, so she had been tempted to continue through the land of Beryllios, following the river. But she could not bear the thought of coming upon his body, much as she wished to see him again. So her next choice was home. And the closest she had been to home was at her entrance into the clearing those many moons ago.

The low-growing, multicolored flowers on which Sultan trod eventually gave way to the cut gemstones she remembered at her arrival. As she rounded the last turn of the path, she saw the clearing ahead of her. Not wanting the path to Beryllios to close before she was ready, as the way into Chehalem had, Adriana pulled Sultan to a stop and looked back down the path. But there was no one, and really nothing, to see. Dejected, she trotted Sultan the dozen strides into the clearing and heard a soft swish as the way to Beryllios closed behind her.

The archway into Shahar was exactly where Adriana expected it to be. But across the clearing the path previously unavailable to her stood open and welcoming. She was sure it was the path upon which she had originally entered the clearing, the way back to Ayrden.

Without hesitation Adriana urged Sultan into a canter as tears of relief filled her eyes. She was going home. Over the sound of Sultan's hooves on the ground, she heard what sounded like clapping, first soft and quiet, then growing in volume. Slowing Sultan, she looked around and finally up. The trees of the clearing were swaying, their leaves, like hands, clapping.

Applause.

Adriana smiled and continued on to the path toward Ayrden, thinking of Redbud and the communication of the trees, confident that Redbud knew she was completing her Journey and returning home. The path behind her remained open, much to her surprise. And in far less time than she would ever have imagined, she saw the end of the path where it opened into the groomed expanse of Ayrden's castle grounds.

Just as they were about to exit the path, Sultan balked, stopping so suddenly he almost unseated Adriana. She urged him forward. Nothing. She could not get him to budge.

"Sultan!" Adriana said sharply. "We are home! What ever is wrong?" Adriana dug her heels into his sides, but he moved not at all.

Finally she dismounted, hoping to lead him forward and onto the castle lawn. He stood docile and calm as she stepped up to his head to stroke his muzzle. "Come on, boy. We're almost home. See?" Adriana pointed toward the path's opening. "Just through there. Your stall will be waiting. And Beecher will have you fresh water and grain and hay. And Alexander. Oh, Sultan, come on, Alexander is waiting for you."

As Adriana tried to coax him forward, he suddenly reared up. The reins ripped from her hands and his front hooves pawed the air just above Adriana's head. She stepped back and Sultan pivoted away from her. The ground shook with the force of his descent, and he galloped full tilt away from her, back down the path.

And before Adriana could make a sound, he disappeared from sight.

Not because of his speed, but because of the trees, which snapped into place behind him, as if there had never been a path there at all.

Adriana trudged across the vast expanse of lawn, morose at the thought of her failures. She was returning with nothing, not even Sultan. The creamy stone walls of the castle rose up in the distance, and as she drew closer her heart grew heavier. This was not at all how she had envisioned her homecoming. To return in any fashion at all, she had imagined, would be cause for celebration and evidence of success. Instead, all she could see were her devastating losses.

Yet she was glad to be home and yearned to see her family even as she dreaded, with an intensity that bordered on desperation, seeing Alexander and having to explain Sultan's absence. Her eyes fell to her feet. Her soft brown boots, scuffed and worn from her travels, sank into the deep green grass.

Suddenly a clarion trumpeted the sound of jubilation. Adriana raised her eyes to see members of the royal household pouring from the castle doorways onto the terrace. She saw Emaht and Prelechett first, then two little girls with strawberry hair dancing out the door and around the skirts of her mother. Could that possibly be the twins? They were so tall! How long, Adriana wondered once again, had she been gone?

She glimpsed Bess exit from one of the high glass doors to one side of the terrace, Banah gliding along behind her. Banah! How would Adriana approach her to find out about her relationship with Kelak?

And then, like an anvil pulling her heart to the bottom of a deep lake, she saw Alexander. His dark head bent in concentration over Ty, who was pressed close to his side. Adriana's eyes fell once again to her feet and tears welled in her eyes so that she did not see the King run down the stairs to meet her.

"Adriana," he exclaimed as he wrapped her in his arms. "You are home. You have returned."

In that moment Adriana felt her mood lighten a bit. That she had returned, albeit without Sultan and empty-handed, seemed to be enough for her father.

They stepped onto the terrace and Adriana walked toward Ty and Alexander.

"Alex, I am so sorry. Sultan . . . ," Adriana began, lifting her eyes to really look at him for the first time since she had seen him exit the castle with Ty by his side.

But the person looking back at her, with a broad smile and dancing brown eyes, was not her brother. It was Theo, back from the dead.

When Adriana awoke, she was lying on the bed in her chambers. She was so disoriented that for a moment she thought perhaps she had not yet gone on her Journey. Perhaps dreams and reality had mixed so completely in her mind that it was simply the day after her sixteenth birthday and she had yet to leave.

But when she sat up and saw her boots, scuffed and stained, still on her feet, she knew none of it had been a dream. Memory flooded her. Theo was alive—where was he? Had that been reality? What was going on? As she leaped to her feet, her eyes skittered around the room and she noticed the door. It was partially open, and she could hear soft voices in the passageway.

"You can see her as soon as she awakes," Adriana heard her mother say.

"I am awake," Adriana said, opening the door to find Theo standing in front of her mother.

"My dear," her mother said, turning to give her a tight hug. "Are you recovered? No one intended to give you such a fright. We were unsure how to best handle the situation. Obviously we misjudged."

The words washed over Adriana, felt but unheard. She could not take her eyes from Theo's face. He was alive. How could that be?

"Theodore, why don't you and Adriana talk in the upstairs sitting room? It is just along here." The Queen walked with them, her arm linked through Adriana's. She cut her eyes toward her daughter, a look of concern on her face. "Does that suit, Adriana? Or do you need some more time alone?"

"That suits perfectly, Mother. Thank you," Adriana said. "But what of Alexander? Where is he? Why wasn't he on the terrace when I arrived?"

The Queen leaned her shoulder against Adriana's for just a moment. For the first time in Adriana's life, her mother seemed to be seeking comfort from her daughter rather than giving it. "Alexander is on his Journey. We can discuss it further after you have had an opportunity to speak with Theodore."

Once they arrived at the sitting room, the Queen closed the door behind the two of them. At the metallic click of the door fastening, Theo took Adriana in his arms and they both began talking at once.

"I am so sorry I frightened you—" Theo began.

"How can you be alive?" Adriana asked, her voice fraught with emotion.

Theo dropped his head to hers and kissed her lips. "I love you, Adriana. I loved you in Beryllios, and—"

Tears of joy sprang to Adriana's eyes, and she gave him a fervent kiss before saying, "And I love you."

He pulled back a slight bit. "I know. I died hearing your sweet words. If I had remained in the depths, it would have been the greatest treasure of all to take into eternity."

"But what happened? How can you be alive?" Adriana repeated her question.

"I was the eldest heir of the twelfth generation. It was my destiny to be the sacrifice that freed my people from the dragon. I was hoping to keep you from becoming too involved, as I knew full well my death would be coming soon."

"How did you know?" Adriana asked. "Your mother said you didn't have access to the prophecy." The two sat down close together on one of the hyacinth blue love seats that flanked the massive fireplace of the sitting room.

"Remember when we were sitting on the rock at the Pools of Lilac?"

"I didn't know that was what it was called, but yes, vividly. That is where you told me you couldn't love me."

Theo nodded. "Remember the question you asked me? If I had any scars? And my reply?" At Adriana's nod he continued, "At twelve I made my trip into Eremia. The journey is not totally dissimilar from your own. Though it is more about fighting temptation. Invariably we are tempted by the dragon—were tempted by the dragon," he corrected himself. "My experience was no different. The scar came not from Zimley, however, but from your brother Ty."

Adriana pulled away, her face conveying her disbelief. "Ty? Theo, if you were twelve that was what, seven years ago? Ty would have been a little child! You could not possibly have seen him in the wilderness."

"I know it seems unreasonable, but I tell you truth. If Ty could speak here in Ayrden, he would tell you the same, I promise you."

"What do you mean?"

"Adriana, Ty visited me in Eremia, an older Ty, perhaps seventeen or so. Visited me and talked to me. He told me you would arrive, that we would free Beryllios, by your courage and my sacrifice."

Adriana was even more confused. Did this confirm that

Ty was a See-er as she had often wondered, or something else entirely?

Theo continued, "And he told me I would break your heart." Theo looked at her. "You have brothers—you can imagine my response to that at twelve. I didn't really care. I didn't even know you. But that knowledge, seven years later? After I came to know you? To love you? It hurt me to withdraw from you, but I hoped to spare you."

Adriana was even more confused. "But how is it you are alive?"

Theo took her by the hand and they walked out onto the portico that wrapped around the upper level of the turret. "Adriana, I don't know. It was as if I woke from a deep sleep, opening my eyes to a dark, moonless sky. I was wrapped in my chimanga, clutching Thebazeli's betrothal box. I was strapped to a burial raft and was floating in that lake of water." Theo pointed to the west, where last light was fading.

"Theo, there is no lake there," Adriana said with assurance, confident in her knowledge of her homeland's topography. But when she looked out to where he was pointing, she was shocked to see a lake of sapphire blue. Crystal water spilled out from between towering walls of jade green, covered by amethyst and violet flowers, and into the lake.

Adriana gasped. "It looks like Beryllios!"

"We, your family and I, are confident it is the way to Beryllios, opened once again. And this time not by a seasonal land bridge, but a permanent one. When I awoke in the lake, Ty was waiting for me. He pulled me from the water and brought me to the castle. But he did not speak. Nor did he seem to hear anything I said. I have not told anyone but you that I met him in Eremia years ago."

Adriana nodded and stepped closer to him. "So what now?" Adriana asked, gazing in amazement at the cliff walls so reminiscent of Beryllios.

"Your father has sent a pair of messengers to ride along the cliffs, hopefully to relay to my family and all of Beryllios that the way is open to Ayrden once again and I am alive. I waited here, in hopes you would soon return. And when you are ready—well, first let me ask you. How did I come to be holding Thebazeli's betrothal box?"

A soft blush rose to Adriana's cheeks. "I asked your mother's permission to place it in your hands. She said it was mine to give to whomever I desired. I wrapped your fingers around it myself."

"And did you intend for it to be a proposal?"

Adriana felt joy rising within her like a candlelit lantern floating into the night sky as she thought of all that had been redeemed in the past few hours. Theo's life, her Journey, even Sultan's running away—perhaps to find and aid Alex on his Journey—all seemed to take on a shimmering, satisfying significance.

"I intended it as a proposal," Adriana said with assurance. "Do you intend to accept?"

CHAPTER 34

THE FESTIVAL OF HOMECOMING

Adriana's Festival of Homecoming began as the moon rose over the woods. A new head maid helped her dress in an elaborate emerald gown of raw silk. Banah had been caring for Bess since Adriana's departure and had requested she remain in her service.

When Adriana sat down at the royal table, a rush of conflicting emotions surged through her. The sight of Alexander's empty place filled her with sadness and anxiety. She missed his teasing and affection. Moreover, what her mother had eventually told her concerned her greatly. Alex's horse, a young mare that he and Beecher had trained together, had returned to the stable before last light on the very day Alexander departed. There had been no sign or word of Alex since.

Her mother looked older, visibly drawn in a way that

Adriana had never seen. Though every time she looked over at Adriana a smile lit her face, it was not enough to mask the sadness in her eyes.

Her father seemed euphoric that Adriana was home and pleased and confident that Beryllios had been reopened to Ayrden under his rule. But no matter how broad his smile, there was a tiny furrow between his eyes. He looked distracted, and Adriana wondered if it was just because of Alexander. She needed to have a long talk with him very soon about his brother, Kelak. The thought filled her with dread. She wondered how her father would respond to her description of her time in Chehalem. Would he be disappointed in her failure to bring Kelak back to Ayrden? Would he be angry at his brother's treachery? Would it make him more concerned for Alexander?

With a sigh, Adriana turned her eyes toward Bess. Another dilemma. She had seemed distant ever since Adriana's arrival, though for what reason was unclear. Was it simple unfamiliarity? Had she really been gone that long? Or was something else afoot? Time enough to discover that, Adriana supposed, as Theo had agreed they should stay in Ayrden until she'd had her fill of home. Then they would travel together to Beryllios to tell his family of their wedding plans.

At that thought joy once again surged within her, and she slipped her hand into his.

"Dance?" he asked.

Adriana arose and they walked toward the dance floor. They passed the twins, soon to turn five, playing mother to Sarian and Emaht's son, a beautiful little boy with clear gray eyes and hair the same red color as the twins'. The three seemed almost like siblings, Adriana thought.

More like siblings than the twins and Ty, she acknowledged with another change of emotion as her eyes fell upon her ever-silent brother. Though he had given her a long hug of homecoming at the first opportunity, he seemed even more detached and remote than he had when Adriana left on her Journey. And what of the story Theo had told her of Ty, older and speaking, meeting him years ago in the wilderness of Eremia? Adriana gave a shake of her head. There would be much to discover, and set to right if possible, before she and Theo left Ayrden for Beryllios.

Pushing thoughts of her family and the Journey she had just completed from her mind, she allowed her thrill at being in Theo's arms to pull her thoughts away from her concerns.

Late in the evening Adriana and Theo walked by the newly created sapphire lake, the tiny crescent moon casting a thin ribbon of light across the water. The sky was full of candlelit lanterns that floated across the sky, creating small pools of light as they drifted over the lake.

"The betrothal box. Do you know if it opens? If there

is anything inside?" Adriana asked.

"Funny, I don't know. You know this is the first one given in twelve generations."

Theo pulled the small jewel-encrusted box from his jacket pocket and held it in the palm of his hand. Adriana reached across and pinched the two rings atop the box between her fingers. The tiny square lid came away in her hand. Nestled inside was a gold band of emeralds and rubies. Theo tipped the ring out into his hand and, as he did so, like from a tightly wound music box, the point-counterpoint melody from their last dance together in Beryllios began playing.

Theo took Adriana's hand and slipped the ring on her finger. It fit perfectly, as if it had been made for her alone.

Acknowledgments

Though my parents are not alive to see the publication of this book, the love and life they provided for me permeate its pages. The fables, fairy tales, and Little Golden Books my parents read and reread to me taught and reinforced much of their worldviews. A positive attitude and a willing spirit can take you far; just ask the Little Engine That Could. Laughter and joy are an important part of life; look at Johnny Go Round, the tan tomcat. A quick, shrewd mind can help you even when a situation looks very bad indeed; didn't Br'er Rabbit escape unharmed? If things are bad today, they are not necessarily going to stay that way; the Ugly Duckling did turn into a swan after all. My parents lived a beautiful life of genuine love that they wholeheartedly shared with me. I am eternally grateful.

This book would not exist without the persistent encouragement of Maureen Ryan Griffin, midwife of writers' dreams, and all the past and present members of our Tuesday morning's Under Construction class. Particular thanks go to Caroline Brown, who inspired Adriana's